A COUNT OF FIVE

Also by Erin L. Snyder

Novels
FOR LOVE OF CHILDREN
FACSIMILE

Short Fiction Collections
TENDING THE FIRE
25 CHRISTMAS EVES

A COUNT OF FIVE

THE CITADEL OF THE LAST GATHERING

BOOK I

BY ERIN L SNYDER

A Count of Five

Copyright © 2015 by Erin L. Snyder
www.erinlsnyder.com

Cover art by Erin Snyder

ISBN 978-0692458174
Idyll Themes Press

Dedicated to Lindsay Stares, my wife and editor.

Special thanks to Jesse LaJeunesse and Bryan Yarrow for their invaluable advice and suggestions.

PART 1

1

Alaji followed Theojin over the ridge towards the drop-off. They crawled across mossy stones and through tangled, yellow grass and dry shrubs. The sun floated behind their backs – they approached from the west, so eyes below would be less likely to see them. They stayed alert for scouts or a party of hunters wandering up from the camp. But they came across nothing of the sort, nor did they stumble across goblins, a bear, a dragon, or any of the other countless dangers they'd dreamt up on the way.

At last, they crept to the edge and gazed over. Alaji plucked a couple brier berries growing near her and popped one in her mouth, squeezing it between her teeth just tight enough to crack the rind, then she sucked on the sour juice inside before spitting out the seeds and leathery skin. They took a moment to absorb the scene. The field below the cliff was covered in tents with figures darting in and out. Among the tents were a hand's count of fire pits where cooks toiled over simmering pots of broth. Elsewhere, women tanned animal skins and tended to the horses and dogs while chickens, pigs, and goats wandered in the fields.

"Start counting tents," Theojin whispered, scratching his thin beard as if it were fuller. "I'll be your third hand." It was silly. Alaji was more than capable of keeping track of a third hand in her head; both of them were. But they'd come together for safety, anyway, so there was no reason not to work together. She placed the second berry in her mouth and started at the edge of camp, moving her left hand slowly over the scene below. As her hand passed the first tent, her small finger curled, and her hand slid onward. The second finger traded for the first as she moved over the next tent, and so on, until she reached five. Without pausing, her fingers sprang up together, while the first finger on her right dipped. The next five on her left were traded for a second on her right, and so on until she'd exhausted all five fingers on that hand. She opened both hands, while her brother dipped a single finger on his left. This continued until they'd counted the camp.

"Four on the third, two on the second, and one," she whispered, before her brother could add it. "How many per tent, do you think?"

"An even hand, let's say. It's hard to tell."

"Then one on the second hand, two on the third, four on the fourth. That's more than the battle of Red Lake."

"That's more men than have ever stood against the valley," her brother replied. "If more arrive–"

"They might not be planning to take the valley. Maybe they really do want to pass us by and make their wars in the east."

"Maybe," her brother said. "I hope so. But Mikhil heard some talking outside the brewer's, speaking of Hollik ruling the lands from the steppe to the sea. Forging a kingdom to last a hundred years."

Theojin had used the northmen's word for a hundred. Alaji spit the remains of her second berry on the ground. She hated hearing the term from her brother's lips. It was as if he was dignifying their twisted system of counting or acknowledging the importance of the number. She knew he hadn't meant it that way: he was quoting them, and besides, it was quicker to speak it in their tongue. Still, she raised four fingers on her left hand and bisected them with three from her right.

"Does Hollik plan to live forever?"

"I think he wants his empire to outlive him."

"The Vesjin Alliance never made it to a third hand. And that wasn't half the world. Hollik wants it all."

"That's not what dad's afraid of. You know what they're saying, don't you?"

"I know." Alaji began crawling backwards away from the cliff. "The fifth sign. The last war. Dragon shit, isn't it?"

"Maybe. Dad believes it. So does Arahm."

"Well I don't," she said quickly. "Hollik's just another barbarian. He's strong now, but when his food runs out and his furs are gone, what will he do? The northmen are loyal to no one, not even their own. If they don't turn on him and slit his throat, it'll be because he runs off in the night. If he doesn't—"

"If he doesn't, I'll kill him myself," Theojin said, cracking a smile. "Unless the world ends before I have a chance." He laughed, and Alaji hit him on the arm.

"Shut up! We don't know who's near!" But by then she was laughing, too. They rose to a crouch and ran hunched over across the hill.

—

"So many?" Arahm asked. The old man was seated on a stump. The sun was setting over Boars Lake behind them. A handful of fishing boats were still on the water, hauling in their catch. He spoke only to Theojin, though Alaji stood beside her brother.

Theojin cleared his throat and spoke in the deep voice he used when there were elders around, particularly those he wanted to impress. "We're sure. Of the tents, at least. At five men per tent—"

"Yes, yes," the old man said, turning to look out over the water. "I understand the math. There weren't half as many before last moon waned."

"We should act," Theojin said. "Before any more arrive."

"What can we do?" Arahm asked with a shrug.

"Stop selling them food," Theojin suggested. "They'll have to move on. Or, at the very least, they'll be weak when they choose to attack."

"Take away their food, and we'd give them reason to attack."

"Then take more in exchange, at least. Leave Hollik less livestock to bribe his mercenaries."

"The more we take from them, the more incentive they'll have to take it back. Our best course is to continue bartering as we have and trade for weapons in the east. Maybe align with Yelmin and Kiffim. And keep watching."

"Okay. I'll take my sister home and come to the meeting in the square."

Arahm nodded, still looking out at the lake.

—

The walk home was a long one, but it took them along the bank of Boars Lake. Theojin paused to skip a stone across the surface. "Sometimes, I think he's more afraid we'll be left out of the Last Battle than he cares whether we'll win."

"No one wins the Last Battle," Alaji said.

"Yeah, well this isn't the first fight they've called that. The battle of Red Lake, when they tried corralling goblins as footmen, they said that was it, too. Goblins fighting alongside men and beasts, signs of the end. But it was just a fight, and a stupid warlord who lost half his men in a stampede, because he didn't realize goblins and dogs don't mix."

"I don't think we'll be as lucky with Hollik," Alaji said. "He's different. His men stay in line, don't even start fights at the brewer's or steal."

"A tyrant with manners," Theojin said. "Should we just lay down our weapons and pledge him our allegiance?"

"That's not what I mean. Just that he's smart, that he knows how to bide his time." Alaji paused a moment. "Theojin, what's this meeting?"

"It's nothing. Just to discuss some things. Training mostly. Hollik isn't the only one who knows how to use time to his advantage."

Alaji bit her tongue but said nothing.

2

Alaji woke the next morning and went to her chores. Her parents were still asleep while she worked. She didn't see her brother, so she did his work as well, as best she could. There were animals to feed and eggs to gather, then she made three trips to the stream to collect the morning's water. After that, she brought firewood to the pit beside their hut.

There was a fireplace inside, as well, but they only used it in the winter and rain, and then sparingly, since the smoke pooled inside as often as not. She arranged the logs quickly, setting the last stick aside. Once the rest were in place, she grabbed this off the ground, held it in front of her, and concentrated. She gripped the bottom of the stick with one hand and with the other she brought her thumb to her smallest finger. The others danced through the air while Alaji whispered words her mother had taught her years before. She brought her fingers carefully to the branch. Beneath them, the bark singed. Smoke trailed behind her fingers as she twisted the branch, spiraling it upward. When she was a third of the way down, she withdrew her fingers. The top of the branch burst into flame, and she shoved it beneath the logs. The fire expanded in a flash of blue light, before settling to reds and yellows.

She licked the tips of her fingers to relieve the heat. With a glance over her shoulder she checked that no one was watching from the windows. Her mother expected a certain level of decorum when invoking the spells of women. If she'd seen, she would have made some remark about Alaji needing more practice. A woman is expected to have calloused hands to match her husband's. And Alaji had reached the age of marriage, though little had been done about it.

She set the cooking stone beside the fire before ducking back into the hut to get the ingredients she needed to make the bread, returning with a few small jars and a hollowed gourd full of flour. She picked through the flour first, pulling out a number of small bugs which had found their way in. She flung these into the fire without a thought. When she was satisfied, she added water to the gourd and mixed with her hands. She added a pinch of salt next; not too much, since she'd no desire to hear her parents complain about having to trade for more. Finally, she added some ground herbs she'd gathered and dried earlier in the season.

The mixture sizzled as it landed on the stone and began to harden. She sat, watching the first piece cook. She dipped her hand into some of the leftover water before retrieving the bread with her hands. She dropped it onto a small mat woven from reeds before measuring the next part.

"I'll take that," Theojin said, startling her.

"There'll be eggs soon." Alaji was used to him sneaking up on her and offered him no satisfaction. The spells of men included one for moving silently, but it was meant for the hunt, not games. "And the next piece will be better. That one's burned."

But by then he'd already snatched the bread from the mat and was tearing into it. "It's fine," he said. "Better than that. It's as good as mom's."

"Don't say that in front of her. I don't need the competition."

Theojin laughed and tousled her curly hair.

"You're acting strange," Alaji said. "What is it?"

"I'm tired. I was out all night. We were wrong about Arahm. He knows exactly what he's doing."

"I don't remember saying otherwise."

"Fine then. I was wrong about him."

Alaji poured more of the mixture over the stone. "What were you doing all night, anyway?"

"I'm not supposed to say."

"Worried I'm a spy?"

He laughed again. "No. It's just… Arahm wants to avoid talk. You know how things get around. Rumors are where we get most of our information from."

"Suits me."

Theojin broke off a corner of his bread and rolled it into a tube. He chewed at the end absentmindedly. "We're following the northmen around. Watching them. They come near the village at night, you know. To gather information, we think. I'd feel better if they tried to steal something. But they're just learning the land. That's not a good sign."

"It's happening, isn't it?"

"Something's happening," Theojin replied. "They're getting ready for a fight. We don't know if they're set on one, but they're getting ready regardless."

"Are you scared?"

"No. Yeah. A little, I guess. They come from a hard land. And I don't believe what everyone's saying about their magic, that it's a sign of weakness they don't respect the divide."

"Men shouldn't use magic that isn't theirs," Alaji said. "They shouldn't even learn it."

"I know. Believe me, I agree. The gods had reasons for their laws. But I'm not sure the gods will defend those laws. And I'm not sure we can."

"It's not right. Men were the gods' favorite, so they let them choose which magic they could have. And the first men chose the spells of the hunt."

"Yeah," Theojin said. "But I think those men were damned idiots." His gaze lingered on the burning fire.

3

Alaji hadn't noticed the tear in Theojin's shirt, but their mother, Shaji, spotted it immediately. She decided she was too busy to fix it herself. "Besides," she added, "Alaji requires experience."

That meant gathering twine-reeds from the stream, and they were hard to come by so late in the season. She made sure to collect a few extra and hide them: they had another use. She crushed the rest between two stones until they splintered into soft, hair-like threads. Then she rolled these beneath her palm and chanted softly, invoking the weaving spell. It was simpler than the fire spell, but she had far less practice. Even so, she felt the fibers twist beneath her hand, shifting and binding into thread. She repeated the process until she had a handful of short pieces, then she began laying these out on the torn shirt. Then the spell again, though it was harder now. She commanded the pieces to intertwine with the fabric from the shirt, which was made from the crushed inner bark of saplings. The thread took, but not evenly: she had to unweave and re-weave the strands by casting the spell forward and back several times.

Once she was finally finished repairing the shirt, she began her cleaning. Then there were the goats, which had to be counted to ensure none had run off or been killed by predators.

It took Alaji half the day to finish her work, but there was still enough time left. She told her mother she'd promised to spend the afternoon with Mil, a friend who lived beyond the western hill. Her mother made her clean herself and fix her hair, then sent her along. Had it been another friend, her mother may have decided they needed more wood gathered or that there were other garments in need of repair, but Mil had a brother Shaji was fond of. While Alaji's father may have resigned himself to the end of the world, Shaji was always one to hedge her bets. And if the world didn't end, she wanted to live to see her daughter married.

But Alaji had no interest in seeing Mil or her brother. She doubled back to a grove just south of her home where she'd hidden her remaining pieces of twine-reed, then hurried along towards Hawk's Fall Cliffs. It was a long walk, and she almost abandoned her plan for fear of running out of daylight. But she couldn't escape her thoughts. Her conversation with Theojin, who was now sleeping out the day, followed her and made her sick.

Part of it was Hollik, the warlord. The would-be tyrant, who dreamed of ruling the world, from the far-off north to the seas. Five hands of five generations of freedom would end in subjugation. Better for the world to end quickly than that. Better for the gods to undo what they'd wrought than leave their people enslaved to the whims of a conqueror who stole the magic of women.

There was more, though. Alaji was afraid of more than the warrior. She kept a secret from even her brother: if the northmen were guilty, then so was she. And her crime was far greater.

They'd stolen only the spells of women; she'd taken a spell from the gods.

The sun had reached the fourth finger of the sky by the time Alaji reached the caverns. She looked around before going on. This was a holy place, and by rights she shouldn't be here. But she had crossed that boundary years ago. Once she was satisfied no one watched, she went on towards the crevice.

When her people first reached the valley, they had come here. The holiest of their kind descended alone into the dark against the judgment of his sons, who feared there could be goblins – or worse – lying in wait. He was gone for three days and nights. His sons nearly speared him when he emerged, so sure were they that their father had died. But they stayed their hands long enough to realize it was their father who had returned, and not whatever they'd imagined must have devoured him.

He told them that he'd entered the world of spirits, and that he'd learned the mysteries of the hand and of the world. More importantly, he told them that they'd finally reached their destination, the center of the world, where the gods had intended them to settle.

Every year on the winter solstice, would-be seers and clerics traced his footsteps into the cavern. It was forbidden for anyone but them to enter, and only on that day. The penalties were severe, but nothing Alaji thought she couldn't endure. Besides, if no one was permitted here, no one could be here to catch her.

It had been a child's logic. She'd only been a girl when she first snuck into the caverns. Of course, she hadn't gone far that time. It had been a thrill, a quiet challenge to the world. Then she'd gone back a second time. And a third.

By then, it was something else: it was a place to escape the summer heat. It was a place of peace and reflection. It was a secret.

As she stepped into the cave, she drew out a twine-reed. The seers who entered on the chosen day had no need of such thing, since they knew a spell for invoking light. Alaji had never understood what that had to do with the hunt, but then she was not a man and would never understand the secrets the gods shared with their sex. Just as they would never understand those given to hers.

With a twist of her fingers, she lit the reed on fire. The flame died down but cast enough light to illuminate the path before her. She was careful to hold it in front of her as she pushed onward, squeezing through the tight, rocky outcroppings and through the winding corridors. When the first reed had almost burned away, she brushed her hand over it to extinguish what was left. The spell for creating fire had always come easier to her than its reverse, but she was capable enough. She slid the stem into a pouch, not wanting to leave evidence, then withdrew a second strand. She lit it like the first and continued onward.

A third of her reeds were gone when she reached the opening, and she cursed herself for not gathering more. She set aside another third for the trip back, and lit one of the remaining strands, so she could admire the cave.

The walls were covered with designs. Lines expanded into five segments, which in turn branched out again and again, always in fives. She understood the significance of this place and felt its magic. Some of the designs were the work of the first seer; the others were from those who'd come after. Every generation had added something, and – if the world did not end – every generation after would no doubt do the same.

She knelt on the ground and looked up at the ceiling, where the lines changed direction and descended on the other side, until they finally became a single line once more. She breathed slowly and closed her eyes as her strand burned out. Her heart beat, and she counted it. One. Two. Three....

No. Her eyes opened, and she stood up, brushing off her legs. She should not be doing this. The first time had been an accident; magic she'd stumbled on. She'd sworn to herself she'd never invoke it again. She'd sworn that more times than she could count, and she'd always broken that vow.

She could make all the vows she wanted – it wouldn't change why she'd come this afternoon. She backed up until she felt stone behind her. She lit another reed and placed it in a crack in the wall. It was enough to illuminate the passageway. Then she shut her eyes and listened to her heart beating. One. She took a small step forward. Two. She took another. Three: a third. Four and five.

The cavern air was different now. She could feel it in her lungs and in her blood. She could feel the air shimmering, like the flickering light or the surface of a lake. She felt her heartbeats, all five of them. And she focused on the first. She reached for it, but did not move. She called for it but did not speak. That moment was hers once again. The moment she counted one was no longer past but present.

She turned around and saw herself stepping forward with eyes closed. She was outside of herself, but she was whole. Her reflection was stepping forward, mouthing, "One. Two. Three. Four…."

Only it was no reflection. She had moved back in time as one steps backward along a trail. She was reliving a moment she'd just experienced.

On five, Alaji reached forward to her reflection and touched her shoulder. The reflection seemed startled, but still stepped forward nonetheless and vanished as she did so.

Alaji felt faint. Her shoulder was warm, and she reached for it instinctively. A dull pain formed in her head. She remembered the touch. She remembered breathing. It cut into her head, but the pain only lasted a moment. Then it was gone.

She laughed briefly without knowing why. It was reckless. It was something she should not be doing, and she received nothing but the satisfaction of knowing she was experiencing something no one else could. But, for now, that was enough.

Later, she knew, she would feel the fear. The doubt. She would swear never to do this again. Later she would remember.

The penalty for coming to the caverns was five lashes. The penalty the northmen would have faced for learning the magic of a woman, had they been subject to the town's laws, would have been five times that.

The penalty men had set for learning the magic of the gods, be it on purpose or through blind chance, was death. What additional price the gods might exact afterward was only hinted at in myth.

4

The attack came sooner than any expected. Only it came from the wrong direction and source. The northmen, whatever their intentions, kept to themselves and repeated their claim: that their goal of unifying the lands would be accomplished peacefully. If they knew they were being watched, they offered no objection.

But no one was watching the marshlands to the south, and the goblins took advantage. Their strike was more organized than usual, and the toll was greater. They left four homes burning along the banks of Clulin, the shallow river which fed Moon Lake, after killing the families and stealing whatever they could carry.

As was their custom, they left behind a tribute. This time, it was mostly meat, impaled on spikes in the ground near the farm houses. Who, exactly, they hoped to placate with such offerings was unclear. The idea gods or men would accept such a feeble gesture as payment for murder and theft was absurd. But then goblins were not known for reason.

When Hollik heard of the atrocities, he offered assistance in hunting the creatures. Arahm declined his offer but found his people stretched thin. Between spying on Hollik's troops and maintaining the town's normal activities, he had few men to spare. Quietly, he'd sent messengers to Yelmin, the nearest neighboring village, to plead for aid, though they'd yet to reply. There was still bad blood between the two towns, though Arahm had hoped they'd lay old feuds aside in the face of such dark times.

He maneuvered his people as well as he could, but there were only so many young men he could rely on. In the end, he had to turn to women and old men to watch the northern hills, so he could send his warriors south to avenge the slaughter.

Alaji heard about this from her brother and went to volunteer at once, first to accompany the hunters after the goblins and then, when her request was flatly denied, to spy on the northmen. This offer fared no better. While Arahm had looked the other way when she'd accompanied Theojin on his mission, he told her simply she was too young to be doing such work.

Theojin was sent with a hunting party into the swamp. They'd been given instructions to camp in set locations, so Arahm could send messengers if he needed them called back quickly. Before he left, Theojin's father lent him his best bow for the task. He promised to use it well and to return with it.

———

There was a great deal of work to be done in her brother's absence, and Alaji had little time for herself. She was almost glad of it. She felt the pull to return to the caves daily now, and was relieved to have the option taken out of her hands. The idea of trying her spell elsewhere never occurred to her. She only felt safe in the caverns; anywhere else was too exposed.

Shaji sensed her daughter's frustration and compensated by giving her even more work to accomplish. She pushed her harder, as if daring Alaji to defy her, but she did not. This went on for three days, and then, one morning when she was in the middle of milking the goats, Alaji heard her mother calling to her.

"You'll have to do your work later," Shaji said. She offered no immediate explanation or emotion, but studied her daughter's face for a moment. "You are still soft," she said.

It was an odd remark, even for Alaji's mother, who was an odd woman. Alaji said nothing and waited for something more. Another insult seemed as likely as an apology, and neither would have comforted or hurt her. All her mother added was, "Walk with me."

There were times Shaji acted solemnly as a pretense. There were many such times, in fact. So many, Alaji had grown accustomed to hiding a sneer until her mother's back was turned. But she didn't sneer now, because this was not an act. When Shaji moved or spoke, it was almost always with authority. But this time there was fear, as well, and uncertainty. There were few who could have told the difference, but Alaji knew her mother's mannerisms. This was the way her mother had spoken when she'd first showed her the spells of the hearth. This was important to her.

The fields were quiet, and Alaji briefly felt the urge to tell her about the excursions to the caves and the spell she'd taken from the gods. She didn't, of course: Shaji would be obligated to reveal her or face death, and Alaji didn't really believe her mother would die for her.

Alaji followed into the woods, where Shaji silently collected a handful of sticks, and from there they walked to a small clearing. "Your spells are coming along adequately, save your ability with healing magic. But you'll always be able to find another woman who can mend a cut, should you need their aid. Most of them obsess over it to the detriment of their other spells. And of course you're too young to have learned the spells of childbirth. But those are really little more than extensions of healing, no matter what the elders say. You can mend torn cloth, and you can guide animals competently. If these were better times, I think that would be sufficient. But times are not better, are they?"

Her mother paused and drew a breath. "It's time you learned how to use your magic to full effect, Alaji. It's time you learned how to kill."

Alaji swallowed. The idea wasn't new to her: she'd given a lot of thought to how she might use her magic if pressed. From time to time, she'd hoped the northmen would force her hand. But she never imagined her mother had even considered women's magic in such a light. "The northmen use fire, too," she said.

Her mother smiled, which was rare in itself. "Do they? For its practical applications, I suspect. Or to inspire fear. Men are predictable creatures, which I suspect is why the gods elected to entrust this to us. Don't look surprised. If they'd wanted men to have it, they'd have offered it alongside spells of the hunt." She handed her daughter a branch. "Show me how you'd use it. Come on now."

Alaji nodded and stepped back. She lit the top half of the branch, and gripped the bottom half tightly. She braced herself and swung.

"No. You're thinking like they do, trying to mimic your brother. You're not as strong as he is, and you never will be. And the men from the north are stronger by far. Don't match your arm against theirs. Match minds. Be what they expect. Timid." Shaji slipped her hands behind her back and hung her head, as though ashamed. "This is how they see you. Practice it in your face, practice being afraid. If you're no threat, they won't kill you, not outright. They'll close in. Let them."

It was so fast, Alaji never saw her mother's hand move. But in an instant, it had shot out, and a flurry of smoldering embers and charcoal flew from her open palm. She aimed to one side, but a few scattered sparks drifted off course and singed Alaji's skin. If she'd been standing directly in front of her mother, she'd have been blinded.

"The eyes, child. When you're using fire, always go for the eyes. Then, forget magic." Her other hand rose, holding a knife. "Fire doesn't kill quickly. It takes too long. But if you take a man's eyes, his strength's nothing." She handed over the blade. "You'll want to make it quick. The throat's good, if he's fool enough to show it. Otherwise, whatever you can get at. The stomach or chest. Just put some weight behind the blow. Strike with the force of a punch. Make it stick, then pull it back and stab again. Forget everything I ever taught you about gutting fish. You don't want the cut clean or neat."

Alaji felt sick, but she forced herself to stay upright. Still her voice wavered when she asked, "Your hand?"

Her mother showed her the palm she'd used to enchant and throw the cinders. It was red and blistered from the heat. "It's not something you'll want to practice," Shaji said. "But you had to see how it's done. Shall we test your skill at healing before we move on to the next lesson?"

—

The spells Alaji had learned to repair torn cloth, it turned out, could be used to bind an enemy's sleeves to his sides. And her mother had some nasty ideas for guiding animals if Alaji ever found herself facing a rider. But, in the end, most of her teachings returned to fire. "Don't think small. You can set a grove on fire in a few minutes if you choose the right tree. Just be sure your enemies are downwind."

Or, "Smoke is a better tool than fire alone. Never forget, a man who can't breathe loses whatever advantage his size lends him." And finally, "If you're forced to fight by their terms, go for the hair. It burns like dry straw."

Afterward, Alaji's mother had one more lesson to impart. "If you should have a daughter, teach her what I've taught you. But never share this knowledge with another woman. These tricks are worthless if your foes have seen them used or heard them described. The raw magic may have been given to us all, but these tools are for our family alone."

Beyond that, her mother would tell her nothing of how she'd learned to fight, nor would she say whether she'd ever had to rely on such knowledge. She brought Alaji home and told her husband she'd burned her hand trying to fix one of her daughter's fires. For what it was worth, she spoke highly of Alaji's progress with healing magic.

Later, after Alaji extinguished her torch and drew the bearskin curtain concealing her bed closed, she lay down and shuddered. She wasn't sure what bothered her – that her mother knew so much about fighting, that her own ideas on using the spells of the hearth against the northmen weren't as original as she'd thought, the look on her mother's face after scalding her palm…. Perhaps all, perhaps none. But she found it difficult to sleep.

Her mother hadn't exactly surprised her. There was little Shaji did that could still startle her daughter, who'd grown up having every action or movement scrutinized by the strange woman. She wasn't like Mil's mother or any other woman Alaji knew. For her entire life, Alaji had cursed her luck. But today, she felt relief. The other women of the village may have treated their daughters better. They may have held them closer or offered advice and lessons with a more measured temper. But Alaji was certain none of them would have taken their daughters to the woods to teach them to kill.

For the first time, she was grateful Shaji was her mother.

5

Hunting goblins through the marshes was less exhilarating than Theojin had anticipated. Three days of bug bites, leeches, and wading through filth, and they'd yet to find a single one of the creatures. On the second day, they'd located an abandoned pit covered with a leaning roof. Theojin had tried to sort through the belongings inside in search of signs the creatures might return, but he'd given up after the smell made him retch. They tried to set fire to the enclosure, but had to give this up after a few hours. Everything in the swamp was damp, and none of them were adept at building fires. Finally, they knocked over the small roof and smashed it with stones.

As the risks of danger became more distant and the cold set in, Theojin began wishing his sister had been allowed to accompany them. He slept poorly that night, no thanks to a bunch of fleas he'd picked up destroying the goblin nest.

The next day seemed more fortuitous after they spotted tracks. Using the spells all men know, they silenced their footfalls and continued on, readying other enchantments should they be needed.

They managed to spot a goblin at the far edge of a bog, but despite their silent approach, the creature spotted them as well, howled out a warning, and darted into the woods beyond.

"At least that means there are a lot of them," one of the hunters pointed out.

They tracked into the afternoon and came across numerous tracks. Forms seemed to appear and vanish in the distance, but nothing within range. Finally, taking a break, Theojin fell against a tree and threw his head against the trunk in frustration. Above him, in the branches, a pair of eyes stared back.

"They're hiding in the trees!" he shouted, readying his bow. Another hunter was quicker with a spear, throwing it into the canopy. It didn't hit its mark, but the goblin reacted and lost its grip, dropped to the ground, and broke a leg. It hollered in pain and tried to crawl away, but one of the hunters brought his club down on its green head.

It got messy after that. Goblins started sliding down the trunks with shrill cries. Some were armed with stolen stone knives, spears, or throwing stones; others weren't armed at all. Theojin loosed arrows where he saw green flesh, and a few hit their marks.

From branches above, other goblins began hurling whatever they had at the hunters. Rocks, branches, clay pots, and pieces of meat came raining down, along with a few primitive spears. The goblins lacked sturdy footholds or leverage, so their aim was far off its mark more often than not. No one was seriously injured by the onslaught, though most of the hunters were bruised, and Hejkip, the largest of the group, got a long cut on the side of his face from a sharp stone.

Theojin's attention was torn between the fleeing goblins and the ones still in trees. He took half his shots at each group, though he had more luck with the running goblins than he had shooting overhead.

When the goblins ran out of possessions, they began throwing down smaller branches. As their numbers dwindled, they became more desperate. A few of the remaining creatures tried to leap and make a run for it, but the hunters caught up with most of them.

Hejkip, recovering from his wound, charged one of the thinner trees and struck it with such force it began shaking. One of the two goblins fell from the impact, and the other wound up dangling from the branch he was clutching for dear life until one of Theojin's arrows rendered the point moot.

By dusk, the last of the creatures had either escaped into the bog or lay dead or dying. If any remained in the trees, they were hidden too well to bother with. The hunters circled the grove, finishing the grisly business with spears and knives. Dwillith made a point of rolling the wounded over so he could look them in the eye before plunging his spear in. "This is for Gothij," he'd say, cycling through the names of the farmers who'd been killed. "This is for Thuithal's children!" When he rolled over a goblin to find it waiting with a knife in hand and received a cut on his ankle, Theojin had to bite his tongue to keep from laughing.

"Hey!" Hejkip shouted. "Take a look at this!"

The others hurried over to him. As he approached, Theojin knew from the cries what he was going to see. Still clutching the body of its dead mother, a goblin whelp lay on the ground, very much alive.

"So?" Dwillith shrugged. "You want me to do it?"

"It's a baby," Hejkip said. "I mean, couldn't we let it live? Doesn't seem sporting to kill the thing."

Another hunter answered, "It'll grow up like the rest of them, do what they do. You hear about the carnage at Gothij's farm?"

"Heard nothing," Dwillith said. "I saw it. Dead women, dead children. Don't make no difference to them." He motioned at the weeping baby while he spoke.

"Still not sporting. Still don't seem right," Hejkip said.

"Leave it," Theojin said at last. "Just leave it on the ground. Hej is right. Warriors don't kill infants, not even on a hunt."

"You want to explain that to the family that thing leads a raid against someday?"

"That isn't leading any raid," Theojin said. "Because nothing's coming for it but some wolves or a bear. Goblins aren't like us. They let the weak die, and they don't come for their sick." He had no idea whether or not this was true, but for some reason he couldn't stomach the idea of watching Dwillith skewer the creature, especially over the body of its mother. He knew it was wrong to hope the baby would live, but he did regardless.

As they finished their work, Theojin came across a knife lying on the ground. He snatched it up and called the others. "Did any of you drop this?" he demanded. One by one they denied owning it.

"Must have been thrown by one of them. From the trees." Hejkip suggested.

"Yeah, but look at the blade." He handed it over.

"Just bone," Hejkip said, feeling it.

"Whale bone," Theojin said. "It's from the northmen."

"What's it mean?" Dwillith asked.

"It means we've killed enough goblins."

6

Arahm spent several minutes looking over the knife before nodding. "It's one of the northmen's," he said. "But that doesn't mean it was given to the goblins freely. It could easily have been stolen."

"Goblins never raid beyond the lakes. Never. The only way they could have gotten this is if it was given to them."

"I have a knife like this one," Arahm said. "I got it from northern traders. A lot of us have things from the north. Maybe the farmers did, as well. Maybe the goblins stole it from them. Hollik could easily dismiss the evidence. Besides, we have no claim over him."

"We don't need to give him a chance to explain anything. If we can convince Yelmin that Hollik's arming the goblins to weaken us, they'll come to our aid and give us a chance."

Arahm thought silently for a moment. Then, scratching the side of his beard, he admitted, "It might work. I'll send a messenger warning them of our suspicions. Maybe they'll find similar knives, as well, if they're looking." There was a subtle smirk on Arahm's face. He was saying less than he was planning.

"I'll go," Theojin offered, but Arahm dismissed the notion with a wave.

"You'll rest. And practice. We may need warriors soon. I'll send one of the younger boys."

—

Theojin's mother greeted him warmly – though she rarely showed emotion to her daughter, she was always kind to her son – but she didn't embrace him due the smell that preceded him. She blocked the entrance to their hut and directed him to the stream to clean himself.

Some time passed, and Theojin's father joined him by the water's edge. Kuljin was a large man, bulky and muscular, though he walked with a limp and suffered from a pain in his back, a price he'd paid earlier in life for joining an expedition to bring down a mad dragon which had mauled oxen and set fire to a handful of huts by Red Lake.

By now, Theojin was naked in a deep pool. His feet rested on the bottom, and his lips were pale from the cool water.

"Your mother asked me to bring these." Kuljin dropped a bundle of clothes on a large rock by the running water. "She was afraid if you brought them yourself, they wouldn't have been clean by the time you got here. You can leave your old clothes on the rock. She'll attend to them when she has a chance."

He started to leave, but Theojin called him back. "When grandfather was young, didn't he capture a goblin once?"

Kuljin stood, staring at his son for a moment. He chewed on the bottom of his lip and nodded. "Years ago. Before I was born, anyway. It was after a raid. Why?"

"I just wanted to know more about them," Theojin answered, trying to strip all emotion from his voice.

"You kill one on the hunt?"

"More than that. A lot more," Theojin said.

"Good," his father said, but he seemed neither happy nor sad to hear it.

"Did grandpa ever talk about it?"

"All the time. Not many took the time to listen. Heard a few men say he was crazy."

"Who?" Theojin asked.

"Doesn't matter. Had words with those men myself. Never heard them say it again. Matters like that, once settled, should stay settled. Like I said, it was a long time ago. But I'll tell you what I remember of my father's stories if you'd like.

"It was after one of their raids by the Black Lake. Your grandfather used to have a hut down there before he married. Anyway, the goblins didn't plan well. When they get away, it's because they attack people too far from anyone to hear. But there were quite a few men in the area, and when the call went out, they flew in. There was a fight, but goblins don't make much of themselves unless they've got the advantage. There were more of them than of our people, the way I heard it, but not by enough to make much difference.

"When it was over, the goblins were driven off, dead, or on their way. Your grandfather was helping to quicken their passing when he found one that wasn't badly hurt, just unconscious. He got to thinking that if he could learn their language, maybe he could get it to tell him where the others were. He tied it to a tree and set some hounds to keep watch. Said the thing was terrified of those dogs.

"Took him halfway to harvest to learn its speech, but he got it eventually. No matter how many times he asked where the others were, it never gave them up. Didn't matter how much he threatened or bribed it. It just kept claiming it didn't know, that goblins move around the marshes, and they never know where they're stopping until they get there. Don't know if it's true or not, but that's the only answer he ever got.

"But it started trusting your grandfather. Or maybe it was just lonely. It talked to him, told him of its peop… of its kind. They aren't like us. Goblins don't pray to the gods, like men, but they still believe in them. It's strange thinking of them having faith, but they do. They believe the word is made of song, that the gods sung it into being. Have you heard them singing on the plain in the fall? They think the words are the same somehow. Your grandfather asked the creature why their songs sounded so pitiful. The creature said this was a pitiful world. I've always liked that.

"Your grandfather tried to teach it the truth, but the creature did not understand. Goblins don't understand numbers, not like we do. They can count, but they can't grasp meaning behind the numbers or see the world for what it is. Five fingers. Five ages. Five gods, five lands, and five magics. The difference between men and lesser beasts is the power to see the patterns. It sets us apart. It is the one aspect of themselves the gods placed within us that they gave no other creature. All things have magic. That does not make us special. But knowledge of numbers. Of adding and subtracting. Of dividing a whole into fifths. These are things beasts and goblins and dragons cannot see."

Kuljin held up his own right hand. "The secrets of the world are here. The ages of the world. The age of spirit. The age of fire. The age of ice. The age of beasts. And finally the age of men." He'd reached the last finger and his face was pale. "I'm sorry. The world is old, and this age is nearly ended. Your mother and I were greedy. We should not have had children. Yours is the fifth by fifth generation to live in this valley, by most counts. It will be the last."

"I don't believe that," Theojin replied. "The northmen don't think the world is ending. Our own people don't, not all of them. And mother—"

"Your mother is a good woman," Kuljin said. "But she is a woman. A woman's way is different. They do not look truth in the face, not always. I hope I am wrong. I hope the count is off, that there is time for a few more generations of our people. But there have already been signs. A blue mist rose over the lakes while you were gone, a sign of spirit. A fire was seen burning in the east, but the fields were untouched. Ruclin came across a patch of ice in the sun three days ago, just beneath Iomorn Hill. Watch and you will see a sign of beasts."

"And then of men?" Theojin asked. He was angry, though he did not know why.

"The sign of men is clearest of all. It will come from the north, it will be Hollik's war. Spear will strike arrow; ice will burn. Magic will shake the earth, and it will crack open. You know the prophecy."

He was about to leave, but Theojin called him again. "What happened to the goblin? What did grandfather do?"

Kuljin shrugged. "What could he do? He killed it before winter. It was that or leave it to freeze. Even a goblin deserves better than that."

"Of course," Theojin agreed, climbing out of the water to dry in the sun. His lips were almost blue now, but he bit down so his teeth wouldn't chatter.

7

Hollik knelt on the grassy plain, picking at a tick that clung to his ankle. His gaze lay fixed on the north, and he seldom blinked. Behind him stood a handful of his advisors: Jusl, the tracker he'd known since he was a boy; Kilfa, who'd mastered the arts of healing, could find the flaw in any plan, and was his favorite of four lovers; Brimire, the butcher, who served as Hollik's personal guard; Drista, his aunt and former teacher; and lastly, Yemerik. Yemerik, the strange, small, thin man they'd found on the plains dressed in peculiar robes. Of the five, Hollik trusted four with his life. In the case of Yemerik, Hollik had come close to impaling him on a spike and leaving him for the birds to pick at. This wasn't something which occurred once: the urge to kill him had become a daily occurrence.

But Yemerik had something to offer that was rarer and more astounding than anything the others could accomplish. By some power or trance or skill, he could foretell the weather. He'd been with them for three months, and his accuracy was uncanny. He insisted there was nothing supernatural about it, that it was merely a matter of knowing the signs and where to seek them out. But his claims wrung false; Hollik had followed him on one of his readings. Yemerik had wandered the fields, poking at mushrooms and peeling back moss before announcing, "Three days heavy rain, followed by two sunny with rain the second night, a violent storm the next day leading into a clear night." Such knowledge, Hollik was reasonably sure, wasn't written on the back of moss.

Moreover, Yemerik carried a bag with him at all times. When startled, his hand always dipped inside. Hollik had seen its contents only once, when he'd asked and Yemerik showed him the statue. There wasn't much about the thing: it resembled a large egg, perhaps, with some symbols carved in the edges. Hollik suspected a connection between Yemerik's vision and the object, though he could only guess as to what it was.

Whatever his secret, it was more than enough to place his life in jeopardy. The lake folk were far more superstitious than his people, and they'd cut Yemerik's throat for fear of angering some god or another. Even the eastern hillfolk would kill him for displaying power men weren't supposed to command. Strictly speaking, Hollik was under the same expectation, though he'd have little trouble staring down any of his men questioning his authority on these matters.

Still, he'd worked to keep Yemerik's secret as quiet as possible. Hollik wanted the people of the south divided, and even a rumor he traveled with such a man would give the desperate people cause to gather. He felt relatively comfortable that he could defeat them all if necessary, but he wanted as large an army as possible before his enemies were unified. He wanted to conquer the world and create an empire that would be remembered until the end of time; taking risks was foolish.

"The Grulti aren't here," Hollik said. "Pinfoll swore his support."

"He'll be good to his word," Brimire said.

"I'm not so sure," Drista said. She stood between Hollik and Brimire, a blatant gesture. Drista's was a brilliant strategic mind, though she'd always lacked subtlety.

Jusl approached but did not kneel beside Hollik. "Does it matter? You are stronger than any who have ever marched over these plains, with or without him."

"It matters to me," Hollik replied. "If he does not honor our agreement, he is without honor. And, when I've taken the south and east, I will return and finish him."

"He may be ruler of the north by then. When you're gone, he may take your own land from you. It may prove difficult to take back."

"I claimed the north once," Hollik said. "I can do it again if I must."

"We could send a messenger," Brimire offered.

"I won't remind Pinfoll of his word," Hollik said. "A man who can't recall his oath is as bad as one who swears falsely." He turned to Yemerik, who almost seemed bored. "What of it?" he demanded of the seer. "Can you predict what he'll do?"

Yemerik sighed. "I can only tell the weather. And even for that, I'll need to travel the plains for a few hours."

"Then go and find out. Stay near, though. If you run into trouble, scream for help." He snorted, certain the small man wouldn't perceive his words as the insult they truly were.

True to form, Yemerik smiled, nodded, and hurried off.

"It's the totem, right?" Jusl asked.

"I could kill him," Drista suggested. "I'm reasonably sure any magic he could learn, I can quickly master."

"No," Hollik said, forcefully. "If his power becomes more than rumor, there will be calls for his head. Giving in might placate the eastern villages."

"And deprive us of an advantage," Brimire pointed out.

"I like keeping options open. Besides, we don't need him,"

Hollik said, before adding under his breath, "Though he is useful."
He looked up at the sky. Cloudy but dry, just as Yemerik had said.
Knowing when to move men and when to order them to set camp
had cut sickness and fatigue to a fraction of what he had expected.
With Yemerik's council, Hollik could ensure scouting parties were
always hidden by fog. And these were trifles compared with what
he'd be able to accomplish once the fighting began. The very weather
was his ally; he could count on the sun to break free and blind his
foe or for the rain to muddy the field. He was growing reliant on the
strange foreigner, an idea which injured his pride. But even so, it was
true.

8

Theojin was silent. Several days had passed since he'd returned
from his hunt, and he'd been out every night. He sat with his
morning bread and meat, and picked at them slowly.

Alaji sat cross-legged beside him. "What's Arahm making you
do?"

Theojin shrugged and kept at his food. "I'm not supposed to
say." He chewed on a charred piece of meat, then spit it out into the
fire. "I was in the fields," he said. "I followed them past the hills."

"What were they doing?"

"They were spying. I mean, they must have been. I didn't see
them until they were past the mark, but there's nothing else they
could have been up to. After that, they just continued back until they
approached their camp. I dropped off after that. Then…." He
stopped talking. "I shouldn't be telling you any of this, so just forget
it."

Alaji just sat still and waited.

"I shouldn't tell anyone. I didn't even tell Arahm."

"You didn't tell him about the spies?"

"Of course I told him about the spies. But I didn't tell him everything. There was… a woman… in the field. An old woman in the field."

—

He wasn't sure where she'd come from. Theojin could have sworn he was alone one moment, then when he turned back, she was there. The crone in a black dress, walking across the plain with the help of a staff in the dark of night. There was just a sliver of moon in the sky and even that was veiled by thin clouds. But she looked at him as if she'd expected him.

She hadn't been worried, or at least hadn't seemed it, and she moved with strong strides. There was something strange about the clothes she wore: the fabric didn't hang right, like it was too light or thin to be real. She wore strange jewelry, and there was a feather woven in her hair. He'd never seen anyone but children do anything like that, even among the northmen.

Theojin went for his knife without thinking and held it raised in his hand. She laughed and ceased her approach.

"Are you to kill me? An old woman in a strange land, unarmed and without provocation?"

"Who are you?" Theojin demanded. Quickly, he stole glances behind him and to each side. He expected there to be others lying in wait, but he could find no trap.

"I wasn't planning to harm you, if that's what scares you. I was merely out walking the plain and desired some company when I saw you."

"Where are they? Where are the others?"

"The northmen planning an ambush? There aren't any, I'm afraid. At least not tonight. So if you're planning to kill anyone, it will have to be me."

"I don't kill women," he replied. "Not unless I have to."

She laughed again. "Then I've little to fear, unless you consider me threatening." She set down her pack in front of her and began rustling through it. After a moment, she dug out a wine skin and drank. She offered it to Theojin, who approached and took it carefully.

"This is amazing," he said, after a gulp.

"It's a drink from the north. They call it Verow's Brew," the crone told him. "It's named after a flower."

"I didn't know flowers bloomed there at all."

She grinned. "Flowers grow all over."

He tried to return the wine, but she refused. "I'd like to give you something and have nothing else that seems appropriate. Keep it."

"I'm no thief," Theojin protested. "You startled me. Otherwise, I wouldn't have drawn the knife."

"I know," the crone said. "You're a spy, not a thief. But even so, I'd like you to have the wine as a gift."

"Thank you. But… I'm not a spy, either. I was only–"

"I understand the games men play. It doesn't matter what you are. You've given me a few moments to speak with someone. And don't worry. I've no intention of telling Hollik or anyone else about meeting you here. Besides, he knows his men are being watched. He's playing a shrewder game."

"He wants this land, doesn't he?"

"He does. The land and the allegiance of its people."

"He can't have it. We'll drive him out."

"You may," the crone said. "Though, if I told you it would be better for you to lay down your weapons, would you?"

"The lakes have been free for five hands' generations. We will bow to no oppressor."

"I thought as much." The old woman spoke in a whisper and looked at the ground. She retrieved her pack and added, "Thank you for a few moments' company." She nodded once. "Goodbye, Theojin of the Lakes. It was well making your acquaintance." With that, she started away, leaning on her walking stick.

—

Alaji listened intently. The instant he'd finished his tale, she asked, "Did you finish the wine?"

Theojin sighed and dug through his belongings. He handed over the skin. His sister took a sip and handed it back. "It's good," she said. "I had no idea the north was good for anything but ice and horses."

"Yeah. Well, I guess there's something good in everything," he said, before heading in for bed.

9

"Don't eat those," Brimire said. "They'd kill you."

Yemerik looked up at Brimire, as if he might be joking. Then, with a shrug, he tossed the mushroom he'd picked to the side. His attention wandered back to the ground, which seemed to fascinate him to no end.

Drista shot Brimire a stern look, as if demanding to know why he'd spoken up. Brimire, in turn, looked to Hollik, perhaps hoping for some vindication, but his lord seemed as irritated as Drista. Not that Hollik had relented in refusing the many offers he'd had to rid their company of the troubling seer.

The sky was turning dark; the red was all but gone. There were clouds blocking the moon but a dry bite to the air, all as Yemerik had predicted. Soon it would be pitch black.

"I do not like it," Jusl said.

"You liked the solitude well enough in the hills by Heyvin," Hollik said. "Just as many wanted our throats then as now."

"But that was only personal. These people think they have a cause."

"If they'd any sense, they'd join us," Kilfa said. "A new era is dawning."

Yemerik chuckled, then transitioned into a forced cough, as though it would cover the outburst. He was poking at a spider with a reed now.

Drista locked eyes with Hollik and motioned towards her knife. Her eyes pled for the chance. But Hollik just sighed and raised his hand. Restrained, she crept back and sat on the ground. She drew her knife and began using it to clean her fingernails instead. Occasionally, she'd gaze at Yemerik and her grip would tighten on the hilt.

"No one's around," Jusl said, watching the horizon. "At least no one I can see."

"Then this is the perfect chance to murder me and blame the wolves," Hollik replied. "The easiest army ever claimed."

"They'd never believe it," Brimire said. "The wolves in the north, maybe. But here, they're like pups."

Hollik broke a smile, which was rare for the warlord. "Then I suppose we can speak freely," he said. "Have we scouted the grove west of the bend?"

"We could hide a third our men there. We couldn't move them onto the field, though, not without them being seen."

"Heavy fog in the morning," Yemerik spoke up. "It'll drown out everything from the crevice to the hills. At least for the next three days."

"If he's wrong…." Drista hissed.

Hollik nodded silently. Part of him hoped the seer would be wrong, that the battle would prove costly and they'd win by sweat and blood and force, the way he'd intended to take the land. If that happened, he'd leave Yemerik's body to the birds, along with the rest of the dead. But he knew better. Whatever the source, the seer's predictions were perfect. Which begged the question, which of the two men would truly be responsible for the coming victories? Who was really fated to conquer the world?

His musings were broken by a hand placed on his arm. It was Jusl, the tracker, who didn't need to say anything or even look at him: the hand was enough.

Hollik tilted his head back and looked up at the sky. "How many," he whispered under his breath. The others seemed to lose interest, though with the exception of Yemerik, they reached for weapons. Yemerik, completely oblivious, simply continued agitating the spider.

"Just one," Jusl said softly. He pointed up into the sky at a star overhead. Whoever was out there would be in the opposite direction. "He's out a stretch. Must have been there the entire time, hiding in the grass. Won't take a moment."

"Press him toward the camp," Hollik said.

"Could be an assassin," Jusl said.

"I hope it is," Hollik replied, grinning. Then, loudly, he said, "Drista. A fire!" Jusl stretched and started away, staggering, as if drunk or tired.

"Make it yourself." Drista said. "I don't share your bed."

"Dog!" Kilfa screamed, pulling a knife. She swung it upward, stopping a foot from Drista's face. Just as fast, Drista leapt off the ground with a handful of long grass, which burst into flames with a move of her wrist.

The two women pretended to struggle, while the remaining men gathered around. Once again, the exception was Yemerik, who leapt away, startled and confused.

The show went on, while Jusl left the clearing and began circling around. By the time the two women were lighting fire to a dead bush, he was nearly standing over the spy.

What happened then happened quickly. The spy either heard Jusl coming or saw through the ruse. He leapt to his feet, and the women fell into line, standing together in front of Hollik with weapons drawn.

The spy, to his credit, did not break to either side and make Jusl chase him down, which the tracker could easily have done. Instead, he ran forward with his knife in hand and his gaze locked on Hollik.

He never came close. From the left, Brimire caught his arm with one hand and stuck him in the side with the other. The spy coughed once and collapsed. He screamed in pain, while Brimire wiped his knife clean. In a moment, the others were around him, save Yemerik who was staring on in stunned silence.

Hollik pushed his way past Drista and Kilfa, who didn't try to stop him. "Damn it," he said to Brimire. "He couldn't have heard a thing from back there."

The butcher didn't reply, but instead looked down at the spy. He was really only a boy.

Hollik had started to kneel when Jusl reached them. "Wait," the tracker said. "He still has his knife."

"And if he can find the strength to overtake me with it, I say he deserves his prize," Hollik answered, his voice rising. "I was once thought capable of defending myself," he added, his voice somewhat softer. He placed a hand on the shoulder of the spy. "You showed courage. And I don't have many men who could have hidden from my best tracker so long."

The spy looked back confused, hurt, and frightened. His hands gripped his side, but he could do little to slow the flow of blood. He was still clutching his knife, and he started, as if to use it. But the instant his hand left his side, the pain increased, and he whimpered. The weapon dropped from his grip and landed beside him, and he grabbed at his wound once more.

"My arts could save him. If you're really sure he heard nothing," Kilfa said.

Hollik considered the offer for a moment, and he looked the boy in the eye when he answered. "No. He knows who I am, and he knows what we were discussing was worth more than his life. That's too much." Then he added, "I am sorry, though. Courage is rare in this life."

The boy tried to speak, though none of them could make his

words or even their tone. Whether they were threats, a plea for life, or a message for his family, they were lost on the field.

"Take his pack, knife, and boots," Hollik said, standing. "Try not to disturb him more than you need to." Within moments, they were gone.

10

When she saw Arahm approaching early in the morning, Alaji knew what had happened. She'd imagined it often enough, when her brother was out at night. She abandoned her chores and went to meet Arahm, before he could call out to her father, who was still in bed.

"Alaji," Arahm said, softly. "This morning, on the plain—"

"Was his body defiled?" She locked eyes with the old man.

Arahm stared at her for a moment, unable to respond. This was a man's question, not a woman's, and certainly not a girl's. "No," he said, after a moment. "They stole from him, but that is all."

"The northmen are thieves. What will we do?"

"We've sent word to their leaders. We're demanding they answer for the crime," Arahm said.

"Will we strike back?"

He paused to consider his answer. Under normal circumstances, he'd never discuss such things with a girl. But then he'd never thought a girl would demand such answers. "We need to consider if that's what they want. If they want to be met on the field while they are still strong, before the seasons change and they run low on food. I'm sorry, but we must wait until the time is right. But I do not think it will be long now. Now, I must speak with your father."

Alaji nodded. "Yes. Go tell him his son has been murdered by

Hollik's men." She walked past the old man and started towards the tree line. "And tell him his daughter has run off, distraught."

—

She was sick to her stomach and thought she'd throw up. Whatever strength she'd displayed in front of the elder abandoned her as soon as she was out of sight, and she fell to the ground weeping. She thought of her brother and wondered if he'd suffered. She thought about his fear and what his last moments must have been like.

Her tears did not last nearly as long as she expected. Soon, she wasn't even thinking of her brother; her thoughts instead turned to Hollik. "I'll burn you," she whispered, but she knew at once she'd never be able to do it. The warlord had guards who'd be ready for anything she could do.

Almost anything.

They'd be ready for the magic of a woman, as they'd be ready for that of a man. And of course they'd be prepared for a battle of arms, which she had little knowledge of, anyway. But what of the magic of the gods?

It would mean her death. Hollik's men would no doubt avenge his death. Even if they did not, her own neighbors – possibly her own family – would execute her once they learned her secret.

But her brother was dead, and the world may not be far behind. And something else: there were said to be signs in the last days of the world. Perhaps the magic of the gods being brought against the tyrant was the last sign. Perhaps she hadn't learned this magic by accident, after all.

Alaji wandered deep in the woods. She considered going back to the caverns, where she'd be safer, but she no longer cared for her safety. Instead she found an empty grove where the trees were thick.

Her heart was beating quickly. She focused her attention and forced herself to calm down. She shut her eyes and she began her count. Her heart beat once, and she stepped forward.

Two… three… four….

She stepped back in time to two and said, "Open your eyes." She remembered the words as she spoke them, just as she now remembered looking as she counted and seeing herself standing there. She spun around and looked herself in the eye until her double vanished. Her head hurt, as she tried to sort out what had happened, but she did not try too hard. The details did not matter, nor the order of events or the implications. What mattered was that she could step back and make changes.

Her head hurt, but she shook it off. She had another test to perform. Alaji drew her cooking knife from her apron and clenched it in one hand. Then she lifted a leaf up from the ground. She stood before a tree and released it as far overhead as she could reach, stepping away as she did so.

One; the leaf drifted down. Two; it floated right before the tree – she locked her eyes on this point. Three; it spun and fluttered to one side. Four; it dropped to the ground.

Five: she lunged forward, stabbing with her knife as she stepped back to two.

The knife's tip bit into the tree bark, impaling the center of the leaf. It played out differently now; she'd seen the leaf falling, then she'd watched her double appear in front of her and stab it, before stabbing it herself.

It was painful to think about, and it didn't make sense to her, not completely. But she didn't care, because whatever it meant to her memory, the leaf hadn't reached the ground. What she did had consequences. And that would hold no differently for a man's heart than a leaf.

11

"Your father suggested killing you," Alaji's mother said, in a matter-of-fact voice she'd used as long as her daughter could remember to discuss chores or household decisions. She did, however, look up to see how Alaji reacted to the news, before looking back to the roots she was washing. "It is because he loves you," she went on, still in the same conversational tone. "With what's coming, he thought it would be easier for you to escape the last battle, and it would certainly ensure you were never taken by the northmen."

"Where is he?" Alaji asked, trying to match her mother's demeanor. The conversation had begun as soon as she'd walked through the door, without so much as a greeting.

"He's gone to trade," her mother went on. "And, so you don't worry, I talked him out of it. Not even Arahm can say with certainty that the last day is close. Besides, there will likely be some warning, some time to act, if more drastic measures are called for. Would you like something to eat?"

"No," Alaji replied, shaking her head faster than she'd intended. "I'm not hungry."

"That's foolish. You're going to want your strength, no matter how things turn. Theojin's death doesn't change...." It was instantaneous: one moment she was speaking, still in her constant, forceful way, and then she was in tears. The bowl she'd been using to wash the roots tipped, and water splashed across the dirt floor, which turned to a dark smear of mud.

Shaji's fingers clawed against her face, covering her mouth. The mud reached her knees, dirtying her skirts, but she didn't move until Alaji reached her side and took her arm. Slowly, she helped her mother up. "It will be okay," she whispered, though she knew better.

"Your father... stay away from him," Shaji said, gasping. "I don't think he would ever... but please. Avoid him when you can. And... if he ever looks at you oddly, think of an excuse. Run if you have to."

"It will be all right," Alaji said again.

"He does love you," her mother said. "He loves you so much. That's why I'm afraid. He's scared of what they'd do to you. The world is no longer the place it once was. It's not safe any longer. I used to think this business was all games, this thing with the fifth-by-fifth generation. It seemed like something the men said to test each other. But things are happening now, Alaji. And I think it's really the end."

Shaji regained her balance and wiped her eyes with a clean patch of her apron. She shut her eyes and slowed her breathing. "I am going to clean up," she said, opening her eyes. They were still bloodshot, but they'd regained their focus.

"I'll help," Alaji said.

"No. I want you to stay out tonight. Stay with Mil. If her father tries to refuse, tell him you can't bear to stay in this house. Tell him it reminds you too much of your brother. Can you pretend to cry?"

"I... I wouldn't have to pretend," Alaji said.

Her mother nodded. "Good. I'll come for you when things are safe." She placed a hand on Alaji's shoulder and squeezed tightly. It hurt, but Alaji felt better all the same.

12

Kuljin did not cry, because crying was something men did not do. Nor did he display emotion while he walked with Arahm. It was late in the day and the sun shone down on them while they traversed the plain.

"Did you tell your wife of this?" Arahm asked.

"I told her I was going to barter for meat," Kuljin responded. "If she knew otherwise, she'd have demanded she accompany us. Women can be difficult," he concluded.

"Yours more than most," Arahm added. When Kuljin sneered at him, Arahm added, "It was not a criticism. Your daughter is strong. If it weren't for the way of things, I would take her as a soldier. And her mother, even more so. There are men who fear her when she's angry. Proud men, even."

"Women aren't supposed to be like that," Kuljin said.

"Heh. With what's coming, I'd rather more were. If the gods wanted them otherwise, they shouldn't have sent such times." They said no more until they reached the encampment of the northmen, where they were greeted by a man of medium build wearing clean clothes. There were other guards around as well, but the well-dressed northman barked orders, and they left the lakemen alone.

"Hello. I am Telmik." He offered a hand to Kuljin, who took it with little enthusiasm. "Are you the fallen warrior's father?"

"I am," Kuljin replied, sharply.

"I am sorry to hear of your misfortune, as is my lord. Hollik would like to speak with you, but I'll need you to leave your weapons here."

"We carry no weapons," Arahm said. "Unless you think this a match for your lord." He pulled a decorative knife from the back of his sash.

"It is our way," Telmik explained, taking the blade. Kuljin offered up a similar one. "Thank you. I'll take you to Hollik now, if you'll allow me."

They made their way through the encampment. No one interfered, though it seemed as though there were always a few northmen keeping an eye on them.

They reached Hollik's tent quickly. It was guarded by a large man holding a spear. He exchanged a few quick words with Telmik then ducked into the tent. He returned a moment later and held the flap open.

"This way, please," Telmik said, leading them inside.

Hollik was sitting beside two of his men. Kuljin recognized all three from times he'd seen them in town, always at Hollik's side, but he did not know their names.

"This is Kuljin," Telmik said, motioning to him. "Arahm, we know."

"These men are here by my oath of fire and friendship," Hollik replied. "Make it known." Telmik nodded once, and backed out of the opening. Hollik addressed Kuljin once more. "Are you familiar with our oath?"

"Arahm told me we'd be safe."

"If any harm you without provocation, they will be put to the fire, along with a finger off my hand. This is not taken lightly by my people. They would hold me to my word, if no one else could." He held up his hands to demonstrate they were whole. "As you can see, no man under my rule has ever tested my honor.

"I have been told your son's body was found this morning on the plain," Hollik continued. "For what it is worth, I am sorry for your loss."

Kuljin sat still and remained silent. It fell to Arahm to respond: "The boy had possessions missing." He cleared his throat and waited for a response.

"You think his killer is in my camp?" Hollik asked.

"He's here," Kuljin said flatly.

"It is likely," Hollik admitted. "If you can describe what's missing, I'll send some of my men to look for the possessions. And, with luck, whoever is responsible. You are welcome to search yourself, but my people would be more discreet. If the man you're seeking were to see you first, you may never find him. "

Arahm nodded, and Kuljin described his son's knife and pack. Hollik motioned to one of his guards, who stepped out to order other men to attend to the work. When he returned, he brought a skin of bitter, northern beer, which the lakemen declined.

"We have some of your drink, if you'd rather," Hollik offered, but neither accepted. "It could be a while before we hear anything. If we have anything that would make you comfortable, just ask. I can have food brought. Women, if you'd like company." Once again, Arahm and Kuljin turned him down.

Hollik made polite discussion about the weather and the seasons, and he asked about his guests' lives. He limited his questions to the village's festivals, celebrations, and history, and stayed far from any subject touching on defenses or arms.

Finally, Kuljin grew irritated. "What will happen when this man is found?" he demanded.

"If your son's killer is found here – if a man is found with your son's possessions who can't account for their acquisition…." Hollik considered this for a moment. "It depends on who the man is, I suppose. I won't lie to you: there are men here who I have traveled with for years. There are some men I would not give to you, but I do not believe these men are capable of such action. If it is any but a handful of my men, though, and I am satisfied by the proof, their life will be yours. Otherwise, we will need to find some other recompense."

"There is nothing you have worth what I've lost."

"I know this. But I will not offer my word when I cannot account for the consequences." This was the last Hollik spoke on the subject, before returning to other topics, of his homeland and his hopes that their two people would one day know each other as brothers. As before, Kuljin and Arahm listened in silence.

Before the sun set, one of Hollik's guards returned and whispered into his ear. They traded quick words, then Hollik rose. "I believe we have found what we were looking for."

Together, they walked to the outskirts of the camp, where a man was bound to a standing log and surrounded by guards. Beside him was Theojin's pack; on his feet were his boots. One of the guards handed Hollik the knife Theojin had been carrying.

Hollik looked the man over. "He is one of the Urvim, from the far north and west. A number of their tribe came to us at the start of the season, and we took them on. They are unfamiliar with your tongue, but I can translate if you have any questions. First, though. Will you examine the pack? Please be sure it's what you're seeking."

Kuljin pulled open the pack and glanced through. "I know these things. I'm certain."

Hollik exchanged terse words with the bound man in a lyrical language neither Arahm nor Kuljin were familiar with. "He says he traded for these two nights ago with an old man in the south. Is it possible your son no longer had possession of the pack last night?"

"I saw him leave with it on," Kuljin replied.

"Then I am satisfied," Hollik said. He walked over to Kuljin and handed him the knife, much to his guards' consternation.

Kuljin gripped the handle and looked into the eyes of the warlord. It was obvious what thoughts were going through his head. But he did not act, and almost immediately Hollik had stepped away.

Hollik gestured at the prisoner. "This man does not own much, but I will have it brought here. What you can carry back is yours. Leave the rest on the ground beside his body. Is there anything else you'd like me to ask him?"

"No," Kuljin replied, testing the knife's point with his thumb.

"For what it's worth, I am sorry." With that, Hollik and his men started away.

The Urvim fell to his knees and spoke quickly, though of course neither man could understand him. He held his hands open, made numerous gestures of friendship and pleas for pity, and even began to cry.

"Do you really think he killed Theojin?" Kuljin asked.

Arahm sighed. "No. It is too convenient. A mercenary from

some far off land? He was given these things or they were forced upon him. They chose him because he couldn't tell us more. And, no doubt, because they can do without him."

"Why bother?" Kuljin asked. "Why not toss the pack and boots into a ravine?"

"They want us satisfied. They want us to think them honorable. I need to think on this more. What of him?" Arahm pointed to the bound man, who'd backed away to the edge of his rope. His hands, tied together, were connected to the line tethering him to the pole. He pulled it taut, as if it might break.

"He's still one of the northmen," Kuljin replied, brandishing the knife and closing in. "He's still one of them."

13

Yemerik was wandering the plain when Jusl called out to him, "Hollik wants you back in camp!"

"How did you find me out here?" Yemerik asked, good-naturedly. He started towards the tracker, who just looked him over slowly.

"Hollik wants you back now," Jusl said.

"I see," Yemerik replied. "Secrets of the trade, I suppose." He smiled and seemed pleased with himself. "We shouldn't keep our master waiting, then."

Jusl paused, baffled by the man's behavior. The night before, Yemerik seemed ready to piss himself; now this. He wondered briefly what the next night would bring to the seer, if that was even what Yemerik was. "It's… no. It's THAT way."

Before long, they were once again with the rest of Hollik's war council, which hadn't waited. They met in a tent which had been dragged out of earshot of the rest of the camp. The group was sitting in a circle, with a small fire burning in the center. There was little smoke, thanks to Drista's knowledge of dried plants. What little there was drifted up through a hole in the top of the tent.

"Won't this pacify the lake-men?" Brimire asked. "We need them on the plains if this is to work."

Drista snickered. "Not even fish-chewers would believe the Urvim murdered their boy without leave."

Hollik slammed his fist against the ground and turned on his aunt. "Don't insult them!" he bellowed. Drista was cowed at once by the outburst, and she slunk back. Hollik regained his composure. His voice lowered and his tone became more forgiving. "The man who left here lost his son because we were rash." Now it was Brimire who deflated. Hollik saw the reaction and gestured to his friend that he wasn't angry. "We will not become what these people think we are. We won't flinch when the time comes to take their lives, but we'll leave them their honor. Is that understood?"

No one spoke for a moment. Finally, Drista nodded and said, "You will be a great ruler, when this is over." Her tone was different now, its edge gone. She wasn't looking for some advantage, nor was she competing with the other advisors. There had been a time long ago when she always spoke to him like this, but that was before she had a taste of power.

Hollik leaned in, and the others did the same. "Drista is right that the lakemen won't accept the justice offered them. But more than that, they'll infer weakness from our deceit. If we had dismissed them with nothing, they'd have been angry but scared. But now, they'll be looking for an opening. Tomorrow, we'll show it to them. On the following day, the men of the lakes will make war on us, and we'll wipe them out with minimal losses." He turned to Yemerik and glared into his eyes. "That morning – fog."

"Oh, yes. No question about it."

"You are to stay with Brimire until then," Hollik told him. "You know a great deal now, and I would not want those secrets reaching our enemies."

Brimire grinned – while Yemerik might miss it, he'd just been given permission to kill the seer if the choice came between that and having him fall in the hands of the Lake Folk. He knew it was unlikely such an opportunity would arise, but it seemed a step in the right direction.

14

"Tell him what you told me," Arahm said to Guljir, the brewer. He motioned to Kuljin, who waited quietly. The three men sat together in Guljir's small shop, which was otherwise empty. A few of Arahm's men stood watch out of earshot, with orders to come running if anyone approached. "Tell him what you heard."

"Some of the northmen have a tongue for my beer, even if they can't drink it right," Guljir said. "They've been coming here since the army arrived. Since it started, I've been reporting back to Arahm, but there hasn't been much to report. Until now. This morning, they came in looking agitated. So I tell them a drink's on me. Then a second. Pretty soon, I've got them talking. Seems there's trouble in Hollik's camp. Some of his men, some Urmim—"

"Urvim," Arahm corrected him.

"Yeah, that was it. Urvim. Guess they're a tribe or something. They're leaving, and demanding their pay. I don't know what's got them upset, but it's serious. There's talk of fights and threats. The men in here were ready to leave for the north themselves. Every one of them."

Arahm laughed and patted Kuljin's shoulder. "You cut them deeply last night, and that wound may prove Hollik's downfall. The first blow in a war."

Kuljin was not laughing. "It was the second blow."

Arahm's mood grew somber to match Kuljin's. "Of course. Of course they started it. But Theojin's death will not be in vain."

"Could the men have been lying?" Kuljin asked.

Arahm shook his head. "It aligns with what our spies report. A lot of activity, screaming, and groups of men leaving. If this keeps up, a third of Hollik's force will have abandoned him by nightfall."

"That's not enough," Kuljin said.

"Not for us alone," Arahm admitted with a smile. He leaned closer to Kuljin and Guljir. "What I say next cannot leave this room. Yelmin is sending its sons. They arrive tonight, by Black Lake. Tomorrow, we force the northmen from the plains. And we take Hollik's head."

"Why would Yelmin help us?"

"Your son is to thank. Theojin discovered Hollik was selling weapons to the goblins, weapons used on our people. And Yelmin's."

"No goblins have been sighted north of the hills," Kuljin replied. "And how could Hollik's men have found them in the south without being seen?"

"There is much we don't know, but Theojin found a northern blade in their possession. And warriors in Yelmin recently uncovered a great deal more." Arahm's voice was strained, and his tone made it clear that Kuljin was not to delve any further into such questions.

Kuljin nodded. "Then we will attack. And the war will begin."

"It will begin and end in one stroke," Arahm said. "If the gods will it."

"If the gods will it," Kuljin echoed with a sigh. The words were hollow, and he wondered what had happened to his leader. This was a man full of hope. But what hope was there? What future?

Arahm had forgotten the signs. He'd lost sight of the simple truth: five by five generations had passed. There was no hope for the lakes. There was no hope for anything. The time of the world had been spent, and the magic of the gods would soon be unleashed.

Whatever traps Arahm set or whatever traps he fell into – it made no difference. This would end with neither freedom nor conquest of the world. It would end in death.

Just as it began.

—

Mil's parents lived halfway between Alaji's family and Red Lake. Their hut was one of ten in Ashentril Field. The land offered little to look at, but it was among the most fertile around the lakes. They'd welcomed Alaji in without question. Their son, Ejick, was off running errands for Arahm, so there was plenty of room for a guest. Besides, in these dark times, any family counting a young warrior among its number had reason to set a precedent – who knew what help they would need in the days ahead?

For her part, Mil fawned over her friend. After a few hours of Mil crying over Theojin's death, Alaji was so sick of the sound, she discovered she was unable to weep herself. This was good, she decided, as she'd already reached the conclusion that sorrow was utterly worthless in the pursuit of revenge.

Ejick came home briefly in the afternoon carrying news. His expression shifted quickly. One moment, he seemed somber; another, eager. He spoke in private with his parents first, then approached Alaji. Without a word, he took her in his arms, hugged her, and kissed her forehead. "We're burying Theojin this evening," he said, after drawing a deep breath. "He'll be remembered. Arahm said we'd hold to the old ways."

The old ways. Men were buried by men and women by women, and neither were supposed to intrude. It was only tradition, not law, and seldom enforced. But the northmen lacked any such custom, and not behaving like the northmen had become justification in and of itself. The proclamation angered her, but only for a moment. Seeing her brother's body would only upset her more. She had to be focused for what was coming.

"If there's anything you'd like said over his grave… I'll say it," Ejick continued. "Your brother will be remembered," he promised her. "And when this is over, you and I…." Much to Alaji's relief, he never finished this sentence, but rather trailed off and gazed deeply into her eyes. Alaji forced herself to smile quickly, which pleased him to no end.

She felt as though she ought to feel bad for the boy, but she could not manage to dredge up even a shred of pity in her stomach. Whether the world ended or things returned to normal, she knew what he did not: that she would not live long enough to answer whatever question waited on his lips.

It was almost just as well: she'd never cared much for Ejick.

After he left, Mil took Alaji aside. "Something's happening," she explained. "My brother brought orders from Arahm." She spoke the name with pride, as though their leader's commands were rare and it was an honor for Ejick to carry them. "My mother and I were called to the caverns tonight. I think everyone's supposed to go. At least any woman without child."

"Then it's starting. The war."

Mil nodded. "Arahm didn't say why, but… what else could it be? I asked my parents, and they said you wouldn't have to go. If you don't want to. After what happened yesterday, your family's given enough."

"I'm going," Alaji said bluntly. "After what they did to Theojin…."

Mil grabbed Alaji and hugged her, just as her brother had. "Thank you. I'm so scared. Ejick will be out there fighting. They're going to need us to tend the wounded."

"Of course," Alaji agreed.

———

Getting away from Mil, even for a moment, proved extremely difficult. But eventually Alaji managed. It was almost dark when she walked through the woods, alone at last. She found a small, enclosed circle of trees north of the farms and knelt in the center. She'd intended to practice her magic, but she couldn't find the energy. She was exhausted, and soon she'd need to leave with Mil's family to meet with the other women sent to heal the injured and morn the dying.

But she knew she wouldn't be there long. She knew she'd break away somehow and make her way to the fighting. Or perhaps the fighting would come to her. She'd find her way to the field, and she would die there or find what she sought.

She smiled, because she knew she wouldn't die, not at first anyway. She understood. She opened her hand and pressed her spread fingers against the ground, and she whispered the prayer of her people, "I know the count, and I know the way. I fear the five, and I obey.

"You should be able to hear me now. I… I have something of yours. It might be something you gave to me, or it might be something I stole. But I don't think that matters, because it's mine for now. I think this is how it's supposed to happen, that I was meant to unleash your magic onto the world against Hollik. If so, then I have nothing to say beyond, 'thank you.' If this isn't part of your plan, though, please let me kill him anyway. After that, I don't care what happens to me. I know I'll have to die, and I'm not sure the world will get to go on, either. But none of that matters now. All that's important is that I get this. Justice for my brother and my people. And maybe for the world."

She lifted her hand from the ground and slowly stood, brushing the pine needles and dirt off her skirt. She left the clearing feeling better. She was focused now, and everything seemed clear.

15

The sun's light brightened the air, though the sun itself could not be seen through the thick mist, nor could the sky or anything else beyond the tall grass the warriors crept through, armed with axes, spears, and bows. The men of three villages went together; Yelmin had succeeded in enlisting the aid of her neighbor to the south. The hillfolk of Jalin had, at long last, concluded Hollik's army posed a danger to them as well, so they marched with the western and eastern lakemen.

Arahm led them through the fields towards the camp of their enemy, and with a force this large, he'd little doubt they'd finish the northmen. He'd played out various scenarios in his head, as to what they should do with prisoners: set them free in a sign of good faith, force them to work for five seasons to atone for their crimes, or simply execute them on the spot. He'd made no final decisions, of course, as a wise leader must leave room to capitalize on an opportunity. If they lost many men, for example, it would be prudent to enlist some of the northmen, and perhaps eventually absorb them into the community. On the other hand, if casualties were low, there could be merit in setting an example as to the fate of invaders – after all, it could serve a reminder to Yelmin and Jalin, in case either thought of trying to succeed where Hollik had failed.

Despite Arahm's best efforts to get him to stay behind, Kuljin had insisted on coming, as well. His presence was ultimately a distraction and he presented a risk: men bent on vengeance had a tendency of calling attention to themselves – and to those they traveled with. Fortunately, Kuljin didn't seem especially bloodthirsty any longer, though there was no telling what feelings might overtake him once the fighting began. If it came to it, Arahm would send him off to die. It would be a pity, though: he'd grown accustomed to his company.

"It's hard to see," Kuljin whispered.

"The gods be praised," Arahm replied. "They won't see us until we're upon them. With luck, some will still be asleep. This war will be over as soon as it begins."

Kuljin grunted in response. The sound had the makings of an affirmation, but there was clearly little weight behind it.

"We're almost to their camp," Arahm said, motioning for the men to hold their ground until more could join them. They had plenty of advantages, but there was little need to push their luck.

"We should have come across a scout by now, at the very least," Kuljin said.

Arahm shrugged. "There'll be plenty to draw the archers' attention when we reach the camp," he chuckled. But he looked out at the edge of the mist and squinted. Kuljin had a point: this was easier than he'd expected. But then again, the northmen had lost a sizable portion of their troops the day before – it wasn't so surprising there'd be mistakes in assigning guards. Or perhaps guards had been assigned and they'd simply abandoned their posts. Hollik's army was falling apart. Still, it was troubling.

He motioned for the men in front to continue, and he kept a close eye. Before, he'd been dreading their first confrontation, as it would risk their surprise. But now, he desperately yearned for the first snap of a bowstring and the assurance it would provide.

When they reached the edge of the camp – still without incident – he felt a chill overtake him. The mist prevented him from seeing more than the first few tents. He peered in, but could see nothing – no men moving around, no women cleaning the carcasses of rabbits; nothing. It was still and quiet.

He looked to Kuljin, who simply stared back with a blank intensity. At last, Arahm truly understood him: this wasn't anger or fear or hatred. It was acceptance. Kuljin had never hoped for this to go as planned, never hoped they would catch Hollik unawares and slit his throat, because such hope would have been absurd, perhaps even blasphemous. What happened here was meant to happen.

For months now, Arahm had professed those same views, though his actual beliefs had wavered. Now, he truly wondered. Had he days to think on it, he may have been able to reach some philosophical conclusion regarding the will of the gods and the meaning of fate. But as it was, he decided to simply put it to the test.

With a wave of his arm, he ordered the men onward, to – hopefully – find their foes drunk and slaughter them in their sleep.

He hoped they would. But he was not in the least surprised when he saw the first wave of his troops barge into those tents, only to fall back screaming as the enemy poured out. Nor was he surprised to hear a dozen horns bellow almost in unison, to be answered from the west.

16

Alaji waited with dozens of other women, as well as a handful of men serving as guards. She eyed these men carefully, taking note of their number and placement. It was already clear their protectors were of two types: young men too small and weak to be of much use in a fight, and old veterans who could handle themselves but would have slowed the army down. From the perspective of someone planning to desert her post, the mixture was ideal.

The women, on the other hand, could be more trouble. They stood ready, eyes surveying the field below. They were stationed on this hill to offer medical support to wounded soldiers. To either side, Alaji could see similar gatherings on the neighboring hills, protruding from the expanse of mist.

Each group had brought firewood. For the moment, it remained unlit to conceal their presence. When the battle started, the fires would be set to guide the wounded to help. If an enemy soldier made it this far and got past the guards, he'd find the wives and daughters of the lakes armed and would likely find them no more merciful than the men. Indeed, he may find them decidedly less so.

Alaji looked to either side and wondered if Shaji was on one of the neighboring hills. Her mother hadn't been at the gathering by the caves, though that was hardly surprising. She didn't know what to hope for. That her mother would die quickly if the world ended or find some peace if it didn't.

Alaji was lost in thought when she heard the horns blow in the distance. Everyone on the hill froze, their attention now focused on the patch of fog that must be concealing the battle.

"What does it mean?" Mil asked. Until then, Alaji had forgotten she was there.

"It means it's starting," Alaji said. As inconspicuously as she could, Alaji picked up her small pack holding her water skin and knife. There'd been nothing else she'd imagined needing.

Mil didn't seem to notice anything strange about her friend's action. "But… did they reach them in secret? Or was it a scout? What's happening?"

Alaji shrugged. "Either way, it's starting." She kept her gaze focused on the patch of fog in the distance. "Wait. There."

"What? What is that?"

"Light," Alaji replied. "It's fire. It means the northmen are using magic. Women's magic," she added this last point in an angry, possessive tone.

"Then… they were ready," Mil concluded.

"Wait here," Alaji said. "I'm going to get a closer look."

She began walking slowly, though she moved with determination. She didn't get far before one of the older men blocked her path. "Easy, Girl," he said. "Fight's no place for you. Besides, time you got there, the worst of it will be over."

Alaji looked out at the field. "I know," she replied. "I just want to get a little closer, so I can see if there's someone coming. Just to the stone there. Could you come with me?"

"I… no. I need to stay here. Hey!" He shouted at one of the younger guards. "You! Get over here!"

By this time, Alaji had already circled around him and was continuing down the hill.

"Damn it. Go after her!" the old soldier said, and the young man rushed to comply, though Alaji had a head start. She'd picked up her pace as well, and showed no indication of stopping. The soldier started running, and she did the same.

Then, before his eyes, she vanished, leaving only mist circling where she'd been standing.

—

It came from instinct, or it came from desperation. The old man's words, that she'd reach the battle too late, had struck her. How long did it take men to kill each other, even armies of men? Not long, she guessed.

She was counting as she ran, and she cast the spell taken from the gods on five. At once, her memory became jumbled, twisting and contorting: she'd seen herself before herself, running on. Her mind was as clouded as the fog: she'd been there and hadn't been there. It had been both ways.

She caught herself from slowing down. The soldier was still behind her. If he caught her, what would they do to her? Would he dismiss this as a trick of his eyes, or would he recognize magic beyond those spells given to mortals? She ran on, and again she began to count.

It happened as before, though she did not allow herself to slow down, regardless of the emerging vertigo. She bit down on her lip as a distraction and began counting again, this time starting her count anew just as she leapt. And she looked ahead, content that she was there.

And so she appeared, four steps ahead. Alaji moved towards her own back, then leapt, just where she'd appeared. Before her, she appeared again. And before that Alaji, another, each moving in the image of one before, each moving to the same rhythm of the same beating heart.

In the distance, as Alaji counted two, a bird called out. It called out again when she reached four in the following cycle, and she almost lost her count as she realized it was the same call.

The old man was wrong: she would reach this battle in plenty of time.

17

Alaji stopped using her spell when she saw herself stop appearing ahead. By this time, she was tired, disoriented, and nearly ready to collapse. The air carried the odor of smoke, and the sounds of combat – of screams, threats, and of weapons crashing together – were close by, though she couldn't see a thing yet.

"There!" a voice cried out. Her attention snapped to the present, as a pair of men charged at her. Before she could react, one grabbed the other and stopped them both. "Wait! She's one of ours! Come on!" he turned and charged back into the mist.

The other held a moment and looked Alaji over. "Go!" he screamed at her. "Get out of here!"

She nodded, and he left like the others. Then she took a moment to relax as best she could. She caught her breath and began moving. They'd have seen her using her spell if she hadn't stopped. But wouldn't she have seen them at the same time? Then what would she have done?

She'd have stopped.

Her head throbbed. This power was wrong, unnatural. But what would she expect of the magic of gods? It was power over time, over the order of things.

She should have practiced more, should have learned what she was really capable of. In the caves, she'd never even used it two times in a row. What else hadn't she discovered yet?

She began her count and started walking. She willed herself to appear before her, but nothing happened and she forgot to even step back. No, that was wrong. She forgot to step back, because nothing happened. One event led to the one that caused it. How had she done it running on the plain? She hadn't meant to at first – it had happened after she found a rhythm.

She counted, took one step forward and one back in time. She did this again, focusing on the count and not her shifting memory. A third – a fourth. And the fifth appeared before her.

"Don't try to resolve it," her reflection said aloud to her. "Ignore it, and focus on the task."

In the back of Alaji's head, the count went on. She followed her reflection and stepped back in time reflexively when the time came. Another image appeared before both, and Alaji said, "Don't try to resolve it. Ignore it, and focus on the task." Five steps later, and the same words were repeated behind her.

After a few moments the reflection ahead of her froze and dropped to the ground. "Get her!" she heard a voice scream. A northman emerged from the mist, ax in hand.

Alaji had reached five, and instinctively she leapt back. The northman had vanished, as had the other Alajis. She dropped to the ground as a sharp pain shot through her head. It passed quickly, and she looked up to see a northman stumble into view, look around, and leave. She waited to see if he'd return, and when he didn't, she stood up and brushed herself off.

She began to circle the battleground, conjuring her duplicates in time and following their lead, ducking back – both in time and into the mist – when one told her to do so. Once, one yelled for her to run. She slipped back in time and did so, never learning what danger she'd avoided.

She saw numerous bodies of wounded soldiers who'd tried to crawl away from the battle itself, only to die alone on the cold earth. She kept a count at first, but once she'd filled her second hand, it seemed a waste of effort. Some of the dead were those she'd known; others were men of the north, or even their women.

As the morning wore on, the mist began to dissipate and with it her protection. But it also meant the end of his: Hollik would have few places left to hide. She ducked into the grass and looked out while the fog burned away, revealing distant fighting. Spears, aided by spells of the hunt, glided through the air and buried into the chests of young men. Burning torches scorched flesh, while stone hammers cracked bone and axes split skulls. It was horrible, yet somehow not as bad as Alaji had imagined.

She tried to determine who was winning, but from so far back it was nearly impossible to tell whether a dying man was from the lakes or the north. Besides, this was just a portion of the field: there was no guarantee it represented the whole of the battle.

If any of the soldiers approached, they would likely see her. And, if they persisted, she may have to use the gods' magic to elude them. The thought terrified her, though she couldn't say why. There was no going home for her – she knew this already. Even if the world persisted, she'd used her magic to escape her post on the hill. Besides, with Theojin gone, her home would never feel right. Hollik had to answer for her brother's death, and it was quite possible the world had to, as well. Further, she expected the gods would need her to answer for using this power. She doubted that the fact they seemed to have given it to her for just this day would mitigate their fury.

She considered simply using her power to cut through the battle. She'd be seen, but she'd likely find who she was looking for. At least then it would feel done. She feared the act of revealing herself more than she feared the repercussions, anyway.

Before she could act – or even decide how she would act – events made the question moot. Near the fighting, she saw an old man appear dragging another. She squinted to get a better look.

The limp body was that of Arahm. And the one carrying him away from the conflict was her father.

18

He was a danger to her, but then so was everyone else. And, with luck, it was possible he might aid her. She searched around for something to throw and came across some berries growing in a clump of bushes. Then she moved closer, staying as hidden as she could to avoid being seen by anyone else.

She was close enough to the fighting to see clearly the faces of the men and to hear the whistle as spears and arrows cut through the air. Her father looked resigned, sadder than Alaji had ever seen him. She watched him for a moment, then threw the berries.

He cringed as they spattered against his back, then he turned, dropping Arahm as he did so, drew his blade, and looked frantically around. He put his other hand to the back of his head, where one of the berries had hit, touched it, then brought it to his face. He smelled his fingers then licked them. At the taste of the juice, he lowered his knife and looked further out.

Alaji rose up briefly and waved to him. Then, without looking to see how he was reacting, she dropped down and started crawling in his direction. When she'd gone about two thirds of the way, she heard her father's voice whispering her name. She stood up again, and saw him standing close to her, again looking around frantically. Arahm was still unconscious and was leaning against him. Now Alaji could see a spot of dried blood caked to the side of his head. Both men were badly bruised, as well.

Kuljin carefully laid Arahm down and ran to his daughter. He wrapped his arms around her. "You shouldn't be here!"

Alaji pushed him back gently. "I had to come," she said. "I'm needed."

"The healers were supposed to stay at the hills," he said.

"I came alone," she replied. "When the fighting started."

Kuljin looked past her at the hills and considered the distance. He touched his head, then looked over his shoulder at the rising sun.

"Father," Alaji was adamant. "It does not matter. We should get Arahm away from here, then talk." She lifted one of Arahm's arms and waited for her father to do the same. He did so, reluctantly.

They moved in silence, until the fighting was well behind them. "We need to stop here," Alaji said. They set Arahm on the ground as gingerly as they could, and Alaji looked him over. She took out her water skin and poured some liquid on his lips, but she couldn't tell if he was swallowing any.

"Can you help him?" Kuljin asked.

"Not without more time than we have. Even then, I've never worked on someone so injured. I'm not sure if my magic would help him or kill him."

"It makes little difference now," Kuljin said. "I don't even know why I saved him. We're losing, Alaji. They tricked us. They used… they used Theojin's death to deceive us. Made us think their army was falling apart, when it was really sitting in wait."

"Father. Do you know where Hollik is?"

The question caught Kuljin off-guard and he looked at his daughter in bewilderment. "What? Why?"

"Hollik must answer for what happened to Theojin," Alaji said. "He has a lot he must answer for."

"You should not have come here," Kuljin said again.

"Mother told me what you said. About killing me."

Kuljin covered his mouth and began to cry. He knelt on the ground and gasped. "Alaji," he managed to say, "I could not. When Theojin died – when I saw what the northmen could do–"

Alaji placed a hand on his shoulder. "It's okay. I understand what's happening here. I know what this means."

"You couldn't," he said. "You are… you are a girl, and do not know what men do. I don't want you in their hands."

"Listen to me," Alaji said. "If I can find Hollik, I can kill him. I can kill him before his guards can stop me."

"But... how?"

"It does not matter. I know I can do this. There have been... signs. Theojin's death was the last. After that, I understood."

"His death," Kuljin whispered. "Yes, it was the sign of man, wasn't it? The murder of the last generation of men. And you share his blood. Blood that was spilt." He looked away for a moment, first at the ground, then at his fingers.

Alaji grabbed his hands, and he looked into her eyes. "Where is Hollik?"

Kuljin nodded. "He... I saw him, with his guards. Two hands' throws," he pointed.

Alaji began backing away. "Thank you. Goodbye. I love you and mom. Tell her." She turned and ran.

Kuljin leapt up. "Wait!" he screamed, the wonder now gone from his voice. "Wait! You can't go!" He charged after her. Then, to his astonishment, he realized he chased two of Alaji, one running before the other. He froze in shock, just before the closer one disappeared.

19

Alaji's heart pounded as she tore through the field. She stepped back, and the reflections appeared in front of her. Yes – stepping back was the right word. The world around her deteriorated into short flashes of repeating sounds and events. She had little reason to worry about the fighting. If a spear was coming near her or someone was trying to grab her, she had plenty of time to react. She had four chances, in fact, to determine the right course.

Not that she needed them. The soldiers, northmen and lake-folk both, were too shocked to act. She briefly wondered what it must have looked like from their perception – a row of five identical girls, with the last constantly vanishing and a new one appearing in front – but she stopped trying to imagine it after she nearly lost her count.

She charged through the battle, darting around the soldiers as she sought out the warlord. She ran past guards who could never catch her, as they were caught in a loop of motion, almost as if they were dancing. She went into the northern camp, where women tended to their own dying and warriors caught their breath.

All of them paused to look at the girl, though there was nothing they could do to stop her. A few loosed arrows, but she was moving too fast – a full five times their pace – so the few who managed to fire had no hope of hitting her, even if they'd known which to aim for.

When she saw him, he looked afraid. His men were shouting from all sides, and his guards were as confused as he was. This was good: it was right he should be afraid.

She watched as the first of the Alajis drew a knife. The spinning count in Alaji's head struck five and she leapt back. The second drew her knife, and so on. When it was her turn, she did not even think. The knife was in her hand, and she ran after her duplicates. She spiraled in to prevent his guards from blocking her, and she got past them easily enough.

Hollik had time to get his knife in his hand and step backward, but that was all the time he had. Alaji watched as the first of her reflections leapt, plunging a dagger into his throat. The count hit five, and the second followed. Then the third and the fourth. And then, as she approached the dying man, her count hit five a final time and she leapt back to one. The scene reset, and it was her turn to lunge, knife in hand.

Only to be stopped in midair.

A hand, which had not been there – which could not have been there – had grabbed her wrist. It belonged to a man who now stood in front of her. His other hand was buried in a small cloth bag at his side, which he was holding away from them. He was small compared to the other men around. He was even small compared to the northern women, two of whom were screaming and pointing at Alaji. Under normal circumstances, she may have been able to overpower this man, but something else was happening.

Waves of pain crashed against her head. It was from all sides, pressure building, as though her skull would split. The knife dropped from her hand, and the man who'd stopped her let go. He looked surprised at her reaction and tried – unsuccessfully – to catch her as she fell back. Alaji wiped her lip beneath her nose. Her vision was a blur, but she could make out the color of blood when she withdrew her hand.

The man who'd stopped her opened his mouth. "That was amazing!" he screamed. "Look. Just take it easy. You're out of sequence. You'll be alright, but–"

The red smear on her hand drew further and further out of focus, and the sounds of combat started to blend together. Behind the man who'd stopped her, someone else screeched, "Kill her! Kill the girl!"

"No!" the man shouted, "Preset fifteen, me and the girl, eight hundred years! Now!"

The world spun and unwound. She was falling unconscious, but that wasn't all that was happening. Everything was turning around her. The screams and shouts and smells were gone. She tried to focus, to at least see her end coming. But she couldn't keep her eyes open.

As Alaji passed out, her head leaned back to the ground. But the ground was different.

PART 2

1

It was all wrong. The ground was wrong, for one, beneath her head: it was too soft, too wet. The air was wrong in ways Alaji could never have articulated, even if she weren't a hair's breadth away from falling back into unconsciousness. The fact there was no light ebbing through her eyelids was wrong, too, as was the fact her skin wasn't burnt from lying on an open field. The smell was wrong, as well – it was the muggy stench of a bog instead of the fragrant odor of grain or even smoke from the battle.

And then there was the fact she was alive. Every blade of long grass that had whipped by and left a welt she'd ignored in the adrenaline of the battle now seemed to holler at her, and the pain in the back of her head, while greatly diminished, still lingered on. She doubted such pain would last beyond the lands of the living, though having never been dead, it was really just supposition.

But there was something else wrong. Something beyond the air and earth. Things had a different resonance here; they felt different in a different way. The flow of numbers in her head and of blood in her veins was different. Their weight was wrong.

She opened her eyes and found herself staring at the night sky. Her heart pounded as she realized she was being watched. Her gaze settled on the face of the one who'd somehow caught her, who'd stopped her from ending the life of the tyrant.

Her hand shot to the fold in her dress where she kept her knife, but it was gone, having fallen to the field. The face observed her with fascination but did nothing. Alaji sat up and checked around her on the ground, but the blade was gone.

So was the field.

Her nose hadn't deceived her: she was sitting on a mossy patch in the middle of a swamp. A tree was standing to her right, and the strange man was to her left. He wore strange clothes that didn't look like those of the northmen and carried a sack unlike any she'd ever seen. The fabric looked stiff, and at a glance she couldn't tell whether it was some strange skin or woven from some plant or tree she'd never encountered. The man himself was just as odd. His complexion was pale, and his features looked nothing like anyone she'd seen. His age was difficult to gauge. He carried no scars or age spots, leading Alaji to briefly wonder if he was only a hand's age older than herself. But the wrinkles around his eyes were closer to those of her father's. It was as if the years had been kind to his skin, but left him looking unnatural.

Alaji pulled herself up quickly and leaned against the tree. In the back of her head, her count matched pace with her heartbeat. The numbers felt clunky, though she thought she was gaining a hold on them. She didn't dare try to step back after what had happened last time, though. Not unless she had to.

"Hi," the man said. He kept one hand inside his bag, just as before. "That was really impressive. It's been a long time since I saw short-range transference performed without an anchor."

Alaji just stared at him. She had no idea what his words meant, nor what sort of leverage he hoped to gain or what game he was trying to play. Was Hollik here? Was there anyone else?

"Hm. You don't know what I'm talking about, do you? That means you really are from the... er.... the lakes?" He spoke the word strangely, like it didn't fit in his mouth. "Listen, my name is Yemerik, and I'd like to help you."

Alaji just stared at him. "Where's Hollik?" she finally asked.

"Hollik," Yemerik laughed. "He can't hurt you here, if that's what you're worried about. That lout hasn't even been... Listen. You were tossing around some sophisticated magic in the battle. I wasn't really sure what to make of it, and wanted to ask you some questions." He approached Alaji at a slow pace, keeping an eye on her.

"You're with the northmen," Alaji said. She pushed her back against the tree and tried to appear helpless, pitiful. Her nails bit into the bark behind her.

"No, not really. Well, I suppose I was traveling with them, but that's all. It really does get complicated, and I'd rather not get into the details." He was only a few arms' lengths from her. His hand was still clutching whatever he had in his bag.

"You stopped me," Alaji replied.

"What? Oh, the fight. No, it was just the best time to pull you out, before things got bad. There were about to be a lot of bodies and lot of blood."

"He killed my brother."

"And the rest of them? Not that I mind. I really have no stake in any of it, and I didn't like Drista, Brimire, and the others any more than I like Hollik." Yemerik said. Alaji just looked back, confused. Yemerik nodded. "That part wasn't planned, was it? I'm figuring this out, I think. You were taught, what, five sequences? I think I counted five. By the way, who taught you to do that?" He'd stopped moving and simply stood ahead of her.

"You don't understand what you did," Alaji said. "He'll destroy everything. He'll enslave the world."

"Who? Hollik? I promise you, he won't. Half this continent at most, and that's if he's lucky."

"I was given this magic for a reason," Alaji said. "I need to stop him."

"Yes! Exactly! Who gave it to you? Did they tell you their name?"

"The gods," Alaji said, peeling a clump of bark from the sick tree behind her. She shifted forward, invocations of fire already on the tip on her tongue. But she never got to throw it, at least not from her perspective. Because Yemerik suddenly vanished and reappeared a few feet to one side, screaming in pain and surprise. His face was dotted with a dozen small burns; nothing serious, but more than enough to break his concentration. He covered his face, scratching at the still-burning embers.

With both hands.

Alaji dove for the bag, catching it while Yemerik was preoccupied. She twisted it, so the straps crossed, and she pulled. Yemerik kicked violently at Alaji and connected with her shins, but she didn't relent.

She held the bag tight, and she chanted quickly. With his free hand, Yemerik covered his head. Then he fell back, as the straps on his bag unwound and split. Alaji turned and ran, bag in hand, and Yemerik started after her.

But the count had never stopped cycling through Alaji's head. She slipped back in time and kept running. She half expected Yemerik to appear in front of her as he had in the battle, but all she heard was him shouting behind her.

She charged into the shallow, murky water and trudged on, stepping back every five beats, while Yemerik's cries echoed on. He begged her, threatened her, and shouted things she did not understand, but it made no difference. He'd stopped her from saving her people. Or perhaps he'd simply interfered with the end of the world. Either way, he served Hollik. He was the enemy.

Now, if Alaji guessed right, he was an enemy without power.

If she was wrong, she expected she'd be dead shortly. She ran on into the dark, so distracted she didn't even notice than when she stepped back in time, there was no mirror image behind or in front of her.

2

Yemerik sat on the small island of moss and grass and wondered if everything the girl had said had been an act. He picked at the newly formed blisters on his face and tried to parse out how he'd been outmaneuvered. And, as something of an afterthought, he wondered if he was going to die here and, if so, if anyone would ever realize what had happened to him.

On the ground beside him, he found a small handful of crumbled tree bark. He picked up one of the larger pieces and looked it over. It wasn't even scorched, of course.

From his perspective, the fight had gone far differently. Alaji had tricked him into approaching. When he saw her move to attack, he reacted instantaneously, commanding his talisman to roll back a few seconds to put him at an advantage. He might have invoked a different preset: a few minutes, a few hours, years, decades… it would have been just as easy. And, had he still been on the plains with the pack of delusional barbarian conquerors, he'd have played it safe and done just that. But, as he was confronted with what seemed to be a scared girl who'd been taught a few elementary tricks of magic she didn't appear to understand, he wasn't as concerned as he should have been.

So, preset four it was: a few seconds to regain composure and prevent the escalation from ever happening. But, unfortunately for Yemerik, the girl was faster than he'd anticipated. Between starting and finishing his command, she'd cast some archaic fire spell and hurled a fistful of burning cinders into his face. She'd done a number to her hand, as well.

Yemerik's command finished before he realized how bad a situation he was in. By the time he understood what had happened, he'd already started reacting. And, what was worse, he'd moved back right before she'd burned herself.

She'd known to go for the talisman, though she hadn't known how to use it. If she had, she wouldn't have bothered with the same silly temporal jumping spells she'd used in the battle: she'd have jumped centuries instead of seconds and simply left him to die here.

That meant she was being manipulated. Whoever had trained her had told her to get the talisman, which carried with it two frightening prospects: either someone wanted it or they wanted him left without its protection.

Had he been lured to the lakes for just that reason? And, if so, what did that mean? Had it all been a ruse? The book and the Second Gathering might not exist: the clues that led him here could have been planted. Or perhaps it was all real and simply not as benevolent as he'd hoped. If that was the case, he'd almost welcome the long road to the jar.

He needed answers. He needed to know who'd taught the girl temporal manipulation hundreds of years before its invention. And most of all, he needed the talisman back, because without it, he was stuck here and most likely dead within a week.

3

The swamp ended at the edge of a hill to the south. It took Alaji until morning to reach it. She stared up at the top as the sun rose, she studied the hill's shape, and she swallowed. She wasn't especially surprised to find she knew it, nor the one next to it. She wished she was wrong, but she knew better. The way the numbers felt as she'd counted, the way the world felt... she hadn't gone somewhere different; she'd simply gone *before.*

She climbed to the top and looked out over the valley. The five lakes stretched before her, though their shapes were slightly different. There were no houses scattered over the land, nor were there boats on the water. There were no fields for pigs or goats to be heard or smelled.

Five generations of five generations of her people hadn't arrived yet. The forests hadn't been trimmed back, and the gardens hadn't been planted. Their fights with neighbors in all cardinal directions hadn't started, and they hadn't traded goods and ideas before finally coalescing into the culture they'd become.

A distant howl made Alaji shiver. It was a sound she'd heard only a handful of times, but she knew what it meant: the dragons hadn't been driven out. She turned her head skyward and looked around. There were no shapes overhead, but she'd have to be careful, assuming she wanted to survive here.

Frightened, hurt, and tired, Alaji found a large rock to sit on. She removed her boots, which had been all but destroyed by the mud. She cleaned herself as well as she could and tried to stay calm. Was this the punishment the gods had chosen for her? To linger alone here in the wilderness? So close to her home, yet robbed of any comforts.

No. This couldn't be the will of the gods, because the gods had better sense than to work through men like Yemerik. This was magic; magic she couldn't understand, but magic nonetheless. Not the secret magic of gods, but something else. The way Yemerik had spoken to her before she'd gotten the upper hand was that of an adult speaking to a child. It was the way the northmen discussed the lake folks' customs when they traded.

It meant that whatever was in Yemerik's bag was beyond her understanding, but not beyond the understanding of mortals. Alaji opened it carefully and looked inside. She found several rolled-up sheets of thin material almost like leaves in texture. She unrolled these carefully and examined them. They were covered in strange markings, so fine she couldn't imagine how they'd been made. She replaced these and turned her attention to a strange, egg-shaped stone. It was smoother than anything she'd ever seen and it contained a number of symbols inscribed around the edges. Like the symbols on the rolled sheets, Alaji wondered how such fine work had been possible.

She also came across a small, wooden box. When she slid the top open, she found stacks of small disks, some containing the likenesses of men and women, others depicting trees, the sun, or animals. These were beautiful and displayed craftwork beyond imagination. They were as hard as rock but made of something else. Something smooth that shone like water. She looked them over before returning them to their box. She suspected these might carry some power, but the fact they were hidden away meant Yemerik couldn't have been using them before he lost the bag. The sheets were possible, but they seemed too flimsy and weak to house great magic.

That left the stone.

She held it in her hand and stared at it for several minutes. It was pleasant to look at and she wondered about its creation, but it didn't seem to be doing anything. She felt around the edges, but still could find nothing of note.

She held it close to her head, shut her eyes, and tried to relax, not an easy task under the circumstances. Somehow she managed. At first, there was nothing. Then there was a strange sensation, like she felt in the holy caverns. She opened her eyes.

In the back of her head, she began to count. One. Two. Three....

It was faint, but she could feel the stone echoing her count, pulsing with each of her heartbeats. It seemed to push her and pull her at once, always gently, like the ebb of the waves at the edge of a lake. She cleared her mind and whispered, "Can you take me home?"

Nothing happened.

Alaji shook the object, attempted to twist it, ran her fingers over the runes etched into the sides, tapped it with the golden and silver disks from the box, licked it, held it close to her heart, and said prayers to all five of her peoples' gods – even Gelji, He Who Waits for the Fall – but none of it had any effect. Finally, she returned the stone to its bag and put it all in her pack. She finished what little remained of her water and returned the empty skin, as well. She'd examine the stone again later, but for now she wanted to start moving. She had no food or water, Yemerik would likely be after her, and there could well be any number of dangerous creatures about, including dragons. Staying put didn't seem like her best option.

She put her boots back on, grimacing as they brushed against blisters, and began to push ahead. Briefly, she risked a stop at the top of the hill to gather some brier berries, but she grew wary out in the open and hurried on. Besides, she'd need something more sustaining.

Unfortunately, Alaji was no hunter. Had Theojin been here, he'd have been able to bring down birds with stones plucked from the ground: such was the training and spells bestowed upon men of her village. Alaji had never really cared that she'd been forbidden from learning such things, but she found herself wishing she had those techniques now.

While she knew nothing about spells of the hunt, she did have one tool at her disposal: if she got an animal close enough, she could guide it. It was one of the odder spells in her arsenal, and few women paid it much heed. According to legend, there was a time when her people were riders on the plains, and in those days it had been the woman's job to break the horses.

The idea that those days of legend had not yet passed made Alaji feel queasy, which she was almost grateful for, as it dismissed her hunger for a time.

Of course, even if Alaji could enchant an animal, she'd be hard pressed to kill it without some kind of weapon. She located a strong, straight branch and brought it with her. She thought of looking for a sharp stone to bind to the end before realizing she had nothing to bind it with. If she found some reeds, she could make some rope, but that would take time. She decided it wasn't worth it, at least not yet.

She went down the hill, stumbling over roots and cutting herself on thorns. Growing up, she'd been up and down these hills dozens of times and had never realized how cultivated they'd been.

She was so tired, she almost cheered when she came across a path in the woods below. Until she began wondering who could have made it.

4

According to everything Alaji had been told, her people were the first to inhabit the Valley of the Five Lakes: before them, nothing but beasts and monsters lived there. But someone had been here. Perhaps her people were older than she'd been taught or perhaps some tribe of nomads had lived here in some forgotten era. It didn't make sense with what she'd been taught, but neither did her own presence.

Assuming it was still in use, whoever had made the path might be nearby and could well be dangerous. But Alaji doubted her ability to survive long on her own. If someone was nearby, perhaps they'd have access to food or tools. She had little to trade with, but perhaps they'd take pity on her.

She felt she had little choice, so she pushed onward. The path was small and overgrown: no one had bothered trimming back the branches hanging at head-level, so Alaji was constantly forced to push these aside or crouch under them. If she did meet up with whoever had made the path, perhaps she could teach them how to maintain a proper trail in lieu of trade. Perhaps there was a great deal she could teach them. She was from a civilized age, one with great knowledge about the world: surely there were things she could show a group of primitive explorers. Assuming they didn't kill her on sight, of course.

The path weaved, and she almost lost it several times. But she managed to find her way again, in part because she realized where it was heading. The route was a little different than what she was used to, but this was the way to Boars Lake.

Alaji stayed focused on the distance and kept a lookout for anyone. That's likely why she didn't notice the things above until one leaped down, latched onto her back and buried a mouth full of needle-sharp teeth into her shoulder.

She screamed in pain, fell back, pinning the thing on her back to the ground. She looked up and saw them at once: dozens of goblins hanging in the branches far above. They howled, and another – almost right above her – let go.

Alaji managed to duck to one side, so it missed her. The first had let go of her and now stood up, its mouth red and grinning. The two on the ground spread out, ready to jump at her as soon as her back was turned. Several nearby scampered down tree trunks to surround her, while others overhead shimmied out to the tips of their branches to position themselves over the girl below.

Alaji looked around frantically. "Help!" she screamed, hoping someone would hear her. But as soon as she said it, she knew no one was coming, because there was simply no one to come. The path she'd followed hadn't been overgrown: it was simply made for creatures smaller than herself.

The count started in the back of her head, but they didn't let her reach five. Before she reached three, another jumped down and bit into her arm. She screamed again, and lost her concentration. She swung at the goblin, but it jumped back with others.

Their smiles widened, and they crept closer. Alaji swallowed. It was a horrible way to die. Given the choice, she'd have rather it had been a dragon. Goblins are cowardly, and they'll wear down their prey, injuring it from behind. Then, when the fight is gone, they'll devour it, one bite at a time. They don't always wait for it to die before starting.

Alaji gripped her branch, the only weapon she had, with one

hand and ran her fingers over the other edge. She wouldn't be able to defend herself against so many, but she wanted to hurt a few of them first, maybe even kill one or two.

A small fire exploded at the tip of her branch, and she waved it in front of them. The goblins fell silent immediately, and every one on the ground backed off. One toward the front grabbed another's arm and began shaking. It shouted something in their tongue; a single word which the others began screaming, as well.

Alaji tried to parse it. She knew a few words of the language, and this was familiar, common. She remembered after a moment and stood back. The word meant, "Dragon," and the goblins were terrified. A glance above revealed that the ones in the trees were no less frightened: none seemed interested in pushing the attack.

It took her a moment to figure it out. Hundreds of years from then, the goblins she'd known had mastered tools and would burn their victims' homes to the ground. But these were unarmed. They hadn't picked up knives or spears from murdered families: they were fighting with their teeth and claws. And, apparently, the only source of fire they knew were dragons. It wasn't a tool to them: it was only death.

And, by extension, so was she.

Most started running, though a few, too scared to take their eyes from her, stood their ground. Some of these were knocked over by others dropping from trees in a mad dash to safety.

Now the count was cycling through Alaji's head, but she didn't need to use it. She lit a few saplings on fire for good measure, and the rest got the message and ran off.

Save one.

5

He was smaller than most of the others; both in height and in weight. He lacked the round belly shared by many of his kind, and his green skin showed numerous scars. He didn't try to hide or run, but he didn't advance, either. His mouth was shut, and his arms were folded.

Alaji stared at him for a few moments, then threw a burning stick in his direction. The goblin jumped back a few feet, then froze once more. Alaji found another stick and lit it on fire. She walked towards the goblin, who stepped back, matching her pace.

She threw the second stick. This time the goblin didn't even dodge as it landed several feet away. He turned back to the girl and waited for her next move. His arms now hung at his side, but he didn't flash his teeth or make any other threatening gesture.

He was learning.

Alaji decided that was at least as dangerous. She found a third branch and cast her spell. She held it like a torch and locked eyes with the goblin, who began backing away the moment she stepped forward. He matched her pace, but it didn't do him any good: when the count in her head reached five, she stepped back.

From the creature's perspective, she vanished and reappeared closer. Then she took a step and vanished again. He turned to run, but she was already beside him.

The burning branch crashed into the center of his back, knocking him to the ground. He rolled over to see her standing above him. Her clothes were bloody from where the others had bitten her, and the branch rained red embers down at him. Each bit into his skin like a mosquito, and he whimpered. She raised the branch up, and he covered his face.

She hollered, but didn't bring the club down on him. He lay panting on the ground for a moment. The girl kicked him once sharply in the side and swung the branch in the air between them. He fell back while she swung again. Neither came close to connecting. She bellowed again, and the goblin rolled over onto his knees, scampered to his feet, and ran off.

Once he was gone, Alaji began to cry. Her shoulder and back hurt more than anything she'd ever known, and she wondered if the bites would get infected. It was certainly no less than she'd have experienced in her own time if she'd killed Hollik and had to answer to his people or hers. She'd considered the notion of losing her life, but hadn't thought through the rest of the price. There was pain and fear in death; more than she'd imagined. How much worse would it have gotten before the end?

She leaned against a tree and tried to use her healing magic, but she was never adept at such spells in the best conditions. Here, without water or food or medicine, trying to cast on herself was all but impossible. She attempted a few times, but stopped when she became worried she'd do more damage than she'd fix. She gave up, climbed to her feet, wiped the tears from her eyes, and breathed in deeply. She clenched her teeth and started towards the lake, pausing only to replace her stick.

6

Alaji had been four when her mother first took her fishing on Boars Lake. There had been dozens of small boats on the water. On the shore, others stabbed at the surface with spears or cast nets, as they'd come to do.

Out of the blue, Shaji had said, "It's because of the Lord of Boars. That's why this is Boars Lake, why it's named that." Alaji hadn't asked, nor had she ever given the matter much thought. She'd grown up hearing the lake's name so often, it had simply settled into her consciousness without question. The fact the word matched the name of an animal had never even occurred to her.

She said nothing of any of this, of course. She simply looked up at her mother, who stared back. Alaji could feel her judging her, but she was used to this and paid it little mind.

"Do you know the story of the Lord of Boars?"

Alaji knew better than to lie, so she answered, "No."

Her mother gave a sigh of disappointment and began. "When the gods first made the world, before they created women or even men, they created fields and forests. Then they created the first of the animals and beasts. They were nothing like the things you know. The first creatures were as large as the hills. The first rabbit could even leap over the tallest tree. But nothing, not even Jur, the first dragon, was so large as the first boar. His name was Urimi, and mountains fell beneath his hooves.

"The five gods looked down on their creations with wonder, and gave them gifts of magic. To the first bird and the first dragon, they gave spells of flight. They gave spells of burrowing to the creatures of the earth and spells of speed to the first deer and the other creatures of the plain.

"They had planned on giving the spell of fire to Urimi, but the gods were tricked. Jur, the first dragon, convinced Urimi to take a nap beneath the hot sun. Then, while the boar slept, he took his place and claimed his spell.

"When Urimi found out, he grew angry, and kicked at the ground. He left a great hole, which filled with water. This is that very hole, Alaji. It is the Boar's Lake."

"Did he ever get a spell?" Alaji asked.

"Of course. The gods pitied him and gave him the spell to act beyond death. That is why a speared boar can still strike down his killer. And it is how Urimi finally took his vengeance upon Jur. But come. We've wasted too much time, and have fish to catch."

—

Eight hundred years earlier, an older Alaji dug the water skin out of her pack and waded into the lake to fill it. She had water now, but little food. She knew she could find some roots and mushrooms in the forest, but that would take time and leave her at the mercy of the goblins and whatever other creatures lurked within. Of course, she didn't know whether she was truly much safer here in the open, but she felt less scared.

She eyed the lake. Beneath the surface, she could see flickering tails of silver; more fish than she'd ever seen in any of the lakes. Of course, this was before her people came, before they'd harvested the waters.

With a net, she could have caught dozens. With a spear and an hour, she could have had a few. If she wanted to eat, she'd need something more than sticks and her hands.

Or would she? The count seemed to appear in her head on its own. One... two... three.....

Alaji found a small peninsula extending into the lake. She went out to the tip, which ended in a series of stones, dropping off into the water. She waited until a fish came near, then she reached in, right where the fish had been. As soon as her hand broke the surface, the fish whipped its tail and vanished.

But Alaji stepped back and clamped her fingers around the startled fish, who'd never had a chance. She pulled it out of the water and laughed. Then she stopped laughing as she realized she was alone.

Where was her duplicate?

7

Cleaning the fish without a knife was a difficult endeavor. She found a sharp stone which made do, but it was hardly the blade of flint she was accustomed to. By the time she was done, half the meat was a pulpy mess. She impaled the rest and cooked it over a fire she started on the shore.

She devoured it and could have gone through five more, but she was too tired to catch them. The sun hadn't begun to set, but Alaji was exhausted. How long had it been since she'd slept? She hadn't had a chance the night before the battle. She'd stayed up with the women preparing medicine and bandages. Then she ran the plains. How much time had that taken? Not long as the sun measures, but longer for her. She grew dizzy thinking about it. She didn't have the words to think of time in this way. Her people measured it in fifths and fifths of fifths of the sun's arc. They had no words for one who moved outside of this. They had no concept.

And that was before her abduction. She'd arrived here at night, long before the dawn. The sun hadn't cared – it rose regardless – but it had been that much longer since she'd slept.

She considered her options, and they were mostly bleak. She knew of a few caves near the lake, but that was in her time. Would they even have formed yet? And, worse yet, would they be inhabited?

Alaji decided she was better off facing the cold. She cleaned her wounds in the lake, using what magic she could muster to prevent infection. Such magics were easier when used on others, but she managed to soothe the pain for the time being. Then she returned to the woods, where she found a fir tree with dense branches but enough room to lie underneath. She curled into a ball and tried to sleep.

It wasn't easy, and she woke shivering several times. Her shoulder and back still ached from her injuries, and her dreams tormented her. Hollik appeared in several, as did packs of goblins and a dragon. And of course, there was Yemerik, there to stay her hand and keep her from defending herself.

When the sun finally rose, she was already awake. She was still tired, but she was able to function. Her wounds hurt as much as the night before, if not more, so she set out to search the woods for some herbs she could use to enhance her spells. On the way, she found some berries and roots she could chew on.

She also found something more substantial. A hare was moving through a clearing, picking at some grass. Alaji eyed it, but it caught wind of her. The animal's head turned so one of its eyes was pointed at her.

She charged forward while the count began in her head. The rabbit turned to run almost immediately, but as soon as Alaji reached five and stepped back, the hare was where it had been. It started fleeing again, but didn't get far before Alaji's spell moved time backwards a second time.

Now she felt it. A sense of freedom and power. There were no duplicates, but it was more than that. There was no price, no pain in her head. No confusion as to the order of events. Each time she stepped back in time, the hare was set back. She was almost upon it before it had built up a lead. While it was fast, Alaji flickered into existence, appearing only one step in five. The animal never had much chance.

She grabbed it by the scruff of its neck and lifted it in front of her. It kicked violently at the air, but Alaji held it away. Then she turned it to face her, and tried a spell of enchantment. The first didn't take, nor did the second – she was never as good at such magic as she should have been – but the third attempt stole its gaze. The hare stopped fighting and went limp. Alaji felt a tree behind her with her free hand, and she turned so it was at the hare's back. Then she hurled it headfirst against the trunk as hard as she could.

Cleaning the hare was no easier or more efficient than the fish, but it made for a better meal. She roasted it back by the lake, using the herbs to season the meat. It was still unfulfilling. She'd have done better with some salt, but that wasn't something one found lying by a lake. As far as she knew, it only came from eastern traders; she'd never learned how they came across it.

Palatable or not, eating gave Alaji a chance to think about her magic and to reflect on the change. She wasn't sure what was different, but she suspected Yemerik's egg-shaped statue. After she finished the rabbit, she removed the stone from her pack and examined it again. She tried invoking its power as Yemerik had, but she couldn't remember what he'd said to activate it. She could feel something emanating from it, but she couldn't figure out what it meant. She was more certain than ever it was somehow alive, but that was as much as she could tell.

There was one more thing she wanted to try, however. She held the stone and began her count. She stepped back, and looked around. She was alone: no duplicate remained. Then she set the stone down and walked away from it. She could still feel the stone at first: its energies washed over her. Then, after a few more paces, it stopped.

Alaji swallowed and began her count. When she reached five, she stepped back. Now there was another Alaji behind her. She turned to face herself and waited for her reflection to vanish. When it did, it left her dizzy with conflicting memories of how she'd come to be there.

She moved back towards the stone, expecting to feel the energy once more, but she came within a few feet and felt nothing. She tried her trick again, and turned to find her reflection staring at her.

A thought occurred to her: what would happen if she touched the stone? But she wasn't the only one who thought of it. Both Alajis' heads turned to the stone simultaneously, and both lunged for the object. She – the one who'd stepped, not the reflection – reached it first, an instant before her duplicate would have. As soon as her fingers brushed its edge, the other Alaji vanished.

There was no pain, but neither were there memories. Whatever the other Alaji had thought or been was no longer a part of her. If the other had been a second faster, would she have disappeared instead?

Alaji was horrified by the idea. And yet, was it so different than being on the plains, when she'd slipped her perception back and used her spell to test future actions then left them to disappear? She'd abandoned herself – at least a version of herself – to flicker out, as if it never was.

Quickly, she recovered the stone and returned it to her pack. There was a great deal about this object she still didn't understand, but she thought she understood part of its purpose. Somehow, it protected her from creating reflections. Reflections which could die or vanish like figments.

How many times had she died since playing with this spell? Died or worse. She clutched the bag containing the stone tightly and focused on the energy pulsing out of it.

8

The following days offered little change, save when the weather was less cooperative. Alaji stayed put, venturing out only to hunt or fish. She cooked the meat at the lake's edge, then went inland to sleep. She found some twine-reeds along the lake and pounded them to thread, which she formed into a blanket as well as she could. It offered little warmth, but it was better than nothing.

When she remembered to do so, she cried. It was difficult for her to mourn Theojin, because it was difficult for her to think of him as being dead. In a sense, he wasn't dead at all. Theojin hadn't been born yet, nor had their father and mother. But this wasn't why Alaji had trouble keeping him in her thoughts. The truth was she was too busy trying to keep herself alive, and that drive was stronger than her grief. She hated herself for that fact, but there was no changing it. If Arahm had been there, he'd have said it was her duty to grieve first and survive later, and if the gods did not deign to grant her both, better for her do her duty. But her duty seemed as distant to her now as her village.

She missed it – missed her mother, father, and brother. She wanted to return to them, but the notion was absurd. Her brother was dead, and her parents would be honor bound to turn her over to Arahm so she could be executed. Only Arahm was likely dead, as well. Would Hollik have left anything? Would he slaughter the women? The children? The animals? Or would he simply demand obedience? Perhaps that was no better.

How long had it been? A few days since she came here. Hollik could have burned her village to the ground in that time.

A thought struck her. She was embarrassed it had taken her so long to think it. The warlord hadn't been born yet. He hadn't raised his armies or lured her people into his trap. And he certainly hadn't killed Theojin.

The idea washed over her, its conclusions following in waves. If these things hadn't happened, could they be stopped? Could the future be changed?

Would the gods allow it?

It was nothing but supposition unless she could unlock the secret of Yemerik's stone. But it was something she'd lost. It was hope for more than the tyrant's death. It was a chance at life. Perhaps even a chance to see her brother again. She'd already proven that the past could be changed. Her presence here demonstrated it. Why not her time? Why not her brother's murder?

In the meantime, she had another world to occupy her attention. It was a new world, fearsome and strange, but also strangely beautiful. On the third day, she caught sight of a pair of dragons, spiraling over the lake, dropping towards the surface to spit fire, then swooping back to snatch the dead fish floating to the surface. These were larger and fatter than the dragons she'd seen in her own time. They were as long as five men laid head-to-foot, and they seemed faster, too. Healthier. She hid in the tree line to watch, and prepared to retreat if necessary, but the beasts either failed to notice her or seemed content with fish.

She felt sure she could elude them if they forced her to. In fact, she felt content she'd be able to outrun anything that came at her, provided she had time to start. Still, she was happier not having to test herself against the monsters. Likewise, she'd yet to cross paths with a bear or anything else especially dangerous. She wound up using her magic only to eat, heal, and experiment with time, though never without the stone.

On the fourth morning, Alaji woke to find a shadow falling over her. She leapt up, only to smack her head on the underside of a branch. Quickly, she scampered around the trunk to put it between her and the shape.

When her sight cleared, she realized there was no immediate danger: the shadow had been cast by a deer pelt dangled from the tips of branches on her tree. She crawled out from under the tree, bringing a log with her. Her count ran through her head, in case she'd need it. She looked all over for some explanation, but there was nothing nearby.

The pelt was far from flawless, but it had been dried and cleaned. It would function better as a blanket than the one she'd made, which was already falling apart. She held the pelt in front of her face and breathed in. The odor was faint but unmistakable: goblin.

Could it have been left by accident? It seemed unlikely – its placement in the tree was too obvious. And the fact it was in her tree couldn't have been by chance, either. Was it a message then? A payment? Some sort of threat?

She almost burnt it on the spot. But that was foolish. It was a blanket, and the nights were cold. She rolled it up and wedged it between the repaired straps of the bag she'd taken from Yemerik. But there was a lesson to be taken, as well. She was being watched here: the goblins were stalking her.

It was time to find a new sleeping spot. She headed east, leaving Boars Lake behind. It took her a fifth of the day, but she reached her destination. Her people would one day call it the Lake of Fire. The name was given due to the water's ability to catch and reflect the sunrise, or so the story went. Alaji had seen countless sunrises over all five of the lakes, and they all seemed alike to her. But as long as the lake's name had nothing to do with dragons, it hardly mattered.

She found an overhanging rock she could fit beneath that didn't seem to house any animals, and she set up her new camp. It wasn't much, but at least now she had the pelt.

The next morning, she awoke to find a freshly-killed eel laid out for her. She could find no sign it had been poisoned or sullied, but she tossed it into the woods regardless. She still didn't understand what these things meant or why they'd been left. There was no clear aggression; if the goblins wanted her dead, they'd have been able to accomplish the deed in her sleep. But goblin "gifts" are a strange thing. The stories of dead animals left behind in the wreckage of burned farms were testament to that.

There were other questions that troubled her. Did the goblins realize they could simply slip in and murder her in her sleep? Were they testing her with these items? Luring her into a false sense of security before they struck?

Mostly, she was horrified how easily they were tracking her. She'd hoped to escape the notice of anything in the valley until she had time to find a way home, assuming such a path through time existed. Goblins were far from her only concern – Yemerik was still out there, and he was far more dangerous. But the goblins had proven they could find her. They could approach her silently.

She would not risk it again. The next night, she would confront them when they came. Last time, she'd simply driven them back, but apparently that hadn't been enough. The next time she fought them, she'd make sure they stayed away.

9

Alaji spent a great deal of her afternoon preparing. She gathered branches, which she sharpened on rocks and stuck into the ground in a semicircle around her dwelling, leaving a few of the largest and sturdiest where she slept. Then she gathered water as well, expecting she would want to wash herself. There would be blood, after all.

After that, she laid down beneath her deer pelt as if asleep. But she watched the forest, waiting for them to appear. It was close to midnight before one did.

She saw the eyes first, reflecting the moonlight, as the goblin closed in. He held something in his hands – a dead squirrel, by the look of it – and stopped to examine one of the branches Alaji had left. He ran his hand over it, then shook it lightly. Then he began to affix the dead animal to the branch, pushing its mouth around the end and working it downward.

One goblin. Alaji had imagined there'd be a dozen. She planned to leave a few alive, so they'd warn off the others. But with only one, that wasn't feasible. She'd have to drag his body back to their trail. Hang it in a tree somehow, so they'd see it.

She began her count and leapt up, grabbing the largest stick. The goblin saw her and turned to run. But of course it was futile: she ran after him, stepped back in time, and was now past him. He panicked – from his perspective, the sleeping girl had vanished and appeared behind him. Alaji lit the branch in her hand and swung it. The goblin leapt to the ground and crawled backwards. But he was crawling into a corner, approaching the overhanging stone.

In one hand, Alaji held her burning branch. With the other, she lit the one the goblin had been working on, right below the squirrel. The branch caught quickly, and the dead rodent's fur flared up.

Then Alaji began her count again, shifting to the next branch, stepping back in time, and lighting it, as well. The goblin watched in horror as she seemed to vanish and appear beside one branch after another and light them on fire.

Then she closed in. She didn't step back, because there was no need. The goblin wasn't fighting. He just sat as she approached. She raised her torch and aimed at the goblin's head. She was still counting, in case he tried to attack. But he didn't. He didn't move at all.

He was far too afraid. His gaze locked on the fire at the end of the torch. She could see the light in his eyes. Up close, there was no doubt. This was the goblin from before, the one who stayed while the others fled. He was smaller, less nourished, and covered in scars. But there was something in his gaze, something in how he looked at her, which seemed less goblin than human.

She hesitated. If it had leapt at her or tried to scratch her, she could have struck it. Even if it turned away to try and hide, she could have killed it. But it just stared ahead. It was scared, but not pitiful.

"But it's a monster!" her mind screamed at her, and she raised the branch again. But it didn't act like a monster. It just kept looking on, bravely facing her. She lowered the branch.

"Go!" she yelled. It didn't move. So she ran back and knocked over two of the standing branches, kicking dirt on them to extinguish the flame. "Go!" she pointed.

The goblin stood and brushed himself off. He took a non-threatening pose and waited. Alaji ran at him, but he held his ground. His arms hung at his side. He flinched while she pushed her torch near his face, but he didn't run. He began to speak, but Alaji couldn't understand him.

"I said, GO!" She said again.

The goblin sat on the ground. He kept looking at her.

"Go. Just go," Alaji said. But she was tired and confused. Goblins weren't supposed to act like this. But then there were many things she'd seen recently that didn't seem to reflect how the world was supposed to be.

"Go away. Leave or I'll kill you."

The goblin simply laid down on the dirt and shut his eyes. Alaji kicked dirt at him and looked at her branch. She inverted the spell of fire and set the branch down. Then she crawled as far from the goblin as she could get without leaving her shelter and wrapped herself in the deer pelt.

She thought she was too excited and too frightened to sleep, but she was wrong. Within seconds, the world around her vanished.

10

It was already light when she woke, somewhat rested. That the prior night could have been a dream certainly crossed Alaji's mind, especially when she looked around and saw there were no goblins in sight. But the charred remains of the sticks, one of which still held a blackened squirrel carcass, suggested otherwise.

This meant the goblin had been here. He'd faced her down, risked his life, and slept on the ground. Then he'd woken up before her and run off.

Clearly, Alaji knew far less about goblins than she'd believed.

She decided it didn't matter. The goblin was gone now, likely biding his time or planning his next move. Would he return again tonight? Would he bring the rest? Alaji shivered. She should have killed it. She should have bashed its skull in and burned its body to a crisp.

And then, almost whimsically, she realized she'd have another chance. The goblin was approaching from the woods. He held a fish, still flapping, in one hand. It was huge – almost twice the size of any fish she'd seen in her time. It was almost too large for the poor creature, who struggled to keep from dragging it. The goblin approached and offered the fish to Alaji, who stared at the display, baffled. As soon as the goblin set the fish down, he stepped away.

Alaji sighed. It was early, and she was tired. Far too tired to want to murder a goblin, let alone one which had brought her a gift. Besides, she was finding the idea of killing him more and more distasteful. Instead, she began to gather firewood. The goblin followed and mimicked her, finding logs a similar size and coloration to the ones she chose. Then he followed her back and set them beside her.

Alaji looked over the pieces the goblin had picked and discarded the ones that were too wet or rotten. As soon as Alaji threw these aside, the goblin went to the sticks and looked them over.

Meanwhile, Alaji arranged the rest of the firewood. The goblin seemed to sense when she was ready to light the fire. To her surprise, he approached to watch more closely. She traced the symbols and whispered the incantation, and the red embers bloomed.

The goblin backed away from the flames. Alaji began cleaning the fish with her edged stone, then she buried the guts and speared the fish. She roasted it over the fire, turning it occasionally. The goblin kept watching while she worked.

When she finished, she removed the fish from the fire to let it cool. Then she tore off a piece and offered it to the goblin, who accepted it after eying it carefully. He didn't taste it until after Alaji started to eat. Then, he started with a small nibble to test it. He gave no indication of whether he liked it or not, but he finished what Alaji had given him.

Despite the fact Alaji knew several goblin words, she made no effort to communicate beyond sharing the food. Likewise, the goblin seemed to have given up trying to communicate with the girl, with the exceptions of gifts and mimicry.

Once the fire died down, Alaji began to head towards the lake. She'd eaten, but she'd need food for later. Besides, she drank most of her water during breakfast and needed more. She caught sight of another hare as she walked through the forest, but she left it alone. She wasn't sure how the goblin would react to seeing her use time magic to stalk and kill the creature, and for some reason she didn't want to startle him.

When they reached the beach, the goblin immediately began to paw through the sand. Alaji stopped to watch. Since he'd given her the fish, he'd shadowed her every movement. This was the first action he'd taken of his own accord, and it fascinated her. He came up with a handful of small, round stones; some were fairly pretty. Then he stood completely still and stared at Alaji, waiting for her to act again.

She shrugged then returned to the lake, moving along the shore until she found a spot where the water was deep. She lay still, watching beneath the water for the flickering tails of fish. She kept count in her head then reached back in time, snatching a fish before it could react. She set it on a rock, then started back towards the shore, only to discover the goblin had claimed her spot. She thought he might be trying to catch a fish himself, but he seemed less interested in the water then the stones in his hand. He sifted through his collection, holding the stones to the light one at a time, until he selected a particularly bright one.

Then the goblin began to sing. It was a simple melody, but there was something solemn about the song. When he'd finished, the goblin set the stone on the bank, just above the spot Alaji had pulled the fish from the water. He hurried away, so Alaji could take her place once more.

When she got there, she paused to look at the stone. The goblin had pressed it softly into the ground and had drawn a simple spiral around it. Before fishing again, she chose a spot a few feet away, because she was bothered by the thought she might disturb the marker.

She took a few more fish, and the goblin left a few more stones as payment. Then Alaji cleaned and cooked the fish. She didn't eat them, but rather took them with her, sticks and all.

She gave one of the sticks to the goblin, who took a bite out of the fish while it was stuck to the end. Alaji laughed and did the same. The goblin laughed, as well.

11

She called him Ejick, because he reminded Alaji of Mil's brother. Mil would have been furious, as would Alaji's mother, but no more so than if they'd known she'd adopted a goblin as a pet.

These thoughts raced through her head as she moved through the woods towards the Lake of Fire, her "pet" moving close beside her. Alaji shooed him away when he began acting strangely, because he was distracting her. She realized too late that he was acting differently because he sensed something. Because something wasn't right.

But by then she'd already reached the lake and stepped into the clearing. And she realized she wasn't alone.

It was an odd sensation. Fear, excitement, confusion. She felt these before her mind even made sense of the scene before her. Standing by the water, an old woman dressed in black leaned on a walking stick topped by a small stone. She was staring directly at Alaji, as if she'd expected her to emerge.

They stood a moment, watching each other. Alaji was frozen, unsure what to do. Beside her, Ejick stood and watched.

"I... Hello. Listen..." Alaji stuttered. "I'm... I'm lost. I...."

"You're not lost," the old woman replied. "You feel lost, but you know where you are."

The old woman began to approach slowly. Alaji instinctively began her count. She thought she'd have little to fear from the old woman, but she didn't want to take chances.

"I've come a long way," Alaji said. "I... I've seen things that—"

The old woman cut her off with a laugh. "You're less than a

day's march from the spot you were born. I've come farther. I've seen the floating falls, the marble caverns, the courts of the elf kings, and the fields of ice. You've seen nothing."

"Who are you? What do you want?" Alaji demanded.

"I'm here for the talisman. The round rock you carry," the woman stated plainly. She leaned on her staff and waited.

Alaji moved back. Ejick, reading her animosity, hissed at the old woman and bared his teeth. "It's mine," Alaji said.

"It isn't. Not really," the old woman said. "And that doesn't matter anyway."

"I'm not giving it up. It's my only way home."

"It could take you there," the old woman agreed. "Would you welcome your execution? Or have you begun entertaining notions of changing the past? Saving your kin, perhaps. But why stop there? Why not steal away Hollik when he was an infant and toss him to wild dogs?"

Alaji stared in disbelief. "Who are you?" she demanded again. "Are you with Yemerik? Hollik?"

"I have no such allegiances," the old woman said.

"Could the rock do those things? Could it let me change my brother's fate?"

"If you knew how to use it as I do. But I haven't come to hold your hand. I told you – I'm here for the stone. To take it from you."

"Then leave before I feed you to my goblin," Alaji said.

"Are you counting yet?" the old woman asked. And then she vanished. Alaji stepped back reflexively, reappearing seconds before. But the old woman was still missing. It made no sense: she'd been here, in this time and place. In this moment. And now she was gone.

The blow seemed to appear from the air itself. The old woman's staff simply materialized inches from Alaji's face and made contact. Alaji fell back, trying to restart her count despite being dazed. Ejick hissed and leapt at the old woman but she was gone as quickly as she'd appeared, and the goblin fell on the ground. He looked around desperately, trying to find her. And then she was back, swinging her staff and knocking him back.

Alaji had crawled along the beach towards a small piece of driftwood. It was still damp, but it was all she could reach. She whispered her incantations and threw the smoldering piece of wood.

The old woman caught it and chanted her own spell. She opened her hand, and the wood fell to the sand. The smoke, however, remained in her hand and flame sprouted, as well. It burned without fuel, and yet it didn't scorch the old woman. She stroked it, as one might a pet. Then she lightly waved her hand from side to side, as if she were sprinkling seeds. Sparks flew out, landing on the ground, and where they did, fire exploded. Alaji just stared in disbelief. It was impossible. It was more like the breath of a dragon than spells of the hearth. This was magic like she'd never imagined.

Ejick stared, dumbfounded. He dropped to the ground, grabbed a rock, and was back to his feet once more. He took aim and raised the projectile over his head.

But the woman spoke. She spoke the tongue of goblins as naturally and as crisply as one of the creatures. The words were mostly unknown to Alaji, though she knew their words for "death" and "fire," both of which were repeated several times. The goblin ran for the lake and dove in.

The old woman shook the last of the embers from her hand, which wasn't even singed. Then she walked towards Alaji. For her part, Alaji didn't wait. She scrambled to her feet and ran, as fast as she could, from the old woman. She began counting and she stepped back on five.

But the old woman's walking stick was waiting for her. It met her head first, and Alaji fell onto her back. The old woman's shadow fell over her. Then she saw the butt of the staff come at her. Alaji protected her face, but that wasn't the old woman's intent.

The witch struck Alaji's pack, knocking it open and sending the contents spilling out. The egg-shaped stone rolled across the ground.

Alaji forgot her safety and clambered after the object. She was only inches away when the staff came down. The small rock on the top of the staff met the larger with a crack.

Yemerik's stone split apart.

Alaji could feel it as easily as she saw it. The pulse from the stone exploded, and she reeled back in pain, clutching her head. The pain lasted just an instant, and then it receded. She withdrew her hand and saw blood on her palm. Whether it was from the old woman's staff or some sort of wound from the shattering stone, she wasn't sure.

She took a little joy in seeing the old woman was as hurt as Alaji. She'd been knocked back onto the ground and seemed dazed. If Alaji's head weren't spinning, she'd have leapt at her now, but as it was, she feared she'd pass out if she tried to stand.

The old woman laughed and used her staff to regain her footing. Then she backed off slowly. Alaji went for the pieces. It had mostly split in three shards, though there were eight smaller parts as well. She wrapped her arms around them and glared at the old woman. "I'll kill you," Alaji swore.

"Come find me," the old woman replied. "In the early days, follow the singing birds to the hut at the towering oak." Then the old woman reached into a pack she carried and withdrew a stone talisman. Its shape was identical to the one she'd destroyed, though its coloration was different. She held it to her lips, whispered a short incantation, and vanished.

Alaji was in tears as she gathered the shards of the broken object and placed them back in her bag. Then she looked at the lake.

Ejick looked back at her. The goblin looked around, frantically. Then, biting his lip, he turned towards the woods and ran, leaving Alaji alone.

PART 3

1

For the first time in three days, Yemerik woke up and began his day without having to throw up. He brushed away the leaves he'd covered himself with for warmth and swatted at the bugs crawling on his arms. Every joint and muscle in his body was sore, and his head ached from dehydration. It was, all things considered, a demeaning and unpleasant state for a man of his station. But, again, no vomiting, so things were looking up.

He knelt beside the stream he'd slept near and dipped his head into the clear water. He swallowed a mouthful then sat up, wiping the dirt from his face. It was likely it was the water which had been making him sick, but he didn't have much choice. He didn't have a way to purify it, and without the talisman, he wasn't protected from the millions of microscopic parasites in each gulp. With luck, his stomach was adjusting on its own now: the water he'd had before sleeping had stayed put.

Breakfast was a handful of berries, seeds, and nuts, which was most of what he'd eaten the past week. He'd managed to catch a few fish in the stream using a fir branch like a net, but each had taken him hours. Besides, he'd been left with the problem of cooking them. He'd spent the better part of an afternoon rubbing a pair of twigs together but had gotten nowhere. Eventually, he came up with the idea of using the rocks at the foot of the hills. By mid-afternoon, the darker ones were hot to the touch. The results hadn't been as appetizing as he'd hoped, but he'd managed to get the fish warm at least.

He wondered how long it would take before he started eating them raw. And how long after that before he went after bugs. He tried to think back to his survival training, but he hadn't paid much attention in the first place. He'd always had a far simpler axiom for getting by: when things get bad, go back to the Citadel. Or at least one of the enlightened ages.

And, should he ever lose the talisman that could bring him back, he'd an even simpler plan in reserve: die quickly. But it was a situation he'd never really expected to be in, and now that he was here, he found that plan less enticing than he'd expected.

Which left him sick, starving, and exhausted in a place no one would ever think to look for him. And if anyone ever discovered what had happened, he fully expected they'd laugh and say he had it coming. He wasn't supposed to be here. No one was without permission. But permission for this era was hard to come by, and he had information. It now seemed increasingly likely that information had been planted as a trap, but that didn't detract from the logic of his original decision.

Besides, he wasn't dead yet. At least not from his vantage point. That's always a dangerous perspective when time traveling, but without the talisman there wasn't much he could do about it.

Which put him back where he'd started a week ago: lost, humiliated, and desperately needing to track down the girl and recover his property. He'd no doubt have managed it by now if he hadn't gotten sick. And if he'd known the first thing about tracking. And, of course, assuming whoever the girl was working with hadn't already shown her how to use it to travel to distant eras.

Yemerik toyed with the possibilities. How much had the girl known? Someone had taught her to slip through time. There was no telling how much they'd told her about the Citadel. She'd known to steal the talisman but not how to use it. She'd asked him about Hollik, so she hadn't known what would happen. She hadn't expected it, at least not all of it, which raised the possibility that whoever had planned this and instructed her to take the talisman hadn't known what was going to happen.

That was extremely good. It suggested that whatever was coming hadn't already played out and that he wasn't already dead.

Of course, it was also possible that everything, from her questions to her misuse of the talisman, had been a ploy to mislead him into this conclusion. If so, then it was all a staged game leading to some horrid end. In that scenario, there wasn't a damn thing he could do to stop it, so there was no sense dwelling on the idea.

Assuming he wasn't marching towards his inevitable demise, there was a chance to get the talisman back. All he had to do was figure out where the girl had gone. She'd have been scared and confused. She would have assumed she was somewhere foreign and would have wanted to get home. She'd have gone to high ground and tried to guess the direction.

High ground. As good a place as any to start. Yemerik was standing near the foot of a hill and he started up. It wasn't particularly tall, but he found himself winded and needed to rest three times. When he finally reached the top, he surveyed the area. To the north was the swamp he'd climbed through; to the south, the valley and the lakes.

Would she have recognized the land? Probably not. He'd seen no evidence she'd learned to move more than a few seconds in time: the idea that centuries could be sidestepped would have been too much. She'd have looked at the lakes and the hills and thought them similar perhaps, but that would have been the extent of it. She'd have tried to guess the direction home, not realizing she was staring right at it.

Then what? Assuming she didn't pick a direction at random, she'd have tried another hill. Then another in a futile attempt to find some indication of where she was. That was a place to start, he reasoned. Try the hills, one by one, and see if there were signs she'd passed through. He looked at the line of hills and squinted.

Wait a minute. There was smoke pooling at the top of one.

2

Yemerik studied the clearing from the tree line. The air was thick with smoke, making it difficult to see. But the girl was there, turned away from him, and she was clutching his bag. With her free hand, she tossed a handful of sticks onto the flame.

He paused to consider his options. The first was to sneak up and try to get the bag away from her before she could act. If he could surprise her and reach the talisman fast enough, he'd be safe. But he'd have to be quick: otherwise, she'd simply shift in time. And she could easily kill him. He'd seen what she would have done to Hollik and his men.

Tactically, it was a sound plan with a handful of minor problems. First, he was neither stealthy nor particularly fast. Second, he was tired from hiking. And he was still queasy. Then there was the throbbing pain in his forehead.

Put together, the girl could likely beat him without her magic. With it, she could humiliate and torture him to death. Which meant the direct approach might not be his best option. There was always the less confrontational method: he could wait in hiding for night, then follow her and steal back the talisman while she slept. He tried to imagine waiting on the hill all day with no additional food or water. He tried to imagine following her through the woods in the dark, tried to picture not tripping over every root and stone when he could barely stand.

His chances of success were low. That left one real option. One desperate chance to reclaim the means to return to his time and set things right.

"Wait! Please!" He shouted as he stumbled out from the trees in plain view. "Please! I can help you – I can get you home!" He held his hands in front of him and moved slowly. "Can we talk?" To his relief, the girl didn't run, nor did she seem surprised to see him. So the smoke had been meant to signal him. Of course, that didn't mean she wasn't luring him into a trap to murder him, but his life represented a cheap bet by this point. "Okay. I'm going to come over there. If that's all right. I'm not going to... I'm not going to try anything." He approached until he was about a dozen feet away, then he stopped and sat down. "I wasn't sure... when I saw the smoke. Whether it was you or a dragon or something." He laughed.

"The dragons mostly stay by the lakes," Alaji replied. She was watching him carefully, and she kept the bag held behind her.

"Oh," Yemerik said. He'd been mostly joking about the dragons. "Listen. I think... I think we got off on the wrong foot."

Alaji stared at him silently.

"I mean, I'm not... I'm really not with Hollik. I was traveling with him, but that's all. I don't have anything to do with him, so I'm not your enemy."

Alaji's expression didn't change in the least.

"And I didn't mean for you to get stuck here. I only brought you here to ask you some questions. About the spell you used. I think... I think there was a misunderstanding, and we've both had some time to reflect on that. But now I really, really want to leave this place, and I'm guessing you do, too. I can get you home, but only if I have what's in that bag. You see, you're not where you think you are. You're... please. I know this is going to sound strange, but you see those lakes? They're your lakes. The same ones. Look at them, please. We're—"

"We're in the past. On the fifth hand, I think, before the lakes were settled," Alaji said.

"The what? Oh. Of course. You use that base-five counting system. That would be... what? Six hundred and fifty? That's the right order, anyway." He saw Alaji no longer understood him. "Never mind. Yes. Yes, we're in the past. The stone in my bag can bring us back to where we were."

Alaji nodded and opened the bag. "Can you fix it?" she asked, removing several pieces of stone.

Yemerik tilted his head, confused. "I don't understand. Where's the original?"

"What original?" Alaji asked.

"The original stone. The one that was in there. I... listen to me. I know someone's been working with you. Whatever they told you is a lie. Probably a lie, I mean. I don't know what they want or why they're doing this–"

"You mean the old woman?"

"What old woman?"

"The one who broke the stone." Alaji waved the pieces in the air.

Yemerik shook his head. "The stone – the one that was in my bag – can't be broken, not without.... never mind. Those pieces you're holding are fakes."

"No," Alaji said. "I saw it. These are still... they're alive."

"Alive? They're rocks," Yemerik said.

"But they have a pulse."

Yemerik looked at her with a baffled expression on his face. "Stones don't have pulses," he said.

"But it matches my heartbeat. I can feel it when I concentrate. I feel it now. It's like... rings in a lake. The little waves. Isn't that how it works?"

"It works by connecting to the... never mind. It works by opening a... a door to another point in time."

"I mean when it... when it keeps me from splitting. When I step back."

"What are you talking about?" Yemerik asked, even more confused and irritated. "What do you think the stone does?"

Alaji took a breath. "When I... when I step back. It makes it so there's just one of me."

"Step back," Yemerik echoed. "You mean when you go back in time. It maintains continuity by... yes. Yes, I get it. That would keep you from encountering earlier versions of yourself by overwriting them. Assuming the stone's had a chance to attune itself to your– wait. Wait! Rings! Waves! The energy pattern! You can feel the energy pattern?"

"Energy?"

"Pulses... like a rhythm. You can feel a rhythm coming from the stone?"

"You can't?" Alaji asked.

Yemerik stood up and approached. Alaji didn't stop him and even handed over the largest piece. He began to examine it. "You're saying the energy pattern now... I mean, the rhythms. The rhythms coming off of this match the rhythms from before? Are you sure?"

"Yes."

"But that's... that's not possible," he whispered. "This can't be the same stone, because there's nothing – absolutely nothing – outside the Citadel that could break one of the talismans."

"I saw it break," Alaji said again.

"That's just not possible. It has to be a fake."

"Alright," she said. Then she vanished and reappeared five feet away. "Then why aren't there two of me?"

Yemerik looked pale. He examined the shard in his hands. The markings were indistinguishable from those of the Citadel. He looked at Alaji. And back to the shard.

There were theories buzzing through his head. Many, many theories. That this was still a trick. That the stone and the girl and the hill were illusions. That she had the real talisman on her and was trying to distract him with the shards. The problem was that each of those theories was utterly stupid.

"Okay," he said with a heavy sigh. "Let's say the talisman is broken." He slumped onto the ground and looked up at the sky. He stared up, almost hoping a dragon would swoop down and devour him whole. But there were no dragons up there. Just a bright, blue horizon interspersed with the occasional cloud. All in all, a beautiful day. It seemed entirely unfair that the sky couldn't at least be bothered to rain on him.

"Can you fix it?" Alaji said again.

"It's... no. I mean, the stones are meant to resonate as beacons for... uh. I don't... I don't think it'll make much sense. But no, I can't fix it once it's broken. I don't even think they could do that at the Citadel. I'm sorry... at the place it comes from. The place I come from. The Citadel of the Last Gathering Before the Falling Stars. It's... hard to explain."

"But the pieces still work. When I step back, they still–"

"Yes, but that's different. They're still attuned to the Citadel. They're part of the Citadel, in fact. Like an anchor. You have those, right? Never mind. Think of it this way. The stone, it does a couple of little things in addition to one big thing. The big thing, the thing it exists to do, is to open a portal in time. That requires it to be in one piece. The rest works fine regardless. I'm sorry I can't explain it better. I keep trying to think of metaphors, but you won't even have the concepts for my metaphors yet."

"You're saying we're trapped here?" Alaji asked, taking out her water skin. She took a quick sip and offered it to Yemerik, who nearly emptied it.

"I'm sorry. It's been so long since I've been able to drink without getting sick." He saw Alaji look at him strangely. "It's... the water here. My stomach isn't used to it. There are... it's complicated, but the stone corrects for the difference."

"But it can't take me home?"

"No. It's like... it's like a broken raft. You could use the pieces as spears or clubs or something, but it wouldn't work as a raft. The stone has enchantments on it that will keep you safe from that sort of thing. That's one of the little extra things it does. I wouldn't last long without it. Diseases adapt too quickly. Poisons are always changing. Those spells are rudimentary. It shouldn't matter that the thing's broken: the magic instilled in a pebble of it would be sufficient. Just make sure you keep a piece or two with you, and I'll do the same."

Alaji nodded. She was going to, anyway. The alternative was far too horrific. "Then we're trapped?"

Yemerik rubbed his forehead. "More or less. I mean, there's a way, but we'd never live through it. I don't know about you, but I haven't found much to eat."

"I can get us food," Alaji said.

Yemerik leaned forward a bit. "You can?"

"Rabbits, fish, and other small things. If I had a blade or a spear it would be easier, but I've managed all right so far."

"That... that changes things." Yemerik drew a knife out of a hidden fold in his clothes. He handed it over with a nod. "Be careful with that. It's—"

"Ow!" Alaji cut her finger testing the edge as soon as she had it. It was light but sturdy. But she was entranced more than hurt. The blade reflected light like a stream, similar to the strange disks in Yemerik's bag. "What... what is it? What's it made out of?"

"Metal."

"Metal," she repeated the strange word. "Is it magic?"

"No. It's not even that good of a knife, as far as they go. Now, unless this was all a clever ploy to get my one remaining weapon away from me, could you get us something to eat?"

She started down the hill, but Yemerik called out, "Wait!" Alaji turned back, and Yemerik said, "When you hunt, do you... do you use your spell? The one where you... step back?"

"Yes," Alaji replied.

"I see. Then, take this." He walked to her and handed her the shard of the talisman she'd given him.

"I thought we were each supposed to keep a piece."

"Yes, well. We are, but... listen. When you're using that spell, you should have all of them or none, okay?"

"I used it before with—"

"I know, I know. And that's done now, but in the future, you shouldn't leave pieces behind. Any other time, we split them up. But, when you're using your spell... it can create... complications."

"What kind of complications?"

"Well… it creates a version of me somewhere that will all but certainly die here." He said this matter-of-factly, as if explaining the importance of knotting a fishing net one way rather than another.

—

It didn't take Alaji long to find a goose. She dispatched it with the knife, slitting its throat. She was back at the hilltop, where Yemerik had attempted to turn her signal fire into one that could be used for cooking. She took one look at the result and decided they were better off starting over. Besides, she didn't like remaining in the open. She wasn't as certain the dragons would keep to the lakes as she'd claimed.

After making do with sharpened rocks, it felt good to clean an animal with an actual blade. The fact it was impossibly sharp with a wooden handle that seemed as if it was made to fit her hand helped, as well. She sharpened the end of a tree branch, then began roasting the bird.

"All right," Alaji said to the startled man. "How do I get back to my home?"

Yemerik had a difficult time peeling his concentration away from the smell of the cooking bird, but he managed. "It's difficult. And it's imprecise. But there's another way to move through time. Something my people set up, sort of a door. The nearest is in a place called Ilpinthi. Well, it's a place that will be called Ilpinthi eventually. It's sort of a trade route through time. We built it to move large objects from era to era, but it should work for us in a pinch, as long as we can get there. It's to the west."

"Then west," Alaji said.

"No. First we should get provisions. Food, clothing. That sort of thing. We'll be lucky to reach the door before winter. Your fire spells will help, but we'll need more."

"There are no people to trade with," Alaji said.

"Not here. But your tribe originally came from the north, didn't they?"

"Yes," Alaji said. "But there's a lot of land up there."

"It's our best chance. We'll go north. Hopefully we'll find someone there. Then, we go to Ilpinthi, and from there, Hathari."

"Where's that?"

"In the east, unfortunately. But it's more important we reach when it is. The Hatharian empire won't exist for a thousand years... a... I don't know how many of your hands. Five or six or something."

"It's okay. The northmen count like you. I know the word. It's further forward than we are back, isn't it?"

"Yes, by two hundred... wait. This is easy. That's just three and a half hands, isn't it?"

"It's a finger on the fourth hand and three on the third," Alaji said. It felt so distant. Five generations was as far as her family's history went before dissolving into myths and legends. This was twice that, not counting the eternity that stretched between the real present and the distant past where she was trapped.

"You should really learn to think in tenths," Yemerik said. "It would make things easier."

"Some of my people thought the world wouldn't last that long. I'd begun to think that myself."

Yemerik started to laugh. "What? Two hundred years?" He laughed harder and harder, until he almost fell over. "It endures a bit longer, I assure you."

"There were signs," Alaji muttered, somewhat embarrassed. "We thought the war was going to end it. Or the gods would."

"Well, you can stop worrying about them. Your gods don't exist."

Alaji froze. "Are you certain?"

"Positive."

She considered this for a moment. "I hope you're right."

"Trust me. If your gods existed, we'd have found them. There are no gods. Well, not yet, and the ones that form aren't really... never mind. It's complicated. But that skirmish won't end anything. And whatever Hollik might have gained wouldn't mean a damn thing. I don't know how long his kingdom would have survived, but whatever legacy he had wouldn't have lasted when the ships came in from the east. It'll take the Hathari less than a decade to capture the continent. I always wondered how they did it so fast, but that was before I discovered your people's fanatical obsession with not learning new spells."

"More conquerors?" Alaji whispered.

"Well, yes. But it's not like that. It's... you'll see. If we live long enough to get there, you'll see what they accomplish. They build an empire. The first empire, the first... well, really the first anything. This isn't the end of time. The Hatharian Empire is considered the beginning. They create it all. They invent things you can't imagine. One of their rulers invents the spells you've been using, the magic of time. They even put a city here, I think. Unless there's another set of lakes I'm getting these confused with. I'm sorry. City... it's like a village but much bigger. You'll see some."

"It's where you're from, isn't it?" Alaji asked.

"No," Yemerik said. "I'm from... I don't think you're ready for that. Hathari is the beginning of history. I'm from a place at the end. The only place at the end."

"But they know you in Hathari?"

"Like I said, they were the first to unlock the secrets of time. Well, they started to. My people came to them because of it. We wanted to open discussions and to bring them into our work. We owe them a great deal, actually. Maybe I'll tell you about that sometime. The important thing is, we've kept that communication open. From Hathari we can contact the Citadel. And they'll fix everything. They'll put you back in your time, back where you belong. Then they'll take me home, too. They'll put things right. It's what they do."

Alaji turned the goose. Then she looked at Yemerik. She didn't fully trust him, of course, but that seemed trivial. It was either help him or die where her ancestors would one day walk over her bones. "Okay. If you'll swear to get me home safe, then I'll help you."

"Yes, definitely. If you can help me reach Hathari, I swear I'll find you a way back to your time. You can kill Hollik and all his lieutenants and live out your days however you want."

Alaji looked away when he brought up killing Hollik. The idea didn't have the same appeal it once had. But she only said, "Good. When do we leave?"

"Tomorrow, I think. The trip won't be easy."

Alaji nodded and unrolled her blanket. Then she took the knife and stabbed it into the middle of the deer skin. Slowly she drew it through, then turned the blanket over and cut to the other side.

"What are you doing?" Yemerik asked.

Alaji handed him half of the skin. "The north gets cold. You'll need this."

"Can't you just... kill another?"

"I didn't... no. It would take too long to cure the skin."

"Oh. Then where...." he muttered, wrapping the skin around his shoulders. "I mean. You didn't have.... Is that...." He scratched his head and settled on, "Do you think the bird's ready?"

3

"I'm not going to keep answering your questions if you don't start listening to the answers." Alaji's ultimatum to Yemerik was overdue. They'd been traveling north for all five phases of the moon (she'd been relieved to hear that other people divvied up the moon into five phases), and she was tired of repeating the same discussions again and again. "For the last time, no one taught me to step back. I figured it out myself. Why is that so hard for you?"

"Because it doesn't make sense," Yemerik answered. She knew him well enough now to tell his voice was strained, even though he was trying his best to sound detached. "Time travel isn't something that gets discovered often. The magics involved are extremely esoteric and difficult to master. The odds of it being discovered twice in a few centuries – on the same continent, no less – are too miniscule to be considered."

"I don't know anything about that," Alaji said. "But no one taught me any of this." They were travelling across a ridge now, far beyond anywhere Alaji – or any member of her immediate family – had ever been. It had been a mostly uneventful journey so far. They'd encountered goblins on a handful of occasions, but never by surprise like the time in the woods. She'd gotten used to frightening them off using fire.

"I believe that you believe that. But there's just no way it's true. There are ways someone could have passed this information to you without you even knowing. They might have given you some sort of theory without actually giving you the method. Or maybe they used a spell to transform your memory of how you came about the information."

"Spells can do that?" Alaji asked, disturbed.

"The right spell can do almost anything," Yemerik said.

"Then why do you find it so hard to accept an old woman broke our stone?"

"My stone," Yemerik corrected her. "And I said almost. The magic of the Citadel is impossible to overcome."

"But it is broken."

"I guess I should have said 'almost' again," Yemerik admitted. "But you see my point about your magic."

"If someone changed my memory..." Alaji paused to shudder. "If someone did that, I don't see how I could know about it."

"Well, it's unlikely, anyway. Those spells are difficult and not common, either. I think it's more likely that someone gave you the underlying idea, then let you figure out the rest. It could even have been slipped into your people's myths, so that someone would stumble on it eventually. Like a riddle or something."

"I don't know. I guess that's possible. What would the ideas have been? What would someone have told me so I'd figure it out?"

"How should I know? I don't even know how you do it. I'm a constructive historian, not a thaumaturgist."

"Yemerik!" Alaji shouted.

"Sorry. I never learned much about magic theory. I mean, how spells develop."

"I figured out what 'magic theory' is."

"Yeah, well, it's still my best guess. Someone travelled back and encoded instructions for developing a temporal disruption spell into your people's stories."

"Who would do that?"

"I don't know. Maybe someone from Later Hathari, during the wars, trying to undermine the empire in its golden age. Sorry. That won't make sense."

"I know about war," Alaji replied.

Yemerik laughed. "No, you really don't. Not those kinds of wars. The Hatharian Empire was reinforced with magic, wisdom, arts, and technology gathered from their own distant future. They grew strong. But the things they gathered weren't simply lost. The empire wouldn't fade on its own. Eventually, their descendants began to realize that, as the past was being changed, their future would continue to shift. They sent emissaries back to demand their own ancestors stop gathering objects and knowledge from the future. In essence, they wanted to delay the use of time travel until their era. But their descendants had the same idea, and none of them had any intention of not using magic to better the empire."

"That's where you want to go?"

"Oh, it takes several millennia before things get out of hand, and – for the most part – hostilities are kept to minimum. It's only after the–" Yemerik's voice trailed off as he looked over the ledge. A small village was sitting in the valley below them on the near bank of a river. They weren't close enough to see the people yet, but the huts and fields looked like the ones in her village. The two were speechless for a moment. Finally, Yemerik whispered, "Do you think they're friendly?"

"No," Alaji said simply. "They're northmen."

"Not the ones you knew," Yemerik reminded her. "Your people came from near here. These might even be your ancestors."

"It doesn't matter. It's the land that makes the northmen hard. The lakes calmed us. At least, that's what I was always taught. Maybe those were just more stories. If so, I don't know much of anything. Like you, it turns out."

"Well, we should be ready for the worst, but with luck they'll be used to visitors."

"Even if they're willing to trade, I'm not sure what we have to barter with. I suppose I could kill some geese, but I'm in no hurry to drag them across the plain. It would take a lot of geese to get what we need."

"No," Yemerik said, grinning. "We'll pay with money."

"Pay with what?"

In answer, Yemerik dug around his bag, which Alaji had given back long before. "Money," he said again, retrieving a few of the small disks. He held them up to examine them in the sunlight. "No use wasting the finer metals. Copper pieces should have the same effect."

"What are they?"

"They're coins. They're... I guess it's rather complicated. They're invented to represent trade. Everyone understands that this is worth, say, the same as a chicken. So it's treated the way you'd treat a chicken in barter. It's always a good idea to have an assortment when you're traveling through time."

"That would have gotten more than a chicken back home," Alaji said. "Much more."

Yemerik laughed. "Good. It's not worth much, but I'd rather not introduce too many anachronisms to prehistory. The fewer we have to spend, the better." He started down towards the village. "Remember what I said about magic. Don't cast anything until you've seen one of them cast it first. Neither of us know what spells these people know or what superstitions they have. Oh, and the language! I almost forgot to warn you about the language."

"The northmen have a different sound to their tongues, but they speak our words until you go far to the east or west," Alaji said.

"A different accent, yes. But that's your time. It will be far more noticeable here. The words may be different or have altered meanings. Even the syntax could have changed. I have a pendant that will equalize my speech, but it might take time to adjust. Until it does, I'll have to make do with body language and tone. It will be awkward until then. Even after that, you won't understand much of what we're saying, if you understand any of it."

"And if they attack us?"

"Then forget everything I just said and kill as many as you can, starting with the leaders," Yemerik replied. He handed over the pieces of the talisman he'd been carrying. "If we're lucky, the others will run. Maybe we can gather a handful of supplies and escape."

Alaji whispered a brief prayer to her gods, forgetting for a moment that they didn't exist.

4

They smelled the rotting dragon head before they saw it. When they came to it, speared on a spike and left facing away from the village, Yemerik stopped to take a look, despite the foul odor and cloud of swarming flies.

"I'm assuming this is a warning," Yemerik said.

"We don't do things like this," Alaji said. "I haven't heard of the northmen doing it, either. But I would say it's some kind of warning."

"Was it young?" Yemerik asked, stepping closer to the head.

"No," Alaji replied, somewhat surprised by the question. The head was nearly as large as she was tall.

"Oh. I'd thought it would be bigger. I mean, I know they get bigger, but I suppose this is an early breed. I guess I never realized they'd vary so much."

"How big are the dragons you've seen?" Alaji asked.

"I've never actually seen one before. At least not one living or even... recently living. The only ones I've seen have been foss.... skeletons. The only ones I've seen have been skeletons that were dead a long, long time. I'd like to see some living specimens. From a safe distance, of course."

"There were several by the lakes. I'd have brought you if I'd known."

"It doesn't matter. We can always visit the zoos in Hathari."

Alaji ignored the words she didn't understand. During their journey she'd discovered it was far easier than the alternative. "We could turn back," she offered. "Look for another village."

"No," Yemerik said. "It's late enough in the year as it is. If we want to reach Ilpinthi before winter, we need to move on."

Alaji nodded, before glancing back at the skewered dragon head. She turned her attention forward and kept an eye out for anyone nearby, but there was still nothing. As they approached, she wondered if the town might be deserted until she saw a child standing along the path. The boy was no more than a finger on Alaji's second hand and two on her first – six or seven, as Yemerik would say. She tried thinking of the boy in these terms but they still didn't feel like numbers, only words. The child saw them and took off towards the village.

Soon, they began passing fields of crops, mostly cabbage and onions, though there was some grain, as well. A middle-aged woman working in one of the fields stopped to stare at them. She'd been trying to overturn large stones using a wood tool, which she now clutched, in case she'd need a weapon. She didn't approach or speak, and Alaji and Yemerik continued on. Soon, there were other farmers.

A few shouted at them, but Alaji could only grasp bits and pieces of their words. Yemerik kept going, so Alaji did as well.

"What are you looking for?" she whispered.

"Someone important," he replied.

She guessed they'd found someone important when they reached a hand's count of men armed with spears surrounding an old man who seemed to be waiting for the pair of visitors.

Alaji grew tense. Her count began running in the back of her head while she considered the implications of using it. She wasn't sure what gods these people prayed to, but she suspected they were similar to those of her people. If they saw her use magic that wasn't given to man, would they react the same? And, if they did, what would she do? Yemerik's words echoed in the back of her head: if they attack, kill as many as you can. It seemed like it should have been a joke, but she didn't think it was.

She'd never doubted she could kill Hollik, because she'd believed her power had been given to her for just such a task. But Yemerik had once said she had been about to kill more. Hollik hadn't been alone: there'd been several others with him. His guards or relatives, no doubt. Once she'd finished Hollik, what about them? She'd seen echoes of herself stab the warlord even if she never reached him, and it looked so easy. As easy as catching fish and slitting the throats of rabbits, ducks, and even deer in the field. When she used her magic, everything around her fell into a dance of repeating steps. She could weave through them, striking at leisure.

For the first time, she realized how easy it would be to slaughter a dozen men. And that terrified her. These people weren't so different from hers. They didn't look any more fearsome or any less wary of outsiders. And there was the possibility that they may even be her ancestors. If so, and if she killed them, how would she be born?

The thought consumed her, and she lost her count. She stopped herself from starting again: if the choice was between dying and destroying her people's future, it was an easy one to make.

Yemerik ignored the guards and stepped towards the old man. A few of the guards stepped between and lowered their spears, though they were more threatening than outright hostile. Yemerik smiled at them, though he was sweating. He raised his hands to show he was unarmed, and then he waited.

The old man said something, but Alaji couldn't understand. Yemerik stood completely still. The old man spoke again. This time, Alaji grasped a few words. These were words her people used, though they were distorted, as if she were listening with ears full of water. She thought she understood the gist, though: "Who are you?" or something similar. She didn't dare answer. Yemerik was silent, as well. His pendant hadn't done whatever it was going to do yet.

By the time the old man repeated himself a third time, he was growing anxious, and the spear-carriers were bracing for action. They weren't asking "who" but ""what." Maybe "What brings you here?" Alaji couldn't be sure, but that seemed likely. She eyed the guards and saw them ready to move.

"Wait!" She said, and the men froze. "Please."

Yemerik turned to her and mouthed, "Quiet!" She ignored him.

"Trade. We've come to trade," Alaji said, speaking slowly. "We're lost," she added.

The old man looked her over and said something. She didn't understand a word of it. He touched the shoulder of one of his guards, who stepped back to converse with him. They whispered back and forth for a few seconds, though the precaution was unnecessary: they could just as easily have shouted to each other and maintained secrecy.

"You should have waited," Yemerik whispered to her. "A minute more, and my pendant will adjust."

"I don't think they would have waited," Alaji said.

"If they don't, use the other option we discussed."

"No," Alaji said. "If you were right, if my people came from here—"

"You picked a bad time to start wondering about the nature of causality. Listen, just be ready. I'll try to think of something to say to explain this. But if they don't listen, you need to make sure we get out of this alive."

"Not at the cost of my people."

Yemerik was about to respond when the leader of the men shouted something to him. Again, they were garbled, but Alaji thought she caught the word for trade in their midst. That was promising. She also thought she heard a curse similar to one the men in her village reserved for spies and assassins. That was a little more worrying.

"Oh, thank the path," Yemerik whispered. "It's working. We'll talk about this later. Just keep an eye out and be ready." Then his speech shifted to match the other men's. He began speaking slowly, and opened his arms to show he didn't have any obvious weapons.

Alaji stood while Yemerik traded words with the group's leader, who seemed less than trusting. She had some luck parsing their words, but only understood fragments of the discussion. Yemerik was referring to her a lot, then added something about animals and speech. Then trade. He was saying that word a lot, which was easy enough to follow. As was the direction "west," but mainly because they kept pointing when they spoke the malformed word.

There was more back and forth. Sometimes there were raised voices and leveled spears, but Yemerik seemed to calm them. Then he reached into his bag and withdrew two of the carved disks, one of which he tossed to the leader, who immediately held it at arms' length. He barked an order to one of his guards, who ran off and returned with a man even older than the leader, who took the disk. The new arrival held it between his fingers and began inspecting it carefully. He said something that placated the leader and all the guards. The spears didn't leave their hands, but they did set their ends on the ground and lean against them. The leader approached Yemerik and stood close to him. Now they were whispering, even laughing. Yemerik turned to flash Alaji a smile.

It cost him four of his coins, but when Yemerik and Alaji left the village they did so leading a pair of horses weighed down with skins of beer, blankets, dried meat, clothing, and other provisions. They had a jar full of salt and another containing a mixture of dried herbs and ground roots. They also had new clothes, as well as capes made from the skin of a bear and shoes. Three spears were strapped to Yemerik's horse, as well.

The animals followed Alaji, who'd enchanted them as best as she could. She'd never used the spell on a horse before. Growing up, she rarely had cause to use it on anything bigger than a chicken. For what it was worth, she was relatively good with chickens.

"What did you tell them?" Alaji asked, now that no one was nearby to hear. She'd said nothing in the village, save a few suggestions as to what they should ask for. The salt and spears had been her ideas, as had a number of the herbs.

"I told them I was a merchant from the west, and that I'd gotten lost and had been wandering the wilderness for most of a year. I also said you were a wild-woman I'd found in the south, and that I'd been around you so long, I'd forgotten how to speak correctly."

"They believed that?"

"I needed some excuse for you not speaking right. From their perspective, I mean. It wasn't easy convincing them we weren't spies."

"Spies for who?"

"Some chief named Guilleve, I think. I don't know. I suppose he's their version of Hollik."

"Does everyone have a Hollik?" Alaji asked.

"More or less. Most of history is someone demanding something from everyone else. If he fails, he's a tyrant; if he succeeds, he's brought peace and stability, or at the very least wiped away an old world. It's... it's just how things are. Everything's pieced together in hindsight by whoever wins the fight. It's rare for a leader to be anywhere near as good or bad as they're described. But it doesn't really matter if Guilleve is a good or bad man. They hate him enough to kill anyone they think is his ally. Which brings us to the other thing we need to talk about. You need to be ready to fight."

"For all I know, I'm descended from those people. If I kill them—"

"Nothing. As long as you stay near the shard of stone from the Citadel, temporal changes won't impact you. You could kill your grandparents before your mother was born, and it wouldn't do a thing to you. And, once we get to Hathari and I can contact the Citadel, I can fix all of this. I'll be able to make it like we were never here. Anyone you kill won't be dead."

"What if we die without reaching Hathari?" Alaji asked.

"We have to reach Hathari. Someone is altering the foundations of history. The implications could be catastrophic to the work of the Citadel. Besides, I really don't want to die here and re-enter the cycle at... never mind. I don't want to die here."

"I don't care about your Citadel," Alaji said. "I care about my home and people. And I won't endanger them by killing people who might be their ancestors."

"I wish I could put this into words you'd understand. Your entire concept of time, of measuring years in factors of five, it's insufficient. Look. Let me try this. Imagine each step we've taken since leaving the lakes was a year. We walked more than a thousand in the first few hours. I mean, the first... finger. Whatever. Now think about how far we traveled to get here. If each step was a year, we still wouldn't be near when I'm from. Not one hundredth of the way. Think of how many civilizations like your village would have had time to pop up and get swallowed. Think of how many people we're talking about. Because it's only a fraction of a fraction of the truth. Everyone in your village – everyone you've seen in your entire lifetime – would fit in a city block of the kingdoms that are coming. When I say this is bigger than your village or this little slice of prehistory, I mean it's inconceivably bigger and more important. These are the scales the Citadel works on. We're trying to change the flow of history, to make sure there's as little pain and suffering as possible."

"I don't believe you," Alaji said, growing upset. Her head hurt, and Yemerik's step metaphor didn't make sense. None of it did. She touched the neck of one of the horses, in part for balance and in part for comfort.

"I know this is hard, but I need you to understand how important this is. If we die here, there's... there's... oh." Yemerik's attention was stolen by a noise behind them. He looked back along the road and saw a group of riders approaching quickly. "Alaji. I don't have time to discuss this. If we die here–"

"I understand," she said, looking back at the riders. There were four of them, all armed with spears.

5

As soon as the visitors had left, the debate began. Prilju, the elder, said they should be allowed to go in peace. They were strangers and were to be accorded the hospitality of Brive, the river god. Khuril, the hunter, disagreed. He called them spies and worse. The man, Yemerik, spoke words any fool could tell were lies. He claimed to be from the west, but no men lived to the west. None could survive in those untamed lands. His story about the girl, that she came from the wild, was absurd for more reasons than Khuril could count. And then there was the matter of their deerskins, which looked no better than goblin-cloth.

Prilju agreed they'd been lied to. "But that reveals nothing but secrets," he'd said. "The strangers were afraid, but not spies. Spies are masters of lies: clearly these two were novices."

This had garnered a laugh, but Khuril wasn't easily silenced, nor did he lack support. "Prilju's words are for soft times," he argued. "With Guilleve's band on the march, we can't afford such sentiment."

"They traded fairly," Prilju objected, "and they left in peace.

We have profited well from the exchange and should leave it at that." He held up the four objects, perfect circles as hard as stone and as bright in the sun as the river. Each bore the image of a man or woman on one side. The crowd gasped at them, each of which must be worth far more than the total given in trade. There were already arguments brewing over what was to be done with them; whether they should be turned to jewelry for trade with neighboring towns or whether they should remain here as heirlooms.

Khuril considered this for a moment. He chose his words carefully. "They parted too easily with their carvings. If these are so rare, then they must have plans to retake them." Khuril grinned at his opponent, who seemed to sense the end was near. "Prilju was wise to stay our hand while the strangers were in our village. The man was small, but had a strange look about him. Even the girl had a dangerous look in her eye. It is better such work happen on the field, where our children will not see it done and our women will not have to clean the streets." He looked at Prilju and waited.

Prilju did not like it. He believed in the laws of the river god, and this felt wrong to him. Still, he knew he'd been beat, and Khuril was offering him as generous a chance to yield as he was likely to get. He nodded and did his best not to scowl when the crowd cheered. "Very well. But it is to be quick," he said.

Khuril nodded and went for his horse. His three brothers came with him, and they set out at once. If the strangers were expert horsemen, it could take time to run them down, but they'd manage: the horses they'd been given were nowhere near as fast as their own.

He was surprised to see the strangers ahead of them on the road so soon, still leading their horses by hand, like children. At the very least, he'd expected them to take the animals aside towards the riverbank to hide their footprints in the shallow water. He half expected they'd have crossed by now, but they didn't seem interested in the water at all. Nor had they unbound their spears.

Khuril tightened his hold on his horse's reins, and the animal came to a stop. His brothers did the same, and they surveyed the scene before them. Yemerik and the girl were standing ahead of them in the distance, arguing. They could see the riders now. The girl began to approach slowly, while Yemerik stayed behind. For the first time, it occurred to Khuril that the pair he was tracking might not be spies, at all, but might instead be nothing more than peculiar travelers lost in a distant land. If things had been different, Khuril might have turned back. Despite his brash demeanor, he had no real interest in murdering innocents.

But things were not different. He'd placed his reputation on the line: to return without his prize would be humiliating. His hopes of succeeding Prilju would evaporate. Besides, his brothers were riding at his side, and they'd go on without him. No. He'd made his decision and would carry it out.

"Spear," he said, ready to have this done with. His youngest brother handed him one, and Khuril spurred his horse on. He charged at the girl and took aim, beginning the incantation that would quicken his spear and increase the impact.

Why wasn't she running? Why wasn't she pleading or screaming? It did not make sense to Khuril. He'd never killed a woman and was starting to wish the argument had gone against him. But it hadn't, so he threw the spear.

And, as he did, the girl was no longer where she'd been. The shock threw off his aim, not that it would have mattered, since she was no longer where he was aiming, anyway. But the spear stuck into the soil while Khuril's horse reared up.

The girl had not vanished, but flickered. She'd disappeared in one place to appear again in another. But she was only there an instant before vanishing again and reappearing elsewhere. It was too quick for Khuril's eyes, and his mind couldn't grasp what was happening. He froze for a moment, then turned back towards his brothers. He looked over his shoulder to see the girl had appeared by his spear and was working it loose from the ground.

"Another!" he commanded, as his brother tossed him a second spear. By the time he turned back, the girl was holding the first. Then she came at them. Khuril rode towards her, as did his brothers, all shouting a battle cry.

But the girl was like a reflection in water. She moved without moving, and she did so faster than anything Khuril had ever seen. One of his brothers threw his spear, but he seemed to be throwing it at random: it landed flat on the ground.

The girl was at the side of Khuril's oldest brother first. She never seemed to strike but instead appeared mid-strike, her spear buried in the side of the horse beside her.

The rider was thrown to the ground as his horse collapsed in a spray of blood. But the girl was already gone. Absently, Khuril wondered what had happened to the spear his brother had been carrying. Then he saw the girl again. He'd never seen her take it, and yet there it was in her hand. As if she'd always had it.

When the girl reappeared an instant later, the spear was burning. An instant later, she was in front of his next brother's horse, throwing the burning spear at the startled animal's face. It didn't quite connect, but the animal leapt back and fled, leaving its rider behind, lying on the ground and clutching his own spear. The girl flickered again, and the man screamed. Now his spear was on fire, burning in his grasp. He dropped it and rolled away, wiping his palms on the ground.

Khuril's last brother began to turn his horse, likely to flee, but then he was falling, screaming. He hit the ground hard and was lucky he wasn't trampled by his horse as it ran off. Khuril dismounted, hoping to remove some of the advantage the girl had from the animal's confusion. This magic she was using was nothing he'd ever seen, and he did not understand what was happening. He gripped his spear and waited.

The girl maneuvered in front of him faster than his eye could follow. Like rings of water appearing beneath a skipping stone, he thought. Then she stopped, about four spear-lengths away. It was the first time he'd had a chance to see her clearly since the fighting began. She was exhausted and covered in sweat and blood. Some of it was from the horse, but there was also a gash on her shoulder. When had she been hit? It made as little sense as everything else. Her breathing was heavy, though. If her strength was far enough gone, perhaps he could finish the fight.

He went through the steps in his mind. He'd charge forward, feint to the right, then dive at her, driving his spear through her heart. Or, more likely, he'd die trying. But perhaps he could give his brothers a chance to avenge him, or at the very least escape. He started to run when the girl revealed her strength wasn't entirely gone after all. She vanished in front of him, and he froze. Then she appeared to one side, closer. He began to turn to face her, but she was already gone, now at his back.

He felt something bite into his hand the same instant he saw her appear beside him. He moved to grab her, but she had vanished, reappearing just a foot away. The pain caught up with him, and he screamed. There was a deep cut along the back of his left hand. The spear fell from that hand, though he still held it in his right. But then she was on the other side of him. He had just enough time to see the blade which was made of no bone or stone he'd ever seen come at him. It cut swiftly, and he screamed again, this time losing the spear altogether.

He pressed the backs of his hands together, more to dull the pain than to stop the bleeding. He could barely move his fingers: he had little hope of lifting his spear. He looked around him at his brothers, who were nursing their own wounds and frantically trying to follow the movements of the girl who could move without moving and seemed to be everywhere at once.

Khuril forced himself to look up, so he'd at least see his death coming: it was the only way for a man to die. But his death did not come upon him. Instead he saw the girl bespelling his horse. "Witch!" he said, though he wasn't sure what he hoped to gain.

The girl looked at him. She spoke a great deal, but he understood few of her words. She was angry and hurt. The cut on her shoulder looked painful, though not as deep as he might have wished.

She finished her speech with a word spoken loudly. He looked at her, confused, so she repeated it. And a third time, louder, while pointing towards their village. He understood this time: "Leave!"

He stood, as did two of his brothers. The third tried, but screamed in pain when he placed weight on his leg. Khuril helped him up, allowing him to lean against him. Then they hobbled back towards the village to tell the story of the girl who moved without walking. After that day, Khuril would never again have a leading voice in village matters, and his family would slip into decline.

6

Alaji cleaned the cut on her shoulder with river water as best she could while Yemerik kept an eye out in case more riders appeared. It was getting late in the day. Since it clearly wasn't safe here, they'd have to travel through the night and hope to get far enough away to avoid future groups.

"You should have killed them," Yemerik said, not for the first time. "Weren't you listening earlier?"

"I was listening," Alaji said, grimacing as she splashed cold water on the cut. "I just don't trust you."

"Well, if you hadn't spared them, you might have avoided the wound. You still don't trust me?" he added, turning to her.

"Not completely," Alaji replied. She tried to shrug, but the pain from her cut turned it into something closer to a spasm. "Besides, I got the cut early. From the fat one, when I ran at him."

"I couldn't tell where you were at any point in the fight. It was over in a few seconds."

"Was it? I couldn't tell. It kept shifting. I'd move to where they'd been, then shift back, only to have them act differently. In some ways, I think it was easier when I had the reflections."

"Well, it's a difference of having sequences present to follow. I suppose it does create a degree of consistency by locking in the time line. Just remember they can see them, too. If you think it works better, just leave the fragments behind next time. Your 'reflections' will be back."

"No," Alaji replied forcefully. "No. Never again."

"Whatever," Yemerik sighed. "How's the cut?"

"Deep. Hand me some of the yuir leaves."

"The what?"

"The dried leaves with white spots on them. We got some from the village before they tried to kill us."

Yemerik opened a saddlebag and began pawing through the jars. He found some leaves fitting Alaji's description and handed them over. "How long will it take?"

"What?"

"How long for you to... cast your spells? On your shoulder. It's getting late, and they're liable to send trackers after us. And next time they'll know what they're up against."

"Not too long. I'm getting better at healing cuts. I never had so many opportunities to practice before. Besides, I don't think there will be a next time. They were scared."

"They might have been, but when their neighbors are finished laughing at them, another dozen will come out to prove how much stronger they are than the first batch." He looked back towards the village and squinted. There was nothing yet, but he couldn't believe that luck would hold. "You should have just killed them."

"They could be my ancestors," Alaji said. "If we don't reach Hathari, I won't risk my people."

"For all we know they could be my ancestors, too," Yemerik said. "Hell, there's a better chance even, given.... Forget it. Just. Listen to me: what happens to these people can be fixed. It will be fixed by the Citadel as soon as we get a message to them."

"I know. But I decided to hedge my bet. You still bet in the future, don't you?"

"Not much in the Citadel. But between now and then, games of chance proliferate. They're mostly played with coins, actually."

"We play with stones from the lake. We assign them trade for the game, say a pinch of salt, then exchange afterward." She considered this for a moment. "That's money, isn't it?"

"More or less," Yemerik said. "Only with real money, the value is more consistent."

"That makes sense," Alaji said. She decided her arm was as good as her limited magic was likely to get it, then she used her fabric binding spell to close the rip in her shirt over the wound. The cloth was still stained with blood, of course, but she suspected it wouldn't be the last misfortune her clothing endured.

"You still should have killed them," Yemerik said yet again. He stretched his legs and looked back towards the village once more. "All right. I think we're safe. I think they must have scared off the others."

"I told you," Alaji replied. "The look on their faces... they were terrified."

"Well, they probably claimed that Guilleve's men showed up and rescued us. And before you get too sure of yourself, that only means the villagers will be back at dawn. Probably every man in the town. And when they come, you'd better be ready to kill more than their horses."

"I could lie about it, if that will change the subject."

Yemerik sighed. "I wish... I wish I could put this into words you'd understand."

"I understand fine," Alaji said. "But I won't kill these people on your word. Can you prove that your Citadel can do what you say?"

"Yes. Yes, of course. Just not here. As soon as we get to Hathari."

"Then when we get to Hathari, I'll kill anyone you want."

"Don't joke about that. It's a civilized age. With laws."

"We have laws."

"Of course you did," Yemerik muttered under his breath,

sarcastically. "Of course you did."

7

"So this is the ocean," Alaji said, once she'd finished gasping at the sight. The rocky shore ran beyond her sight in either direction. The surface of the water was unfrozen and churned as if driven by a storm, but the sky was clear. The wind was strong here, stronger than on the plains, and that had been harsher than anything she could remember.

"Actually, no. This is a bay," Yemerik replied. He was shivering and blowing into his palms. "With the ocean, you can't see the other side. We're still a ways out."

They'd been riding for what Yemerik called "weeks." Two fingers and one on the second hand: the designation struck her as arbitrary, even for people who were as preoccupied with the number ten as hers were with five. He'd pointed out it was a quarter of a full moon, but this only begged the question as to why four was suddenly so important.

The horses were resting and chewing on the grass lining the hill they'd stopped on. Yemerik had dug out his maps – another novel idea, but one Alaji found intuitive. She eyed the sea birds and wondered if it was worth catching one. They still had some meat left over from a warren of rabbits they'd found the day before, and she didn't have the first idea of how she was supposed to clean and cook one of the strange birds.

"Yemerik," she said. "Are there fish in the bay?"

"What? Fish? Yes, of course. But I don't think you'll have much luck getting them. They usually don't swim near the shore. You might find some crabs or clams."

"Some what?"

"Never mind," he sighed. "It's probably not worth the effort." He traced his finger along lines on paper then looked up to stare at the shape of the inlet. He looked back and forth a few times, but finally shook his head. "This would be easier if we could get a bird's eye view. Maybe a mountain or a flying spell," he said, knowing full well there were no sorcerers who could levitate objects nearby, nor would there be for at least a millennium. As for a mountain, it would be far longer a wait for one to grow underfoot.

"We should go south," Alaji said.

"The gate could just as easily be north of here," Yemerik replied.

"Well, we're more likely to freeze to death in the north, so if you don't know which direction your gate is in, it seems like we should go south."

"You have a point. Alright. South, towards better weather and, with luck, a passage out of this damned age. There is one thing, though. We're almost certain to find villages by the water." They'd only encountered people once since being attacked outside the village – a group of riders in the distance on the plains. Either the riders didn't see them, were busy, or had some other reason for keeping their distance. Regardless, they didn't approach. "They may be friendly. They may not."

Alaji sneered. "We're far enough from home," she decided. "If it comes to it, I'll kill. But only if it's necessary."

"Fine. Whatever," Yemerik said. "Just remember, none of it will matter once we reach Hathari and contact the Citadel. I know you don't understand this, but they can – they will – correct alterations to the time stream."

Alaji shrugged and looked over at the bay. It was larger than all five lakes of her valley pooled together. Larger than the valley itself.

"Just remember, we have to get through. It's not just about you getting home. There's an attack being waged against the flow of history. Generations of research could be at risk."

Alaji shrugged again. "I'll help you get to Hathari," she said. "If it means killing someone in our way, I'll do it, now that I know it won't be an ancestor. But I don't want to talk about it. Or think about it, until I have to."

"This from the girl who was about to stick a stone blade into a man's neck and gut several of his lieutenants. If we get into trouble, just... pretend the people you're fighting are working for Hollik."

Alaji clenched her jaw and looked away.

"I don't understand. I thought you wanted to kill Hollik."

Alaji was still. "No," she replied. "When I go back... I won't kill him or anyone else. I... listen. When you send me home, I want you send me back before. I want to go back earlier. A hand's days, maybe. I don't want to kill to him; I want to stop my brother from dying. Maybe warn the elders what Hollik's planning, and let them figure it out. I don't know."

Yemerik took a deep breath. "It's not that simple," he said.

"Why? Because there will be two of me?"

"No. Listen, when the Citadel fixes this, it will fix the damage. All of it. There will be... ramifications. Whoever came back here, whoever broke the talisman, has done things that need be corrected."

"What does that mean?"

"I don't know yet," Yemerik replied. "Look, I don't know how this old woman – and whoever she's working with – arranged all this and caused you to learn Hatharian magic. I don't know what else they did or if my presence in your time impacted events. When this is fixed, there's a chance – a good chance – that Hollik won't have gotten so far. Your brother – there's a good chance he won't be killed by Hollik; even if the battle still happens, they might never meet."

"He wasn't killed in the battle. He was killed two nights before while gathering information."

"He was a... a spy?" Yemerik asked, swallowing.

"He went to the fields and was murdered by Hollik in the night. Or one of his men, I suppose."

"I hadn't realized," Yemerik said. He grew quiet, as well. "It... it might not happen," he added solemnly. "Once it's all corrected, there's no reason to think he'd come across them. They wouldn't be in the same place next time. At least, it's unlikely."

"Still, I want to go back early and try to be sure. I'm not sure if I can stop Theojin from going out, but I can try."

"I... I'll do what I can. I promise." He rolled up the map he was looking at and returned it to his bag. "We should go before it gets any later. Ride south until we can at least come across a stretch of coastline I can use to determine whether we're headed in the right direction. Or maybe a village. If they don't try to kill us, maybe they can help us find the gate."

8

Yemerik hadn't done the ocean justice, nor had the legends Alaji had heard from her people. It wasn't merely vast, but infinite; the sky alone formed its boundary. Wind drove the seawater upon the rocks with the force of thunder and the shattering waves broke into droplets like rain. Pockets of water remained in its wake, and these pools were full of strange insects and crawling creatures. In the lull between the crashing waves, Alaji could see stretches of white foam and black weeds caught at the edge of the sea.

It was the most incredible thing she had ever seen, in her time or this. And, as usual, Yemerik was bored. "We should move on," he said. "There could be a storm bearing down on us right now, and we wouldn't know. Damn sight easier when I could just jump ahead a few days and check."

Alaji ignored him for a minute and stood gazing into the sea spray and the grey waves and gulls circling in the distance. The sky was overcast; for the time being, she could only imagine how it all must look beneath the sun.

"Come on," Yemerik said louder. "It's getting late. I want to get started before we have to go inland to find a safe place to sleep."

Alaji nodded and returned to her horse. She mounted it quickly: it had taken some time, but she'd become a capable rider. "Fine," she said. "Lead on." Yemerik rode south along a cliff that ran beside the shore. The ground was worn; it was likely a path, though not a well-traveled one.

It rained later, though it was neither hard nor cold enough to force them to stop. When they came to a clearer trail, Yemerik followed it without a word. Before the sun had set, they came across a village built on a small hill. Yemerik climbed down from his horse and led it on foot. Alaji did the same while people backed away from them. Quietly, Yemerik handed Alaji his shards of the talisman.

A few villagers showed more courtesy, shouting greetings, a few of which Alaji recognized. She replied in her own tongue, which caused Yemerik to turn and glare at her.

It didn't take long for his pendant to do whatever it had to do in order for him to communicate; less than half the time it had taken in the village on the plains. After that, he began conversing quickly. He took out his 'coins' and showed one around. Soon, the villagers had gathered a small pile of food, pots of beer, and other assorted goods to offer in exchange. They cheered when he nodded that they'd brought enough.

Then he brought out a second coin and moved it around. He made an arch with his arms and spoke more. A few replied quickly, pointing back the way Yemerik and Alaji had come. More words were traded, and Yemerik handed over the second coin.

"We must have walked right past it," he said to Alaji. "We'd have seen it if it weren't for the fog. The gate's not far north of here. They say you can see it from here sometimes. You can handle a boat, right?"

"Of course," Alaji replied. She'd been going out on the lakes since she was young. Then her gaze turned to the west. She could just make out the sea in the distance. "Wait. You don't mean out there, do you?"

But it was too late. Yemerik was trading words back and forth. One of the villagers laughed, stepped forward, and embraced his arm at the shoulder. "I think we've reached an agreement," he said. "We'll stay here tonight and leave tomorrow."

"Is that a good idea? Staying here, I mean."

"They seem friendly."

"The other village seemed friendly, too."

"Well, they seem friendlier. Besides, I get the impression they receive more visitors."

Alaji glanced around, somewhat uneasy. "When you asked if I could handle a boat—"

"Don't worry," Yemerik said. "I got us guides as far as the gate. After that, you'll just have to get us back to shore. It can't be that different. Now, try to smile. You'll make our hosts nervous."

She forced herself to smile. But her count never stopped cycling in the back of her head.

9

There was a feast that night, and they were served cuts of roasted fish larger than any Alaji had seen or even imagined; fish nearly as long as a man. It tasted strange, but she found the experience enjoyable once she got used to the oily meat. She also learned what crabs were, but she couldn't bring herself to try one of their legs, nor did she accept any oysters or mussels when they were offered. But she ate greedily of the fish, had a dish of stew she couldn't identify, and sipped a bowl of beer through a reed.

After, they were shown to a small hut. It was lived in, clearly the property of someone in town, but when she asked Yemerik where the owner would sleep, he simply shrugged. The inside smelled of mold, and the beds, piles of hay gathered together in sacks, were inferior to the ones in Alaji's village. Nevertheless, it was a relief after months in the open. In the morning, she woke, changed her clothes, and left to find Yemerik sitting in the open. The sun was just beginning to rise, and the villagers were beginning to prepare for a day of fishing, net-weaving, hut building, and whatever else they did to keep alive.

"Vuyil said he'd be down with some breakfast. After that, they'll take us to the gate. Probably about half a day's trip. They think we're going there on a pilgrimage. I told them we wanted to stay a few days then come back to the village. It might be a bit longer, though," Yemerik chuckled.

"We should take the horses," Alaji said.

"We can't. The gate's on an island, and they'd never fit in the boats. I asked. We'll just have to buy new ones when we reach the other side. For all we know, we could end up with descendants of the ones we're leaving behind."

A villager, who Alaji assumed was Vuyil, appeared with a clay pot, which he offered to Alaji and Yemerik. On top, they found round pieces of flatbread. The inside held another stew, similar to one from the prior night. Alaji tore off a strip of the bread and used it to scoop out a portion of stew. She still didn't know what kind of meat was in it. Probably some sort of ocean fish, judging by how oily it was. Aside from the meat, the food was close to what she was used to. The roots weren't all that different from the types she used to cook with, and the bread, while made of a different grain, was similar to what she'd baked over hot stones.

Yemerik and Vuyil sat and spoke, but Alaji couldn't catch more than the occasional word or phrase – nowhere near enough to have a sense of what they were talking about. Before long, Vuyil seemed to grow impatient. Yemerik told Alaji it was time to go, though she'd already figured that out for herself. They walked towards the water, where they found two boats tied to an outcropping of rock. One of the boats was packed with the possessions they weren't already carrying.

There were three men waiting. Vuyil and two of the boatmen climbed into one boat; the other helped her and Yemerik into the one that held their strange collection of spears, bottles, blankets, and changes of clothing. They untied the boats, lifted oars, and pushed off. Their boatman offered an extra oar to Yemerik, who in turn handed it over to Alaji. If he noticed the boatman snicker, he didn't acknowledge it.

The waves were unlike anything Alaji had encountered on the lakes, but then the boats were far stronger than anything used by her people. She found it tiring work, but she got the hang of it. She was almost enjoying herself when she looked up and gasped.

The boatman said a word she didn't know, but she understood. Here was Yemerik's "gate," stretching out from a small island to a stone pillar. The distance between them – the length of the gate – was more than three times her family's fields.

10

Alaji could feel it. She'd felt it as they'd approached, but between the churning sea and the fierce wind, she'd dismissed the sensation. But it was there, a pulse like those emanating from the stone fragments, like the beating of her own heart. This was different, though. It was larger, deeper, and yet less obvious. It was subtler, but now that she'd found it, it seemed to permeate the ocean. It came, of course, from the gate.

Only it wasn't a gate, at least not in any sense of the word Alaji knew. It was more like a stone bridge, arching over the water. It didn't seem real – the width of the stone was constant; it had clearly been cut. But what tools of men or magic could carve such stone? What could lift it into the air and fit it in place?

She forgot to paddle for a minute, while she gazed at the site. "I don't understand," she said to Yemerik.

"In a moment," he said.

The boatman brought them to the island, where he climbed out and joined the villagers in the other boat. The three conversed with Yemerik for a few minutes before heading back the way they came.

There wasn't much to the island. It was small, especially compared to the stone arch extending from the cliff. From that side, the cliff rose sharply out of the ocean. The other side met the water in a gentle slope, which allowed them space to pull their boat out of the sea. From there, it rose steeply into the air, broken by jagged crevices and the occasional step. There were dozens of small crabs skittering around the lower part, and a number of gulls circling above. Below them was a mass of seaweed bobbing in the tide. Other than that, there was nothing but insects, bird droppings, and empty shells left over from the gulls.

"I never thought I'd have to use one of these things," Yemerik replied, looking at the form overhead. "Not especially reliable."

"What is it?"

"The Gate at Ilpinthi," Yemerik said, as if it should be self-evident. "I told you, the gates are for moving things. Big things, really. This one was largely intended to move water."

"Water?"

"Yes. Sea levels aren't static. They rise and lower over time. A long time usually, but even an eventful century can see a small shift. In fifty million years, there won't even be a sea here. We built the gate in case we wanted to move it."

"Move... the sea."

"Well, a portion of it. Every now and again there's some use for a deluge. Pop open a portal between a time when the sea's high and low, and you can change the course of a civilization. Turn barren land fertile, open up new trade routes, or simply wash a derelict civilization from the map."

Alaji didn't quite understand, but then she wasn't sure she wanted to. "And... it can bring us to the future?"

"Yes. But it might be tricky. I'll need to ready it for activation.

Try to attune it to one of the shards. I understand the theory well enough, but...."

"You've never done it?"

"Of course not. This isn't remotely the kind of thing I was trained for. And the fragments don't exactly function like the original talisman, so there's likely to be some trial and error. Of course, that's hardly the worst of it."

"What is the worst of it?" Alaji asked.

"We'll need to reach the top to get it started," he said, pointing to the stone bridge. "I think there's supposed to be a walkway along the cliff leading to it, but... I suppose it must have fallen off. Or maybe it just hasn't been added yet. How are you at climbing?"

"Not very good," Alaji said.

"Neither am I," Yemerik replied, forcing himself to smile.

—

They ascended from the inclined side, which was still frightening. The rock was slippery from the mist coming off the sea, and both of them nearly fell. In the back of Alaji's mind, she felt the count spinning, though she wasn't sure what good it would do: if she slipped, stepping back in time would only change when she fell, not how far or how hard she'd hit the rocks below.

She was trembling when she reached the top. There was very little room at the peak; just barely enough for the two of them to stop and catch their breath. The wind whipped at them, tossing their hair around.

The drop at the other side made the climb up look easy. The bridge – or gate or whatever it was – leaned slightly back towards the cliff. The drop between the top of the hill and the surface of the bridge was half-again longer than Alaji was tall. The surface was narrower than her arms outstretched, and there didn't seem to be many options.

"We could try to jump," Yemerik suggested. "It's not so far."

Alaji looked at the distance, and said, "Rope."

Yemerik looked over the edge again. "You might be right," he said, taking a length from his bag. He tied it to a bulging rock near the edge and tugged on it. "Care to go first?" he asked, chuckling at the look on Alaji's face. He looped the other end around his waist and took hold near where it was tied to the cliff. He let the slack drop down, where it swayed in the breeze.

"I could lower you down," Alaji offered.

"No. I think... I think it'll be easier if I climb." He inched towards the edge. "Just... give me a moment." He tested the edge with his boot before kneeling down and turning over. He pulled the rope taut and pushed one foot against the side of the cliff. Then, content the rope was holding, he slipped his other foot over and began slowly moving down the rope.

Alaji moved to the edge to watch. Yemerik was thrashing back and forth, trying to find a foothold while he lowered himself down, inches at a time. He was halfway down, when his foot slipped and the rope swung him into the stone wall. Alaji gasped as he made a sound like a hurt dog. He didn't let go of the rope, however, and didn't seem badly hurt. He laughed briefly and kicked, looking for a crack or small ledge he could use to catch his balance.

Then, pulled against the jagged edge of the cliff, the rope snapped.

Yemerik didn't scream: he didn't have a chance before the back of his head struck the rock below, knocking him unconscious and sending his body spiraling towards the rock below.

Alaji acted on instinct. Her count had just rolled over to one, but she stepped back anyway, as far as she could. She was at two, from the prior cycle. She'd never done this before: until then, she'd always moved within her count from one to five. She was confused for a moment as she looked around.

Yemerik was halfway down the rope. His foot slipped, and he was thrown into the rock face in front of him. Once he caught his breath, he began to laugh at the absurdity of it all and the sheer fact he was alright.

Then he felt the rope shake. He heard Alaji groan, and he looked up. She was lying on her stomach grasping the end of the rope, straining against the weight.

Yemerik grasped his end.

"I can't hold it!" Alaji screamed, and Yemerik began releasing the slack as fast as he dared. He kicked beneath him until he felt the bridge. As soon as he had both feet on it, he dropped down and sat panting on the walkway. Above him, he could hear Alaji gasping for air. He felt dizzy, as though he might pass out, throw-up, or both. He gripped the floor beneath him and leaned against the stone wall until the feeling passed, his breathing slowed, and he felt secure standing. He then untied the rope and wrapped it around his arm.

He stepped back so he could see the peak of the mound. Alaji was kneeling, tending to scrapes on her hand she'd gotten grabbing at the rope.

"Thank you," he said, though he wasn't sure she'd heard him over the wind and waves. Louder, he added, "You can stay there, if you'd like."

"No," Alaji said, "I'm coming down."

"I can throw the rope up," Yemerik offered.

"No. I don't think so," Alaji said. Instead, she gripped the edge of the cliff right over the bridge and lowered herself as far as she could. "Catch me!" she said, looking over her shoulder. She had to build up the courage before she could force herself to let go.

It only took an instant for her to reach the ledge, but it was a long instant. At the bottom, Yemerik caught her and pushed them both back towards the stone wall. Alaji pressed against it before ducking to a crouch, just as Yemerik had. They rested a while, silently staring at the rock bridge. Neither looked out at the endless waves or cloudy sky.

"I... I stepped back," Alaji said. "You had... you have some of the—"

"I know," Yemerik said, plainly. "Don't worry about it. I mean, worry about it the rest of the time, but not right now."

"I did it differently," Alaji said. "I'd finished my count, so I stepped back to the previous count."

Yemerik shrugged. "You do it by anchoring yourself, right? Your count basically works like markers, so until you reuse one, there's no reason you shouldn't be able to use it."

Alaji shook her head. "I don't know. I've always just done it."

"I wish I could help more. Like I said, it's all just theory to me. And it's not something I ever really studied." He looked down the long path ahead. "We should go. Get it over with."

Alaji nodded, and they began crawling along the archway. It was large enough to walk along, but neither seemed inclined to do so. It took them a while to reach the middle of the walkway. There was a section hollowed there in the egg-shape the talisman had been before it was broken.

Yemerik dug out one of the shards he was carrying and placed it in the indent. As soon as he did this, Alaji felt a pulse reverberate through the stone, through her, and into the air around her and water below. It was loud, though she did not hear it, not truly. She thought it might throw her into the sea, but she did not move, save for a jerk as her muscles spasmed from the shock.

But Yemerik did not seem to notice at all. He began tilting and turning the stone fragment, and as he did so, the pulsing energy became uneven. Another pulse shot out, but this time she was ready.

"What are you doing?" she asked.

"Trying to take my best guess," Yemerik replied. "It's been years since I received instruction on a manual adjustment dial. They make more sense if you're using a talisman in one piece, of course. I don't even know if it's having any effect."

Alaji's head seemed to split as another wave of energy shot off the stone. "It is!" she said. "It's... I can...."

"You can feel it," Yemerik said. "I'm impressed, but not surprised. Early time magic was achieved by learning to feel the flow of time. It's how they'll do it in Hathari, which lends credence to the theory that whoever's responsible for your abilities is from there. It's a preferable theory anyway, at least compared with the alternative."

"What alternative?"

"Oh. That whoever's trying to disrupt pre-history is from an advanced civilization with an ax to grind against the Citadel." He twisted the fragment around several times, releasing more waves of energy. Each was different, like a note being sung, though they all sounded strained, as if off key.

Yemerik removed the fragment and returned it to his pack. "Well. I think that should do it, more or less. I hope. We've got several thousand years leeway, so there's reason to be optimistic, anyway."

"The gate is... open?"

"No. It's primed to be opened."

"Then... what? It opens when we go through?"

"Yes," Yemerik replied, somewhat surprised she'd figured that out. "When we go through with the fragments, the gate will open." He cleared his throat then corrected himself. "Should open. I'm still working more from theory than experience."

"And take us to Hathari."

"Well, it'll take us to the era. I hope, at least. Like I said, theory."

"Then there's just one problem. We have to get back to the boat."

Yemerik looked back and sighed. "Yes. That. I suppose we should get near the shore and jump. We're probably better off landing in the water than trying to climb and risking falling onto the rocks."

Alaji nodded. "How cold do you think it is?"

"Very," Yemerik replied. "Freezing. And you'll need to make sure you leap away from the gate. If you're pulled back under, even for a moment–"

"The fragments will open the gate."

"And, depending on the tides, we could be pulled through. We could end up in the middle of winter without our boat."

"Winter?"

"Or summer. I'm not entirely convinced I managed to get the millennium I was aiming for, let along fine-tune the seasons. If we come out in the middle of a storm, we can always try again. But it'll mean climbing back up here." From the tone in his voice, Alaji could tell the idea didn't appeal to him any more than it did to her.

"Then we jump," she said.

"After you," he replied.

11

They sat in the center of the small island wrapped in blankets and shivering. They'd sacrificed a handful of extra clothes and a spear to make a small fire. It was better than nothing, but the heat was negligible.

"That," Yemerik worked out through chattering teeth, "That was the damned ocean."

The cold had been unlike anything Alaji had ever felt. The instant she'd plunged in, it had swallowed her completely. She tried to cry out in pain, forgetting for a moment she was underwater. Saltwater. She could still taste it, even after several mouthfuls of fresh water they'd brought from shore. It had burned her eyes and worked its way into the cuts and scrapes she'd gotten climbing.

She'd had her fill of the sea and wanted nothing more than to be back at the shores of her lakes, to gather the nets with Theojin, gut and scale the fish, and roast them on a spit while he told her stories and they argued which myths were real and which were invented.

"We should move on," Yemerik stuttered. "The gate should

stay ready a while longer, but... I don't really know... just how long. And I really don't want to go back up there."

Alaji nodded and forced herself to stand. The parts of her not numb were still in pain, but she forced herself to the boat, as did Yemerik. They dressed in dry clothes and moved their wet items to the floor of the boat. They readied it and pushed it off the rocks before climbing in themselves, remaining extra careful not to fall in.

They paddled for the gate, remaining close to the island. They passed beneath the shadow first, then the tip of the boat slid under. An instant later, they reached the portal.

There was a break in the count of the world. Alaji felt it, felt the heartbeat of everything skip a beat. And, when it started again, it was different. It moved differently, flowed differently. She had no language to describe the change, but she could feel it. It was like the energy emitting from the control piece at the top of the gate; exactly like it, in fact. The frequencies were identical.

She was so taken by the shift, she almost didn't notice the rest. She was staring at blue sky and sunlight reflected off of a sparkling sea. And then, not a second later, came the wind. It was a torrent bearing down on them. It was storm without clouds. The waves were choppy. They rocked the small craft, as if trying to overturn it. The gusts struck them, and the boat turned.

Again, the heartbeat skipped, and the world was old once more. The winds were still beating down at them, and the waves crashed against them. The boat rocked from side to side. It began to tip, and they leaned back to keep it upright.

Yemerik called out over the noise. "We need to...." His voice was lost among the crashing waves, though the force with which he fought to get the boat back towards the portal made his goal clear. Alaji did the same, and they managed to put the boat back on course.

The energy changed again as they passed beneath the break, but the water swirled beneath them, and they spiraled back.

"We have to fight it," Yemerik screamed.

"I know," Alaji called back, hacking at the waves with her oar.

"You don't understand," Yemerik cried. "I don't know how long the gate will stay open!"

Alaji leaned forward, putting every ounce of energy she could muster with little effect. Her heart was pounding, and her count began on its own accord, while the sea and sky and the very fabric of time spun above and below them. She leaned forward for more leverage when a wave struck the side, tipping the boat. She struggled to right herself. Behind her, she heard Yemerik shriek her name.

"I know!" she yelled back, but she didn't. As she spoke, another wave, far larger than the last, toppled over the side of boat, and she slipped into the water, along with her oar. Unlike the last time, the water was warm.

Yemerik reached for her, but the boat was swinging away. He was yelling something, but all she could hear was the pounding drum of the water as it filled her ears.

Alaji was caught in the whirlpool now, with a thousand years spinning around her. She spit out a mouthful of bitter seawater and swallowed what air she could. Then she dove beneath the water and fought towards the era she was seeking. She could feel the energy shift as each current knocked her one way or another. All the while, the count of five danced through her head.

She was in the future – at least for the second – and she forced herself to the surface for a breath of air. The moment she broke the surface, she saw a dark shape moving towards her. It was the boat, just inches from her head.

On instinct, she shifted back in time.

With a crash of lightning, the portal shut.

Alaji looked around frantically as the waters began to quiet. The sun was gone, as were Yemerik and the boat. Slowly, she began to realize that with a single thought, she'd leapt back five seconds.

And a thousand years.

PART 4

1

The water was still cooling when Alaji pulled herself back onto the rocks, but the air was frigid. She was shivering, joints aching and teeth chattering. She tasted blood and realized she'd bitten her lip – it was too numb to feel.

Then she saw something, bobbing in the waves out of reach. She stared at it for a moment – just a moment – and her breathing quickened. And with a primal, angry yell, she leapt back into the water and swam against the frigid waves. She spit seawater with each stroke and cursed beneath her breath against the salt. She cursed Yemerik for not reaching her. She cursed the gate for not getting her through. And, above all, she cursed herself for stepping back.

Somewhere in there, she remembered to curse her gods while she was at it. Whether they existed or not, they could at least help her this once. But they didn't, so she had to do it herself.

She latched onto the object in the waves, the oar she'd dropped, and began towing it towards the shore. The water was like ice by the time she pulled herself out again, and she fell over, gasping, on the rock. She could barely stand or move. The feeling was gone from her hands and toes. And she wanted nothing more than to fall asleep on the stone. She felt herself curling up, trying to hold on to what warmth she could. And she felt her eyes shutting.

"Alaji! Pay attention!" Her mother's voice. At the side of the lakes in winter. "The fish are as hungry as we are," Shaji said. "Take a stick and cast the spell. When the ice puts out the flame, cast it again, until you're through. Then use the hunger of the fish against them. But if the ice breaks...."

Alaji stood up, eyes open. She tore off her shirt and threw it on the rock face. "Your clothes will kill you before they dry." Shaji was angry. She was screaming. Alaji peeled off the rest of what she'd been wearing and tossed them beside her shirt. She even removed her bag containing the fragments and set it down. Her mother didn't let up: "You'll need a fire. As fast as you can start one. Fortunately, the gods were kind. The woods surround the water, so timber is never far."

There were no woods here: only a single oar. Alaji cast her spell in the center of the pole. The fire weakened the wood, and she snapped it in half. She did this once more, reducing the oar to thirds. It was waterlogged, of course, so the spells took time, but she ignored the cold and pain. She grit her teeth to keep them from rattling and focused on the task at hand. Then she lit the first section of oar on fire, casting over the length. She set it in front of her and warmed herself as best she could over the pitiful flame.

She added the second quarter of the oar, and the third soon after. The fire had grown in size, but it was burning too quickly. She needed more time.

No sooner had the thought occurred to her than the count began to cycle. She retrieved part of the broken talisman from her bag and held it close. She crouched before the fire, slipping back in time every time she reached five. She watched the same sparks float off again and again, the same plank split as the flames ate through it.

She was still cold when the fire was gone, but feeling had returned to her extremities, and her mind was beginning to clear. "Mother," she whispered, realizing she was alone. Her voice was like Shaji's: she'd never really noticed before.

Alaji's clothes weren't dry, but she wrung them out and decided to make do. Then she looked back up at the dark rock towering overhead.

She climbed quickly and with disregard. She almost fell several times – a part of her welcomed the idea she might: it seemed a merciful fate. But a greater part didn't want a quick end. She wanted to get home. And while that was a long way off, she knew the next step.

When she reached the drop, she lowered herself as far as she could and leapt. She'd no one to catch her this time, so she had to trust herself to land. She did, though she hit harder than she'd intended and bruised her leg falling forward. She hurried along the top to the center and placed a fragment of the talisman in the opening.

She felt the waves of energy wash over her, and she twisted the fragment, just as she'd seen Yemerik. But unlike him, she could sense the frequencies emanating from the gate. And she remembered how they felt. They stretched and warped around her as she moved the stone. The slightest movement in any direction would change them entirely. The tilt of the stone was more important than its position, but it all seemed to matter. She worked slowly, fine tuning the position of the object until the feeling was the same, or at least as close as she could hope for.

Then she withdrew the fragment and returned it to her bag. She returned to the area near the island, where they'd jumped before. But this time she jumped straight down. As soon as she hit the icy water, she turned and kicked towards the gate.

As before, the ocean and skies and world split, and she was swallowed by warmer water spilling out of the rift. She struggled against the currents, fighting for every inch. She could feel the energy around her, but she could also feel the water pushing her back. It was as if it wanted her to remain in that time. She surfaced, and the winds pushed against her as well. It was hopeless: she couldn't hope to win in her state, not for as long as the gate would stay open. And she doubted her strength to make the climb a third time.

But she was here now. She felt the count in her head as the waves pushed her back beneath the gate. If she was wrong about her magic, about how it worked, then she'd remain on this side, the path to the future would slam shut, and she'd die on the rocks. But if she didn't try, she knew the gate would close on its own, and she'd die just the same.

So she stepped back to one.

There was a time she'd thought the spell moved her five heartbeats into the past, but this wasn't right. If that were so, she'd have remained in the future when she cast her spell before. The reason she hadn't was that her spell didn't open a door: it set an anchor. It connected her to a moment and allowed her to return. When she'd used it before, she'd set that anchor in the past. A few seconds or a thousand years – it made no difference: she returned to the point she was connected to.

So it worked again. She stepped back to when she was five heartbeats before. And this time, that was a thousand years in the future. And, as before, the gate shut.

The water was choppy. It tossed her back and forth as it settled, but she didn't care. It was warm and the feel of the world was different. Above her, there were stars now: it was night here. This seemed odd to her, but she dismissed it. Again, such details were trivial.

She tread water until the seas calmed from being flung open across time. Then she swam to the island and climbed up. The rocks were different. They'd been worn down a bit by the ocean and wind. She crawled a little higher and collapsed, gazing up at the sky. She shut her eyes and was asleep.

2

She awoke to the glare of the morning sun and a shadow that broke it. The call of gulls surrounded her as she sat up. Her clothes were still damp, and her muscles ached as she moved. She was hungry, thirsty, and dizzy.

And there was a building before her.

The shock made her jump, and something barked beside her.

She yelled in surprise as a creature resembling some sort of cross between a dog and a fish turned to look at her. It yawned, its breath smelling of sea creatures, then laid back down on the rock, apparently uninterested in her presence or that of the large structure in front of them both.

There were men on top staring down. None seemed hostile, but she tried to prepare herself in case that changed. It wasn't a building, she realized slowly, but a boat, larger than any she'd ever seen. It was almost twice her height, with a length more than five times that. Above it was a pole, where a length of fabric large enough to cover the tallest hut in her village was resting. At first, she thought the pole and fabric might be some sort of symbol, but the truth dawned on her.

The fishermen on Black Lake would sometime affix cloth above their boats, claiming they could use the wind to outrun their rivals and reach the best fishing spots first. This was no different, only larger. Much, much larger, as these boats themselves were larger. And the ocean, for that matter.

One of the men called down to Alaji, but the words were foreign. She called back, "I don't understand!"

The man said something else. Again, it was meaningless to her. "I'm sorry," she called back. "I don't speak your tongue."

A second man began speaking. Like before, Alaji shook her head. Then she caught a word she thought she knew. "Shore?" she asked.

"Shore," he repeated, nodding and pointing towards land. He pointed to her, to the boat, then to land. "Shore," he promised. One of the men lowered a thick rope with a series of knots tied along its length. Alaji began climbing, all the while keeping an eye on the men above her. They seemed kind, but she knew better than to trust blindly. But then it made little difference: if they tried to hurt her, she was fairly certain she could deal with them, even in her current state.

Fortunately, they didn't seem interested in conflict. They helped her aboard without touching her and gave her space. She decided they were afraid of her, which seemed as good a turn of luck as any. They brought her bread and a jar of something that smelled like beer. She examined the beverage carefully. They offered no reed, but it didn't seem to need one: there wasn't enough grain floating on the surface to need straining. She'd never heard of beer like this, but she quickly decided she liked it.

The boat sat heavy in the water. Working quickly, they lowered the sails and used oars to move away from the rocks. Once they reached the open water, they opened the sails again. The trip was less like any time she'd spent on a boat than it was like stepping on a jut of land extending out into the water. The ship was floating, carried by the wind. There was food and drink in her stomach, a warm breeze in her hair, and the magic of the vessel to amuse her. Her skin was raw in spots from the course rocks, the dried salt, and the morning sun, but she was happy.

A few hours later, they came to rest at what seemed to be a bridge extending out into the sea. Alaji understood the point of this immediately: it was like the rock peninsulas they'd used to board boats on the lake, but scaled up for this frightening new time. The dock ended in a path, which wound uphill to the first of the buildings.

They were massive, like monuments. They towered overhead, reaching the heights of the trees. How these remained standing was a mystery, as was what need men would have of such dwellings. But Alaji was too tired to admire the craftsmanship, and – despite their friendly behavior so far – she remained wary of her companions.

They dropped the rope to the dock, and the first of the sailors scaled down and tied it to a pole. Then they motioned for her to come down as well. The man on the dock stood back, still seemingly afraid of her. The others waited until she'd reached the bottom before leaving the ship, as well.

Then they led her towards the village, if that was even the right word. There were dozens of buildings in view, with more appearing as they approached. How many lived here, so close together? Where was the farmland and the livestock? It made no sense.

There were crowds gathering now. The men spoke quickly, though Alaji understood none of it, save the occasional word here and there which was similar to one her people used. They pointed towards the gate several times and seemed concerned. The people reacted strangely to what the sailors said. An old woman touched the left side of her face using the back of her right hand and muttered something that sounded like a prayer. A younger woman turned and ran. A man drew a knife – metal, Alaji noticed – and held it up, but he backed away. Several knelt, clasping their hands together, and one fell face first onto the ground and began to cry.

"So," Alaji whispered to herself. "I'm a messenger from the gods." If she'd have been able to communicate, she might have tried to dissuade these people from the idea. Or perhaps she'd have waited a bit. She wasn't entirely sure what she'd have done, and she'd have wanted to consider the matter first. But it was moot, since she lacked a shared language to discuss such complex topics. Instead, she motioned towards her mouth to indicate she was hungry, something she was relatively certain they'd understand.

3

She knew she ought to feel guilty taking advantage of their hospitality under such conditions, but instead she relished it. These people were of the future, hundreds of years beyond her time, capable of incredible feats of construction, of creating buildings with two – even three – levels. And yet, in a sense, they seemed to be the ones who were primitive. They behaved as if she came from a place beyond their comprehension.

She hated herself for loving it. But she loved it nonetheless.

They brought her foods she'd never seen. She finally tried crab, not wanting to seem impolite, though she didn't think much of the texture. There were fruits larger than any her people had known, along with wines sweeter than she'd imagined. The clothes they gave her were made from the hair of strange animals raised in the hills beyond their village. The cloth was soft and flexible, yet they were far sturdier than the garments made of reeds and bark she'd known.

They gave her the use of a building with two floors. The bedroom alone was as large as the hut she'd grown up in. It was on the upper floor, a fact that took some time getting used to, but it helped the bedding, likewise woven from animal hair, was as soft as a hatchling's down and as warm as a bearskin.

For the most part, she was left alone, save when offerings were brought to her. She amassed a collection of bead work and chalices; strange and beautiful, but not particularly useful. There was a great deal she didn't understand about these objects and their construction, but it wasn't as though she could ask. So she simply nodded graciously when such gifts were presented. Perhaps she'd have a need to use them as trade later.

She watched the people of the village go about their days from her window. They were different than her in almost every way. Their skin was a touch fairer, and they kept their hair braided. The practice wasn't new to Alaji, but her own village reserved the practice for weddings, funerals, and a few other occasions. Here, it seemed the default for anyone, man or woman, over a hand's age. She touched her own hair – dark and curly – and wondered if she should attempt to copy the custom. She decided against it, not wanting to inadvertently insult her hosts.

There were differences in their faces and bodies, as well. Their chins were more pronounced, their ears were larger, and their cheeks were less defined. They were also a little shorter than the people she'd grown up around. Alaji had always been small for her people, so she seemed to fit in here in that respect.

Most of those who lived in the village spent their time fishing, which was another commonality. Occasionally, ships would appear and new sailors would arrive, exchange cargo, then depart once more.

Sometimes they'd stay a few days, though they were never brought to meet her. She was able to walk around outside, but she preferred to do this in the evening, when there weren't many others around. When the villagers did cross her path, most bowed in her presence, a custom Alaji was growing tired of.

A woman, just a few years older than Alaji, seemed to be entrusted with looking after her. Alaji was fairly certain her name was Imi, unless that was a title of some sort. The first thing she realized was that Imi was as uncomfortable around her as the rest of her people were. Alaji wondered what obligated the girl to remain with her. Perhaps one day she could ask.

First, she would have to learn their language. She'd picked up a handful of words for items of food, animals, actions, and objects. Their word for "stew" was almost identical to hers, though they pronounced it so differently, she hadn't understood until she coaxed Imi into repeating it slowly. There were other words that matched up, but many more were completely different. Some didn't even sound like real words at all.

The people here were strange. Their customs struck Alaji as arbitrary. When certain birds flew overhead, some villagers would stop, bend down, and draw a picture of the bird in the sand. They seemed to be saying something as they did this, though Alaji could never get close enough to hear it, not that she'd have understood it if she did. Magic was also invoked differently. The incantations and movements were exaggerated if not outright changed. Every spell she'd seen had been cast by old men wearing strange outfits. Even spells to start a fire had been cast by them.

She'd motioned to one when Imi was present, and she'd nodded and spoken a word. It didn't sound familiar to Alaji, though she made a point of remembering it, in case it came up again: "Wizard."

One day, after being presented with a new necklace, Alaji called Imi over to her. Alaji motioned to the jewelry and said, "Necklace."

"Hulthik," Imi replied.

"Hulthik," Alaji repeated back. Imi nodded silently, and Alaji removed one of the smaller shards of talisman from her pack. She held this up to her neck and said, "Hulthik?" Again, Imi nodded. Alaji set the stone on a table, knowing Imi was still uneasy with her touch. Within three days, she was presented with a pendant holding the shard, now embedded in a ring of metal. She nodded, smiled, and put it on.

4

Alaji ventured out onto the sea a few times after discovering the villagers would allow her access anywhere she wished, even onto their boats. On hot days, it was a welcome respite, and the vastness of the ocean was awesome to behold, provided the waves were relatively quiet. She attempted to assist in fishing, but discovered she only got in the way, mostly because the others would stop working and step away when she involved herself in their activities.

There was very little about the sea that reminded her of home. The fish were much larger than those from the lakes and they smelled different, the boats' movement was nothing like those she'd grown up riding, and the wind and salt water were entirely new. But she found the open water exciting.

By the time the moon's phases had cycled, she could effectively communicate basic concepts. Imi had grown used to being around Alaji and no longer flinched when Alaji entered a room or spoke up. Their conversations were hardly complex – they were still limited to basic vocabulary and simple ideas – but Alaji was definitely making headway.

She decided it was time to try for answers, even simple ones. She called Imi to her, and they sat at a table located in the house Alaji was beginning to think of as her own. "Do you know... Hathari?" She asked, before repeating the word again.

Imi looked confused. She said the word herself, then gestured to her clothing and said several other things.

Alaji shook her head. "Hathari," she repeated.

Imi thought for a moment, then gathered some of the assorted objects in that had been gifted to Alaji. She returned to the table and set a carving of a fish on the table. "Elsimi," she said, tapping it. It was the word for the village, Alaji believed, though she wasn't entirely sure whether it referred to just these buildings or the larger area around them.

"Elsimi," Alaji said, nodding. "Hathari?" she motioned toward the other side of the table.

Imi took a beaded bracelet and set it where Alaji had pointed. "Hathari," she agreed.

Alaji swallowed. "Yemerik?" she asked, not sure whether it would get a reaction.

Imi nodded. "Hathari," she said again, tapping the bracelet. "Hathari bal Yemerik."

Alaji touched the bracelet as soon as Imi's hand was out of the way. "Hathari? Yemerik? You've met him?"

Imi shook her head, confused. "Hathari bal Yemerik, elun Elsimi," she said slower. She pointed to the fish carving and traced a line to the bracelet.

"Hathari bal Yemerik," Alaji said back, and Imi nodded. Alaji took a deep breath and spoke. "Hathari bal Alaji." She tapped the center of her chest then tapped the bracelet again to make it clear she understood. Then she paused before adding, "Hathari bal Imi." She felt guilty even before watching Imi's face go pale. The girl nodded slowly.

"Hathari bal Alaji ude Imi, elun Elsimi," Imi said, as though acknowledging her own death sentence. She looked as though she was about to cry. As soon as she'd spoken, she excused herself, leaving Alaji alone.

She hated herself, of course, but knew she'd never find her way without a guide who understood this world and – at the very least –

could speak its language. She'd help Imi return home. Maybe she should could get Yemerik's people to reward her, give her something these people valued.

For the first time, she thought she understood the position Yemerik had been in on the plains.

5

There was little fanfare leading up to their departure. The townsfolk assembled a collection of food – smoked fish and meat, jars of preserved vegetables and even fruit they'd acquired in trade, along with a barrel of their best beer, which Alaji had grown fond of. They gave her other things, as well. There were objects of potential use: new clothes, blankets, oiled tarps, and herbs. There were also piles of decorative trinkets: more medallions, necklaces, bracelets, and rings mostly, though there were also a few statues. There were coins, too; nothing so refined as the ones Yemerik had carried, but they presumably held value.

This tribute was piled into an enclosed wagon, yet another new concept from this strange new world, which was hitched to two horses. The final gift was the only one she'd asked for. Imi was handed over to Alaji by an old man, perhaps her father. He spoke for a moment, though of course Alaji had no idea what he was saying. Still she nodded her head and thanked him, wondering what these people thought of sending two girls into the countryside alone. Did they think Imi would survive? Did they care? Their ambivalence towards her welfare made Alaji less conflicted about taking advantage of their hospitality.

She wondered if she'd asked for guards or additional guides if they'd have sent them. Likely, though she didn't want them. She wasn't sure she trusted Imi, either, but at least she felt comfortable with her around.

There were neither tears nor applause on the day they left, though most of the town came to watch them go. Alaji didn't know if there was significance to their departure, though most looked relieved be free of her presence. Whether she was a curse or a messiah, everyone seemed happy to have her out of their hands.

For her part, Imi seemed morose but not miserable. Perhaps she'd reached some sort of peace with her situation, or maybe her family's willingness to hand her over made her realize it was just as well she was leaving.

The road through the countryside was well-worn and wide enough for their wagon. When they passed another going the opposite direction, an event which occurred twice in their first day's travel, one pulled off to the side while the other went by. Alaji wasn't sure what rules or logic dictated who pulled over, but there seemed to be some unspoken understanding that caused Imi or the other driver to yield. As they passed, Imi would call out a simple greeting, then trade a handful of words. Alaji had learned enough to parse out the general themes – something about the sun or weather or the road itself – but nowhere near enough to understand the nuances or actual meaning. She had a long way before she'd understand the language, but – if the quantity of food they'd been given was any indication – she likely had time.

She spoke with Imi, pushing for more information, and she was no longer content with simple objects and animals. She spoke in sentences as best she could, and managed to get Imi to respond in kind. Within a hand's days, they could communicate well enough to debate the merits of stopping early or trying to move onward. Soon after, Alaji knew enough to discuss more complex topics. She didn't push for what Imi thought of her or where she believed she'd come from – there were nuances there she didn't want to stir up until she felt secure in her ability to convey them properly.

They slept near the wagon when the sky was clear; inside it when it rained. Imi seemed startled the first time Alaji started a fire, but she didn't say anything and her surprise quickly faded. These weren't the spells of women any longer, Alaji decided, though she doubted it made much difference. Imi might not know what Alaji was, but she knew her to be something not of this world and wouldn't expect her to follow its laws.

Moving through the land was strange. For the first few days, their road seemed to be following a similar path to how she'd traveled with Yemerik, though they quickly turned south into lusher, forested terrain, which would have been impractical to navigate without the use of the road. The rolling hills gave way to mountains, which the road twisted to avoid.

The road itself was astonishing. The most heavily used trail in her village's center wasn't so wide or well maintained, and this one seemed to go on forever. It even crossed rivers on wooden bridges, far larger and more intricate than any she'd seen.

Much of the landscape had been reshaped into vast farms. She recognized some of the crops – turnips, onions, and lettuce – but there were other plants she'd never seen. She wondered how many she'd already eaten in stews Imi's people had given her.

Alaji had imagined that Elsimi had been large, that it had been some sort of trading port for this incredible age. But as soon as they began coming across towns, her assumptions changed. Everywhere they went, they came across buildings rivaling the trees' height. Sometimes there were dozens of them close together. A few were even built on stone foundations. There were still smaller huts – some similar to those in her own time – dwelling in the shadows of great halls whose purpose escaped her.

Trade occurred in marketplaces filled with fish, odd fabrics, works of art, and dozens of other marvels. Imi bartered for vegetables and fresh meat, trading a few of the coins they'd been given. She always looked to Alaji for permission to spend the money, and Alaji always nodded. She wasn't sure what any of it was worth, nor did she care. They seemed to have enough for a very long time, and if they ever ran out, she knew how to gather food on her own.

6

The wagon wheels kicked over a stone, and one of the horses grunted. Alaji had been half asleep until the bump jarred her to attention. It was getting late, almost sundown, and they hadn't stopped more than a few minutes since mid-morning, when they'd purchased some beer at a village.

"We... stop?" Alaji asked, speaking carefully.

Imi replied with a sentence which, while short, was still difficult for Alaji to follow. She caught a handful of words: "No... town... men... wolf." She motioned behind them, and Alaji looked behind the wagon. At first, she saw nothing, but after a moment she caught sight of something moving in the distance. "Follow," Imi said.

Alaji nodded. In several villages, they'd gotten strange looks from the men they'd passed. A few had even shouted taunts, but they'd all backed off when Imi shouted back using words she hadn't taught to Alaji. During their stop this morning, there'd been a pair of young men who'd kept looking at them and whispering. They approached and traded angry words with Imi, but they'd simply laughed when Imi's tone grew harsh.

"From village?" Alaji asked.

Imi shrugged. "They... traders or travelers. Or the men from... village." She looked frightened.

"Through...." Alaji thought for a moment. "Through night?" Imi nodded and said something Alaji didn't catch. They traveled on, as it grew dark. The horses were panting, but Imi pushed them on. The road began winding through a thick forest on the side of a hill, and it became harder and harder to see.

The men seemed to fall further and further behind them, then vanished altogether. Imi stopped at a stream to water the horses and give them a few moments' rest. Both she and Alaji peered out behind the wagon.

"I don't... see..." Alaji said, as best she could. She only caught a few words of Imi's response, but it sounded as though she hadn't seen the men, either. "We... rest. Night," Alaji suggested, but Imi shook her head. Again, she said something Alaji couldn't understand. The fact she wasn't taking more care to communicate concerned Alaji as much as anything else.

It began to rain as they went on, barely more than a mist, but still unpleasant. Imi motioned to Alaji then back at the wagon. She was offering to drive on while she slept, but Alaji shook her head. She motioned to the seat and made it clear she wasn't going anywhere.

Time drifted slowly. Without stars or moon, it was difficult to tell how much had passed. Alaji thought it was nearly the middle of the night when they came across a downed tree blocking the road. Imi stopped the wagon. She was terrified, but she leapt down immediately and ran over to try and move the tree. Alaji began to follow.

"Hey!" the voice came from the forest near Imi, who leapt back. Two men came out towards her. They were the pair from the village, which didn't surprise Alaji. She tried telling herself these were Hollik's men, though she knew the warlord was centuries gone. And she couldn't make herself believe the lie, anyway. Hollik's men were disciplined, focused. These were more like the bullies of her own village. But, for some reason, it no longer seemed to matter. She slipped her hand into her bag and felt for the handle of her knife.

One of the men said something and laughed. Imi said something back, but Alaji's rudimentary knowledge of their language covered none of it. She'd given up trying to understand it for the time being, anyway. Instead, she focused on the way they moved. She didn't need to begin the count: it had been cycling since they stopped the wagon.

The men were armed; one with an ax, and the other with a cudgel. Neither were holding the weapons ready; they weren't expecting much of a fight. Alaji was as surprised as they were when Imi tried to give them one.

"Run!" Imi shrieked, leaping at the first man and clawing at his face. She scratched him, and he yelled, leaping back, startled. Her advantage lasted only an instant, however: he struck her with the back of his hand and sent her tumbling. He laughed at the girl and lifted his cudgel.

Then he screamed, and his cudgel dropped away. He clutched at his right arm and found it covered in blood, a deep gash running near his elbow. Imi remained on the ground, looking up in disbelief.

And the other girl, who could not have moved so fast, stood holding the knife that had made the cut. She didn't seem rushed or frightened; she simply waited. "Leave," Alaji commanded the men. "Run!"

The one with the axe held it ready but moved away. The wounded one, however, drew a blade of his own, and charged. Alaji stepped back, first in place and then in time. She stepped in short increments, moving back a second or two at a time, and the man coming at her did so in impossibly slow bursts. His reactions were different depending on where she was, but they were lethargic in comparison to her own.

There were so many things Alaji could have done to stop him. She could have tripped him. Could have cut his other hand or leg. She could have plunged the blade between a joint or cut a muscle. In the hours that followed, she'd think back and wonder why she hadn't, why this one, who reminded her of the sort of young men she'd grown up around, was different.

She was angry at him for following them, of course, and angry he'd struck Imi. She was tired, as well. And there was a strange, intoxicating freedom that came with using her forbidden magic – though Yemerik had implied it wouldn't be forbidden here – for the first time since she'd arrived.

But none of these explained it. It was instinct that drove her hand. She'd become a hunter on the plains, honing her spell and her skill. She'd slit the throats of a hundred rabbits, birds, and even a handful of elk. It was second nature to her, and she forgot herself.

The man dropped the knife and grasped his neck. He fell to his knees, then on to his back. He wriggled on the ground, gurgling. His friend dropped his axe and ran.

Alaji looked at her knife and at the body before her. She turned to see Imi staring in horror and awe. Alaji offered her hand, which Imi took reluctantly. She embraced her as if they were sisters and said everything was alright, trusting the tone to bridge the gulf in language.

Imi was shaking. She pointed to the woods where the second man had run. She spoke quickly. "Village... wolf... men...."

Alaji picked up those words: the rest were lost. "It's okay," Alaji said.

"No," Imi replied. "Men... help men.... Village...." She saw Alaji's confusion and grew more worried. So she pointed, first to Alaji's blade, then to the dead man, then to the woods where the survivor had fled. Finally, back to the bloody knife. Then, with a finger, Imi traced a line across her own throat.

"We have to kill him?" Alaji asked, startled.

Imi nodded slowly. "Kill before...." More words Alaji couldn't piece together. But Imi's was as scared of the man now as she'd been before, perhaps more so. It made no sense. Would the dead boy's family seek revenge against two girls? Was he so important that someone would come after them? They were girls: wouldn't the boy's family be too ashamed? It all seemed absurd. But she didn't understand this world, and Imi did.

"Wait here," Alaji said, before disappearing into the woods.

7

Alaji grabbed a dried branch off a dying tree as she ran and lit it with the spell of the hearth between steps. She'd later realize she'd cast it between anchor and shift, that she'd cast one spell in the midst of another, but for the moment she was too focused on the situation at hand to notice.

The fleeing man had a head start, but Alaji followed the sound of his footsteps and his lead evaporated. He caught a glimpse of Alaji's flickering torch as she approached, and he turned in terror. He raised his hands to protect himself, and he opened his mouth to beg her to stop, to plead for his life. Then Alaji stepped back, and she saw it again. And again.

She drove the knife in twice, but this was an act of mercy. She'd learned this hunting, to anchor herself to the instant before she struck, in case she missed her mark the first time. The second blow plunged into his heart, and she caught him as he fell. Her makeshift torch dropped to the ground and fizzled out in the wet dirt. For a moment, the man held on to Alaji. His grip hurt, though he didn't look angry. He looked Alaji in the eyes, and all she could read from his expression was fear. And then, almost instantly, there was nothing to read at all. He went limp and slipped out of her hands.

"So I'm a murderer," Alaji said. There was little question: with the first, it had been self-defense. No, even with him, she could easily have spared him. She had options if she'd stopped to consider them. She'd handled more men than this – stronger men, better armed, on horseback, no less – and left them alive.

"I'm a murderer," Alaji said again. She said it to punish herself, but the word didn't hurt. She'd dreamed of this moment the night before the battle against Hollik, then dreaded it on her long march into the west, when she'd argued the merits of mercy with Yemerik. But it seemed small now, insignificant. There was a body before her. He could have family, she knew. He could have a sister. Did Hollik's men think of that when they killed her brother?

She sat on the wet ground and retrieved her knife, which she wiped clean on a handful of leaves. Alaji was tired and wanted to sleep. She wished she could step back to the start of the fight and spare the two men, send them off with cuts or maybe a few missing fingers. But it was stupid. They'd come to kill her and Imi. They'd deserved it. Did that matter?

She shook off the doubt and climbed to her feet. Then she looked at the fallen form and tried to muster some feeling, some guilt. But there was little inside of her. She wondered what else that made her.

She returned to the road to find Imi kneeling on the ground beside the first man. Alaji approached her and looked down. Imi's hands were muddy; she'd traced the symbol of a bird beside the body. Imi looked up then wiped the drawing away, as if ashamed. She stood and shook. Then she whispered a sentence, from which Alaji was able to pick out the words, "man" and "dead."

Alaji nodded, and Imi walked to the side of the path, where she collected the fallen axe. She returned to the body at the side of the road and moved his arm with her foot. Then she chopped at the body, burying the axe in the neck and covering the wound he already had. Alaji leapt at the sudden brutality of Imi's action and the seeming randomness.

Next, Imi found his fallen knife and began towards the wood. Imi pointed in the direction Alaji had come from. Alaji nodded, then hurried ahead to lead. She found another branch and lit it. It didn't take them long to reach the body. Alaji watched as Imi bent over and tried lifting the body. She slipped in the mud, but caught herself.

Alaji grabbed the other side of the body, and helped move it towards the road, though she didn't understand what this was about or why they were bothering. It was slow going, but they made it back. Imi had taken care to handle the body, so Alaji assumed this was some sort of burial. It was all the more surprising when Imi dropped the body near his friend's, drew out the knife she'd recovered, and thrust it into his chest.

Imi stood back to look at the scene and nodded. Then, as if none of it had happened, she turned her attention back to the tree blocking the trail. Again, Alaji assisted her, though Imi never asked for help. By the time the road was clear, it was almost light. Imi drove the wagon on. When they'd traveled a ways, Alaji brought up the possibility of stopping, but Imi simply shook her head then motioned to the wagon.

Alaji felt as though she should stay with her, but she was too tired to sit up. She slipped into the back and rested her head. Strangely, she felt worse leaving Imi to drive on alone than she had about killing the two men.

8

Of course the woman from The Sea Beyond the Sea could do such things. The show of power itself hadn't been a surprise; only her willingness to use it to protect an Imi. The thought terrified the girl more than the men could have. What could they do to but kill her and leave her spirit to the night winds? The woman could do far worse. If she wished, she could take her to The Sea Beyond the Sea, where she'd endure forever as a handmaid, forever robbed of breath, never to be welcomed into the world above.

She'd never heard any say Yemerik, the one before, had used such power, or even the simple wizard-spells the woman had used to invoke fire. Though she'd never heard it said Yemerik had any difficulty with the words of the Shore's Keepers, or of any others, for that matter. Quite the opposite, in fact: he'd been described as very talkative.

The Imi drove on for several hours, stopping from time to time to rest, feed, and water the horses. She took her own meal while the wagon was in motion, eating with one hand and holding the reins with the other.

A little after dawn broke, Alaji, the woman from The Sea Beyond the Sea, woke and joined her in the front of the wagon. She said something about sleep, or perhaps sleeping, then motioned toward the Imi.

"Was the wagon all right?" the Imi asked. "Was I driving too fast?"

Alaji gave her the same confused look she'd used since the Imi had been given to her. The Imi tried again, and Alaji said something else. Again, the word for sleep, conjugated incorrectly, with the word, "Imi", and a host of other terms, none of which added up. The Imi bowed her head and apologized for not being able to understand. This confused Alaji more, and the Imi had to force herself not to laugh or smile.

It wasn't that the Imi disliked Alaji. In point of fact, she found her polite, after a fashion, though the fact she didn't understand even the most common of customs and laws made matters complicated.

Nor did she seem to understand the way of the world. It was her right, in a sense, to kill those men, though it was unlikely those of the plains would see it that way. Only the Shore's Keepers understood what she was and where she'd come from. The men of the plains believed only in two heavens; they laughed at stories of the Sea Beyond the Sea. Even those who'd gazed upon its gateway did not acknowledge its importance. To them, it was an oddity somehow left by the waves or – at most – discarded by old gods who'd long since left this world for its heaven, before the greatest ascended to that heaven's heaven.

These men would not be placated by her origin. If they realized what had happened, they would come for them both. It terrified her, because they'd come to put them to death. And she'd already seen what the woman from The Sea Beyond the Sea would do if threatened. She felt little sympathy for the men the night before, but others didn't deserve their fate. Certainly ignorance of Alaji's people wasn't so great a crime.

Fortunately, it was unlikely they'd figure it out and less likely they'd find them. But still, the idea scared her.

Alaji continued to repeat her statement. Finally, she reached over and took the reins from the Imi's hands. She repeated the word, "Sleep," pointed to the Imi, and pointed back to the wagon.

The girl nodded, and crawled into the back to rest. She was worried Alaji wouldn't take proper care of the wagon and horses, and would have rather continued on despite her exhaustion. But she interpreted Alaji's instructions as an order, and she knew better than to disobey one from The Sea Beyond the Sea.

9

So this was a city.

This was Hathari, the empire-city Yemerik had told her about. It lived up to his description, and then some. It was large – impossibly, incredibly large. The experience of seeing the ocean for the first time was the only comparison she might have drawn, and even that seemed trivial in contrast. This was astonishing. Unbelievable. Buildings towered as if they were hills. Some were four, even five levels high. There were statues made of greenish metal standing watch like giants.

Then there were the people. More than she'd ever seen – more than she'd ever imagined. The armies that fought on the field north of the lakes would have gotten lost in the crowds shifting through the streets. People traveled on foot, horseback, and wagon.

Alaji gave a start the first time she saw a goblin hiding in an alley, but no one else seemed to pay the creature much attention. She kept an eye on it, but it didn't seem hostile or interested in the people around it. Instead, it made do with some scraps that had been tossed behind some kind of tavern.

There were smells drifting around her, more than she'd ever experienced. Pleasant smells of roasting meat and pouring beer, baking bread and fresh flowers. And then there was the refuse from human and animal alike, the odor of sweat and vomit, and worse still, the carcasses of rats and other things that had died and been left to rot. Alaji was grateful it was almost fall: she was certain she'd have been unable to withstand such a place in the midst of summer.

It was horrible and awesome and, most of all, beyond understanding. She laughed and sneered and clapped her hands over her mouth, and no one around her seemed to notice or care.

Imi drove on. While she wasn't as enraptured as Alaji, she did seem easily distracted here. She turned to stare in wonder and disbelief at people with skin that looked nothing like her own, her expression betrayed interest when they rode by a cart selling dresses, and she turned in disgust whenever a gust of wind caught some horrible stench and carried it past the women.

Then there were the oddities. A woman behind a cart sold the skins of snakes, some of which were as long as a dragon. A hand's count of children had gathered around another merchant displaying small stones which floated weightlessly at eye level. Elsewhere, a dog with three heads and six legs was being shown to a potential buyer. Imi sneered at the creature, as she did at a caged creature resembling a man, but deformed and nearly twice as tall as any Alaji had ever set eyes upon.

Alaji wanted to ask Imi about the giant but couldn't begin to fathom how to do so. Besides, Imi had stopped to purchase two small, roasted birds speared on wooden stakes. She gave them both to Alaji, who returned one to her. "Thank you," Imi said.

"It is yours... as mine is," Alaji said. She thought for a moment then corrected herself: "This is yours as is mine." It still wasn't right, but it was close.

"It is as much mine as it..." Imi began to correct her then stopped abruptly. "It is not mine," she said quickly. "It is yours."

"I want for you have," Alaji said. Imi shrugged and drove slowly on while both picked at the roast bird. It was greasy and full of bones, but it had a flavor better than the similar meats they'd had on the road. She turned back to see if the giant was still present, but – despite its immense size – she couldn't locate it.

"Where should we?" Alaji asked.

Imi pointed ahead. "We'll go past the wall and look for Yemerik. I do not know how to find him, but we can ask. When we approach, there may be guards." Alaji didn't know the word, but she nodded. Imi continued, "There may be men. It is important you do not make them angry or hurt them. It would... make it difficult to find your friend."

Alaji nodded to show she understood. There hadn't been any other encounters like the one in the western plains, but Imi still became worried when anyone approached them. Alaji realized that they'd avoided several villages on their journey – she'd seen a few in valleys as they passed nearby – and when they did stop, Imi had hurried them out as fast as possible. Alaji tried broaching the subject once she'd gathered enough of Imi's language to manage it, but it seemed to make Imi uncomfortable, so she'd let it drop.

Likewise, Imi never asked Alaji about where she'd come from, though Imi had said a great deal about her own home.

But there was little time for such talk in the city: there was far too much to catch their attention here. It took them a fifth of the day to reach the circular wall, yet another new concept. As tall as all but the largest buildings, the wall circled the heart of the city. As they approached, Alaji caught a glimpse of the fortress deep inside, standing atop a hill in the center of the walled-off section. She gasped in amazement yet again.

The wall itself had several breaks where roads connected the outer and inner city. Two men wearing strange clothes and carrying spears were standing in front of each opening. Their shirts were made of bits of metal connecting wooden plates, which had been painted brownish-red. Over their hearts, they wore a sash bound with a broach, which bore the image of a deer. Alaji reasoned the shirts must be some sort of armor. It looked lighter and less restrictive than the wood and animal skin coverings some of the northmen had brought into battle.

The man nearest to them spoke. His words seemed similar to Imi's though their inflection was so different, Alaji couldn't understand a word of it. Fortunately, Imi seemed to have fewer issues with his speech. She leapt down and handed him three coins, then led him behind the wagon. She pulled back the covering, and began moving objects around at his direction. While they worked, a few other men dressed like those before approached and motioned toward the wagon and the girls. They made a handful of statements – jokes, if their tone was any indication. Alaji decided they didn't sound threatening or even cruel: it was simply as if these men found the wagon amusing. She glanced over her shoulder and saw Imi watching her intently. Alaji smiled and turned away.

Soon, the man inspecting the wagon's contents grew bored and leapt down. He exchanged a few more words with Imi, who then led the horses through the opening. Once they were through, she returned to her seat beside Alaji.

They'd just started moving away from the wall when they heard a voice cry out behind them. "Alaji!" someone screamed. She turned back to see another of these guards running towards their wagon. He stopped running when she looked at him.

He was no one she knew, but she waved, unsure of what else to do. "Alaji," the guard said again. He was an old man, almost out of breath, and he looked startled.

"Do know Yemerik?" Alaji asked, but her question seemed to confuse him.

"We are looking for a friend of hers," Imi explained. "His name is Yemerik: can you help us?"

The old guard's response was difficult for Alaji to interpret, though he was more intelligible than the man at the gate. "I am Ullin Hund, son of Korli." He said this as though it should mean something. He stared at Alaji, waiting for some sort of response, but she only stared back. "I do not know Yemerik," he added. "I am sorry. I think… I must be mistaken."

Alaji turned to Imi inquisitively. Imi, in turn, looked back at the gate. Several guards were looking at them and their wagon.

"We should leave," Imi said, leading the horses once more. Alaji felt strange riding when they were moving so slowly, so she climbed down and walked beside Imi. They pressed on, hindered by a crowd that grew thicker with each step. The buildings were even taller here than before. The areas between were full of traders selling strangely shaped fruits, multi-colored ornaments, barrels of beer, lengths of beautiful cloth, and dozens of objects whose purpose baffled Alaji. Imi was too busy navigating to offer much explanation, so she was left to wonder at the sheer scope of the place, its inhabitants, and treasures.

They stopped at an open spot surrounding a pile of barrels. There was a man in a stained shirt dunking clay mugs into the barrel nearest to him then bringing them up full of beer, which he traded for handfuls of coins he tossed into an empty barrel. His right forearm was discolored from years of this activity.

"Hey!" Imi shouted. "We are looking for someone." The beer seller looked at her and nodded. "His name is Yemerik," Imi added.

"Don't know any Yem'rik," he said. "Can I get you something?"

Imi looked at Alaji who shrugged. Imi raised two fingers, and the beer seller nodded, pinched a pair of cups between his fingers and thumb on one hand, then plunged them into the drink.

Imi handed the beer seller his money, then presented both cups to Alaji, who returned one immediately. It was a bitter drink, nowhere near the usual quality she'd had since arriving in this era, but far better than what she'd grown up drinking.

When they'd finished, Imi returned the cups to the seller, who immediately dunked them back in the barrel for another customer. While they were climbing back onto the wagon, he called out, "What's your friend do?"

"We're not sure," Imi replied. "But he is learned."

"Might try the Gull's Throat. You know the throat?" Imi shook her head. "It's past the pond, 'round the Sun's Mark. You know the Market?" Again, she shook her head. "Just go west out of Lord's Field, till you reach the pond. Keep to the left and turn off at Kirim's Bakery. It's not a horse's gait past there. You get lost, just tell someone you're looking for the Sun. You hit the Mark, tell 'im you're looking for the throat. Gull's Throat: you got that?"

Imi thanked him and started away. Alaji hurried to her side and whispered, "I not understand."

Imi laughed. "Neither did I."

10

It was nearly sunset in the court of Minot-Rin, regent of Hathari. There were no walls in the court itself: it was built in the open air, though there were more than enough obstacles to prevent anyone from approaching uninvited. While there were no walls, there was a ceiling, decorated with the finest metalwork and held up by four stone pillars. There was a garden surrounding the area, lending it the nickname, "the Court of Flowers." Kneeling beside each pillar was one of the court's magicians, who whispered spells to hold back the winds and maintain warmth. They worked for stretches lasting a third of the day – their replacements would come soon to take their place and ensure it was always summer in the Court of Flowers.

Minot-Rin gazed to the west to watch the sky above his city transform to hues of reds and gold no artisan had ever duplicated. He sighed, because he loved the beauty and because he knew it fleeting. The colors would diminish, and the sky would turn to black.

His business was mostly concluded for the day. A farmer who'd been wronged by a corrupt tax collector had his property restored (the collector's life would be spared, but only because Minot-Rin was merciful and the farmer had not asked for the man's head), trade tariffs had been adjusted at the request of King Ollin-To, a day of celebration had been planned for the construction of the city wall, and the family of a guard who'd died protecting a merchant from a gang of thieves had been honored with a generous gift. It had been a long day, but a good day.

"Esteemed Lord," the regent's advisor said, climbing the stairs from below. "A guard of your city has requested an audience."

"It is late," the regent said, plainly.

"It is, Lord," the advisor said. "If it please you, I will tell him to return in the morning."

Minot-Rin's gaze lingered on the setting sun and the city below. The pond always caught the light like a gem, which is why he'd refused to allow his engineers to have it filled. "Is there a reason he's come at so late an hour?"

"He says it's important, Lord. He said only that he has seen someone who will be of interest. With my Lord's permission, I will speak to him and find out more."

But Minot-Rin did not want to wait for his advisor to press for more information. Instead, he asked, "Is this man known to us?"

"He is known to me, Lord, though not well. He has never asked for an audience before tonight."

Minot-Rin turned to his advisor. "He may ascend, provided his business is brief."

The advisor bowed, and hurried down a set of stairs vanishing on the far side of the court. Minot-Rin rose to stretch his legs. He bent down to inspect a pale blue flower and to brush away an insect which had landed on its petal. By the time he'd returned to his throne, his advisor had returned with the guard, an old soldier wearing decorative armor. "I present Ullin Hund, guard of the circle and gate."

"My most esteemed, honorable lord," the guard stammered, clearly unaccustomed to polite conversation.

"Good evening to you," the regent replied. "I understand you have news for me."

"I do, Lord," the guard says. "It concerns a woman, a girl named Alaji."

"I do not know of this girl," the regent said.

"I met her once, briefly, years ago, when I was a boy. More than forty years have passed since. And I saw her again today, Lord, at the gates of the Wall. I swear on my service and honor, she had not aged a day."

The regent leaned forward. Suddenly, he was interested. "You are certain?" he asked in a whisper.

"My Lord, I would not have come here otherwise. I called out her name, and she recognized me, though she said very little. Her servant asked if I knew the whereabouts of a man, Yemerik, and then they left. I came here as soon as I could be made presentable."

"Do you know of this man? This Yemerik?" Minot-Rin asked his advisor.

"I do not, Lord. With your leave, I will make inquiries."

"Yes. Go. And send a rider for Imn Orith. I would speak to him today."

The advisor nodded and hurried away, leaving the regent to ask dozens of questions of Ullin Hund. When he'd answered them as well as he could, the regent stood and walked over to his garden of flowers. He selected an orange one, plucked it, then handed it to the guard. There were no flowers in the world with the same complexion as the king's, so none who'd seen them could ever doubt the origin of another. "Ullin Hund, you have served me well, but I have more to ask of you. You know this woman by sight, so you must seek her out. Go to the captain on watch and present the flower I have given you. Repeat to him my words as they are said to you: he is to place in your command the two dozen men he deems best. You will then take these men into the city and ask for the whereabouts of this woman, so that you might bring her before my court. She is to be treated with respect and is not to be harmed. However, she must be found. Though you've asked no reward, once you have accomplished this, you shall receive twenty pieces of fine bronze in gratitude."

"Thank you, Lord," the guard said. "Thank you."

The regent dismissed him with a nod, then returned to his flowers. He fidgeted with one, though it was difficult to see in the dimming light. When he'd finished, he called for an entertainer. They brought him a flutist who performed so badly, were it Minot-Rin's father still on the throne, he'd have been executed that day. But Minot-Rin's father had been dead more than a decade, and the son did not share his inclination towards such cruelty. Instead, he dismissed the musician with a wave. The man would be paid, as was custom, but the look on the regent's face made it clear he was not to be admitted again.

It was dark when Imn Orith arrived to the Court, though the flowers bloomed nonetheless. He bowed before the regent, then blurted out, "My work goes well, Lord. I... I have made great progress on an elixir–"

"When I first retained your services, there were some who cautioned against it. They said your theories were unfounded. Do you recall?"

"I do, Lord," Imn Orith said, timidly. "But the past four years have only reinforced my resolve. The philosophy is sound; of this, I am sure. We know from the Midnight Songs the world has grown from the corpse of the Self-Sacrificed God, from eternal life made temporal. A wheel that can turn one way, can the other turn; that is written in Tyve's Journal. The capacity for everlasting life is within us all. Given time–"

"Do not concern yourself with time, old friend," the regent said. "Something better than time has come to us. Today, within this city, walks a maiden who has lived unchanged for forty years."

Imn Orith forgot himself, leapt to his feet and rushed to the regent, who raised a hand to stop his guards from acting. Instead the regent laughed as Imn Orith began rattling off question after question. "Is she here in the palace? Has she been weighed yet? Does she eat food and take refreshment?"

Minot-Rin clasped a hand over the philosopher's shoulder. "I have men collecting her now. With luck, she will arrive by daybreak. I need to know, what do you need to replicate the process?"

Imn Orith considered the question. "It depends. If she can be persuaded to give us the formula, that may suffice."

"And if she will not surrender it, or if she doesn't know?"

"There are other methods we could attempt. Perhaps track down the origin, or find the one who created the potion that brought her eternal youth. If that doesn't work… we would need to distill the original potion. Reconstitute it."

"You can do this?" The regent asked.

"It should be possible, though it would be… unpleasant. We would need to remove the blood and boil it down. To remove the impurities. I should hope it won't come to that."

"As should I," Minot-Rin agreed. "But I'm glad to have options."

11

These were not taverns as Alaji knew them. In her time, beer was sold in a brewer's shop. She'd only been to Guljir's on a few occasions, and then only to deliver a message to her father or brother. Once, her father had sat her on the log beside him and told Guljir to bring his daughter a cup and reed. He'd objected – women were not supposed to enter his shop, let alone be served – but Kuljin grunted and Guljir relented. It was less a law than a rule, anyway, and Kuljin thought the experience of drinking fresh beer in the building where it was brewed more important.

The smallest of these taverns was five-fold as large as Guljir's, and women didn't seem in short supply. The beer in these taverns wasn't fresh, though – like all she'd drunk since arriving in this time – it was crisp, strong, and almost clear. In Guljir's, back in her own time, there'd been a pot where the drinkers would pour out the remnants of their cups when done: a thick, muddy mess of grain and foam. This beer of the future lasted to the bottom of the cup. It was miraculous.

They made inquiries as they went. In the second tavern, they met a man who claimed to know Yemerik, though he hadn't seen him in months. In another, they met a woman who said she knew him, but offered little in the way of description before demanding a bribe. At Alaji's insistence, Imi paid her what she asked. The money bought them little of use: the woman sent them to yet another section of the city, where no one they asked had heard of Yemerik.

Imi arranged for a room at an inn in the city, as well as stables for the horses and what she was assured was a secure area to leave their wagon. The room briefly reminded Alaji of the one she'd stayed in back in Elsimi. When she tried to sleep, she discovered the city was very different. She woke several times that night when she heard people walking or even riding through the street. What business they might have at such an hour was beyond Alaji's imagining.

—

Imi was already up when Alaji woke the next morning. Alaji dressed quickly, while Imi gathered the few belongings they'd taken inside. Alaji could smell roasting meat and mentioned this to Imi, who assured her they'd be able to eat once they reached the lower floor, but she was wrong. When they arrived at the bottom of the stairs, several members of the city guard were stationed in front of them. Among them, was Ullin Hund, who smiled and spoke a single name: "Yemerik."

"Where?" Alaji asked. She looked to Imi and repeated a motion that these people seemed to use for money.

The guard laughed when Imi removed a handful of coins. "I will take you to him," the guard explained, speaking slowly. Alaji missed some of his words, but their meaning was clear. If she had looked back, she'd have seen a concerned expression on Imi's face, but she did not.

After assuring them their belongings would be safe, the guards escorted them to the palace on foot. The crowd parted for the guards, so they arrived quickly. The structure was amazing. Constructed from stone and wood, it was built on the top of a small, round hill. The building was taller than even the wall surrounding the inner city.

The guards brought them inside and took them through a series of great halls. From there, they ascended several staircases. They reached a large room full of guards, who spoke briefly with Hund, who then turned to the women. "You must leave any knives," he said. No weapons before the–" he said another word, but Alaji did not know its meaning.

She removed the knife Yemerik had given her and handed it over. Hund gasped when he saw the blade, but caught himself, nodded with a smile, and muttered something about them getting it back.

Then he led them up a final set of stairs, which brought them into a room with no walls. There were beautiful flowers around them and even more guards. There were also men in strange robes chanting. She believed this to be some sort of magic, but it was no spell known to her people. Even with all she'd learned and been through, Alaji still shivered in the presence of the magic of the gods. The knowledge this was mere superstition did little to calm the reaction.

At the far end of the room sat a man draped in the most

incredible clothes Alaji had ever seen. They were white in color and were lined in yellowish trim. To his side, an elderly man stood excitedly.

The seated man in white whispered, "Which of them is she?"

"I present the Lady Alaji," Hund replied, motioning. "And her Imi," he added, almost as an afterthought.

Imi stepped to Alaji's side and repeated their words, speaking slowly so Alaji would be able to understand. Imi added, "He is the regent of this city and land." Alaji didn't know what that meant, but she understood he was their leader. Perhaps more, to have such wealth.

Alaji thought she should give the man in the ornate robes a chance to speak, but after a moment of him simply gawking, she grew impatient. "Where Yemerik?" She asked, and Imi repeated, correcting her grammar.

"My men are out searching for him," the man in the robes said. "He'll be with us shortly. In the meantime, you are to be my guests."

"Thank you," Alaji said.

"It is my honor," he replied through Imi. "Tell me, Imi, has your Master always spoken in such a manner?"

"I am new to her," Imi said. "She learned our tongue when I met her."

"And where are you from?"

"I am from Elsimi," Imi replied.

"And your Lady?" the regent asked.

When she turned to Alaji, Imi had a look of terror on her face. She stuttered out the question a few times, using different phrases. Alaji whispered a response, and Imi repeated it: "The Land of Five Lakes."

"I am not familiar with the region," the regent replied. "Perhaps she can help my scribe locate it on the maps later. But what brings you to our city?"

"Yemerik," Alaji said, speaking for herself. She still had trouble with some of the regent's words, but overall the ruler spoke clearly and slowly enough for her to follow.

"Is he your blood?"

Alaji didn't understand at first, but Imi managed to explain. Alaji said, "No. He and I... travel. I... I know. About Citadel."

"Citadel? I don't understand. Which Citadel?"

Alaji was speechless. She blurted a response, which Imi worked to parse out for the regent. "The Citadel. Before. Stars. Where they are Gathered."

"I'm not familiar with that, either," the regent said.

"It may belong to one of the eastern churches," the man to his side suggested. "I don't recall hearing the name, but it sounds like one of theirs."

Minot-Rin shrugged. "Perhaps your Yemerik can help us narrow it down once he arrives. In the meantime, I would be honored if you would entertain us with tales of your journey. This isn't your first time in our city, unless I'm mistaken."

Imi conversed quickly with Alaji. She understood most of what was said, but wanted to be sure. "This first in Hathari visit," Alaji answered.

This created more confusion. The regent called for Hund, who approached and discussed the matter quickly. Hund seemed adamant about something, but the regent was growing worried. Finally, to Alaji, he asked, "Does your mother live in our city?"

Alaji shook her head. "My mother?" She paused, looking for the words. "No. She... long ago," she added. "Land of Five Lakes."

"What happened long ago?" the regent asked.

"Battle. Men-of-north," Alaji replied.

The regent turned to the elderly one, and he responded with an equally baffled expression. "How long ago was this battle?" the regent asked.

Alaji lay three fingers of her left hand over her open right, then folded her last fingers over this. She spoke a word that none of them seemed to know. The regent stared at Imi, who shook her head.

The regent patted his chest. "Forty-five years," he said. "Years. You know years? I have lived for forty-five years."

Alaji nodded. She'd learned their numbers in her time with Imi.

"How long ago was this battle?" the regent asked.

Alaji was barely comfortable with the word for two hundred in the northmen's tongue, and that was of no more use than her own people's phrasing. Besides, she didn't know if it had been two hundred or three or a thousand years. Yemerik had said his aim might not be precise.

But, looking at her hand, she realized she could at least communicate the basic idea. She raised her right hand, all fingers extended. "Forty years," she said, bending the first. "Forty years," and the second joined it. "Forty years," she said, as her third dropped beside them. "Forty years, forty years," and all fingers were bent. She nodded.

The regent sat back, a look of amazement on his face. "How old are you?" he asked.

Alaji whispered briefly with Imi to verify the meaning and her pronouncement of the answer. When she was sure, she replied, "Sixteen."

The king looked to the elderly man once more. This time, he saw his advisor smiling. "Don't you see? She is multiplying. Sixteen by forty, Lord. She is more than six hundred years old."

"Is this so?" the regent asked the frightened Imi, who attempted – without success – to communicate his question to Alaji.

Alaji shook her head in frustration and repeated her first answer. The regent asked again. The elderly man by his side duplicated Alaji's count, using both hands to try and demonstrate four-hundred to Alaji, but he lost her entirely on the second hand, since his counting no longer made sense.

And none of them noticed a guard arrive, escorting a new guest. "I present, Yemerik, the entertainer."

PART 5

1

"It's you," Yemerik said, still in disbelief. His voice quivered. Then he stepped forward and almost fell; only his walking cane caught him. Alaji stared at him. He was not as she'd hoped, but she'd always known it was a possibility: she had come late.

Yemerik's hair was white. He was thin and sickly. If it weren't for his voice, she was unsure whether she'd have recognized him at all. She went towards him. "They not know Citadel," she said.

"I know," he replied. "It's gone wrong. Something here has gone terribly wrong. Magic hasn't developed right. There's a lot we have to discuss, but not here. The regent's being suspiciously patient with us as it is."

She was disoriented at first. It took her a moment to parse out his words and another before she realized he was speaking the language of her people. It had been months since she'd heard it spoken aloud. She shook off the confusion and replied, "What do they want?"

"No idea. Let's ask," Yemerik replied. He smiled and turned his attention to the regent and bowed, though it clearly caused him discomfort. "My… my Lord," he said. "Forgive me. I was so surprised to see my friend, I forgot my manners. You can't imagine my relief at seeing her again."

"Nonsense," Minot-Rin said, rising from his chair and swiftly walking across the room. Two of his guards converged near him to observe. "I am very pleased to be present at this reunion. It has been some time since you last saw each other, has it not?"

"I apologize for intruding," the scholar interrupted, rushing to join them. "The language you were speaking just now reminded me of one used by Yrurmi tribes in their rituals. What was the dialect?"

Yemerik took note when the regent smiled. He smiled, as well, and answered the scholar. "It does bear a similarity, doesn't it? But you won't find an Yrurmi able to translate it. No, the girl's family hails from Gryin. I've long suspected some lost connection to the Yrurmi tribes, though my theories have been dismissed by more philosophers than I can count. Perhaps we could discuss the matter at some point. To answer our host's question, though, it's been some years since Alaji and I last crossed paths. When her father died–"

"You knew her father?" the regent asked.

"Oh, yes. Charming man. He grew ill on the voyage from Hathi and never took to the climate here. This was… five years ago, I believe. He'd sent Alaji away a few years before that, to live with her aunt's husband in Turthin."

"And yet, you still recognized her," the regent remarked. He was staring Yemerik in the eyes now, studying every twitch and reaction.

"She looks so much like her father," Yemerik replied. "But she has better luck. It is fortunate that she found her way here, or I doubt we'd have ever located each other. I fear that's a debt we may never be able to repay. Truly we are all blessed to live in a city overseen by so gracious a lord."

The regent smiled politely. "Tell me, Alaji mentioned a land of five lakes. Is this in Gryin, as well?"

"No, she's never been herself. Her family left Gryin before she was born and lived for a time in a valley southeast of there before setting out for the new lands. I believe there were a number of lakes there, come to think of it."

"And a battle. She said there was a battle there?"

"I believe that's why they left," Yemerik replied. "Some trouble between a group of traders and the natives. You know how it is in the primitive lands beyond the protection of civilization."

"No, I don't believe that's what she was referencing. She gave us a number, didn't she? Six centuries, I believe."

"No, my Lord," the scholar said. "The battle was two hundred years passed. The six hundred years was for her... I'm sorry. For something else."

"I do not know the ancient history of Gryin," Yemerik apologized.

"It is of no concern. I'll send for a translator to help the girl. I'd like a full history for our library. In the meantime, I was getting ready to eat." Yemerik inhaled to say something, but the regent did not give him an opportunity. "Of course both of you are invited to join us."

"It would be a pleasure," Yemerik replied, forcing himself to maintain a smile.

2

The Imi was fairly certain there was no place in or beneath any of the heavens that she less wanted to be in that moment than at the dining table of Minot-Rin. She knew little about the regent, but he was a lord of the Hathin, the fair-skinned people of the eastern sea. Her grandfather and two of her uncles had died fighting the armies of his forefathers: her people would remember their brutality until the end of time.

She was also relatively certain the invitation for the only two travelers from the Sea Beyond the Sea to this world in an age hadn't been intended for her. But Alaji had brought her along and had motioned for her to sit. Naturally, the Imi had sat silently without touching the food. But this had backfired: Alaji began to dote, asking if she was well. This had attracted the attention of Minot-Rin, who'd feigned concern and asked if there was anything else he could order brought before them, if his cooks' food was not to her liking.

She'd apologized quickly, then almost immediately began nibbling at whatever was placed in front of her. The food was fantastic, with the exception of the fish, which – while better than most of what she'd had since leaving Elsimi – paled to what she'd grown up eating. Still, it was good enough to remind her of home. And, of course, that made the overall experience of sharing a table with two prophets and a tyrannical lord all the more unpleasant.

The situation was so bad that the presence of Imn Orith, philosopher-physician, was something of a mitigating factor. His constant prattling seemed to occupy the room's attention, which meant no one other than the servants paid her any attention whatsoever. She suspected she'd have had a less favorable impression of him had she been able to understand him clearly.

She could understand his tone well enough. He acted kind and laughed in a friendly manner, but he was too eager, too cloying. He badgered Yemerik with an endless string of questions. And through them all, Minot-Rin watched hungrily. They both studied Yemerik's expressions.

None of it made sense to her. They didn't seem to know where Alaji and Yemerik were from: indeed, how could they? The Hathin had little interest in the knowledge of her people. They worshipped their own gods, petty beings of the lower heaven the Hathin alone believed had ascended. So why should Minot-Rin, regent of Hathari, take such an interest in these two?

A servant brought her a bowl of wine and caught her eye as he laid it in front of her. She couldn't tell whether the look was one of envy or pity. She suspected the latter: even in these lands, no servant would want to be seated by a lord.

The questions, at some point, seemed to become heated. Yemerik was doing his best to maintain a calm demeanor, but she could hear his voice straining. He was fidgeting with his food and drink and was looking around much more than before. He kept looking back at Alaji, as if he was worried she might vanish.

Perhaps she would. She'd seemed to flicker into and out of the world the night she killed the two men in the wood. The memory made the Imi even more agitated. Soon, she was sweating and visibly upset. She was worried they'd notice, but she quickly realized her fears were absurd. The attention of everyone in the room, even the servants and guards, was now focused on Yemerik, Imn Orith, and some question between them.

The room, for a moment, was silent. And then Minot-Rin said plainly to Yemerik, "Answer his question."

The Imi didn't breathe. She'd been ignoring the discussion, which was easy when they barely shared the same language. But she could feel the tension. She was anxious, too, but unlike the servants and guards, she focused on Alaji. The girl from the Sea Beyond the Sea looked upset, as well.

—

"You think she's ageless, don't you?" Yemerik finally said. Something had changed in his voice. He was tired of talking in circles and had been pinned contradicting himself about details regarding Alaji's family time overseas. "I promise you, she isn't."

"It is treason to lie in my court," Minot-Rin said. "I say this not as a threat but as a friend. No one here doubts you have spoken untruths. The proof would be no harder to obtain than a translator, unless you still maintain the child hails from Gryin."

Yemerik was silent.

"Rest assured, I have no intention of pressing the matter. However, I believe it is time to speak more frankly." Minot-Rin took a small piece of bread, dipped it into his wine, then bit off the end. "You are a man of great knowledge, Yemerik. I can see that. I would like you to share that knowledge with us."

"You're looking for something I can't give you."

"I am not an unreasonable man, but you will find me persistent.

If the matter were less important, I would let it go. But the welfare of my people is at stake. I have devoted my life to making this city strong, towards turning it into something greater than it is. This city has grown to rival any in the world."

Yemerik began to laugh. It was the sad desperate laugh of an old man. He was tired, and clearly unable to stop. Guards stepped forward – a few reached for weapons – but the regent stopped them with a raised hand.

He waited until Yemerik had regained his composure. "Do you deny this?"

"No, no," Yemerik replied, trying to control himself. "I'm sure there is no greater city in the world than your Hathari."

"Then why do you insult me?"

"I'm sorry, Lord Regent," Yemerik said. "It's just that I remember what Hathari could have been."

"I have never been insulted by a guest," Minot-Rin replied, though this was a lie. He'd been insulted by diplomats, visiting dignitaries, and even members of his family beneath his roof. He'd simply never been insulted by someone so low as an entertainer.

"I apologize. Blame it on the wine or the company or a shift in my strategy. I'd been trying to find a way to leave your fortress and hoped you'd let us go on equitable terms. But I can see there's no way to convince you that Alaji isn't hundreds of years old, which renders the point moot. Besides, that would still leave us in need of a ship and crew and supplies, so that was never a great plan, anyway. So we need your help."

"You are asking for money in exchange for the elixir of life?"

"We don't have any elixirs," Yemerik replied. "But come with us, and I'll make sure you outlive Hathari by a thousand years."

"Give me that power, and I will give you a fleet of ships."

"It's not that simple, I'm afraid. I need something to make this possible."

"Tell me what it is, and I will have it brought to you," Minot-Rin responded.

"This is something we need to do. Only Alaji and myself can do it."

Now it was Minot-Rin's turn to laugh. "I see your game. But I promise you, you will not leave until I have what you've promised me."

"I can't do anything for you from here," Yemerik replied, sipping some wine from his bowl. "Shall we wait and see if the girl ages?"

"I have waited long enough. If you do not cooperate by the new moon, you will force me to take drastic action."

"Like what? You'll discover nothing if you kill us," Yemerik replied.

"That is not clear." Minot-Rin glanced quickly towards Imn Orith.

"Please," Imn Orith began, "I'd rather work with you both to replicate the process. I have no desire to harm either of you."

"Torturing us won't work."

"That's not what I'm talking about. I assume you've read Feltrie's Treatise?"

"No," Yemerik replied. "I don't even know what that is."

"Oh. I'd assumed... never mind. Feltrie was one of the great philosophers who deduced the possibility of the elixir. He demonstrated that the elixir would not decompose using the principle of property identity. Do you understand?"

"You think, what, you can pull a magic potion out of Alaji and use it to gain immortality?"

"No, not pull. The process would require a distillation." Imn Orith paused to give Yemerik a moment to consider the implications.

Minot-Rin added, "I remind you this is viewed as a last resort. But, to protect Hathari's interests, I will do whatever I must. The choice is yours."

Yemerik leaned back. He clenched his jaw, breathed in deeply, then exhaled. Then he smiled. "I can't accept your terms or your options. My final offer stands. If you want access to our knowledge, you will give us transportation. Otherwise, we will simply leave."

Imn Orith began laughing first, and Minot-Rin followed. "You would not be permitted," he reminded Yemerik.

And Yemerik simply tilted his head, grinned, and replied, "You won't be able to stop us."

The laughter was silenced at once. Minot-Rin rose to his feet and planted his hands on the table. He leaned forward and said, "Be extremely careful. Your words could be misinterpreted." Every guard in the room stood ready.

"My dear Lord," Yemerik replied, "I would hate any misunderstanding to arise between us, so allow me an opportunity to clarify my previous statement. You will be unable to hold us against our will, any attempt to do so will be viewed as an act of aggression, and we will respond with force necessary to ensure our wellbeing and freedom."

Minot-Rin laid his hands down on the table and leaned forward. "You are threatening me?"

"I'm warning you. No, no. That's disingenuous. You were right the first time. I was definitely threatening you."

Minot-Rin looked around the room. He looked at his guards – there were seven. He looked at the old man. He looked at Alaji, who stared back. She was tense and focused. Finally, he looked to her Imi, who sat at her side. He saw fear in her eyes. A level of fear he'd only seen in men who awaited sentencing.

"You have committed a grave act," he said. "The penalty for such a crime is severe. However, I am a lenient and merciful man. I will spare your life, Yemerik." He sneered when Yemerik snickered. Then he motioned towards the shaking girl and said, "Their Imi is forfeit."

A guard stepped towards the girls and reached for his blade, but it was no longer sheathed at his side. His mouth gaped open before he felt the pain. By then, he was clutching at his stomach. His eyes bulged. He was looking at Alaji, covered in blood, with a look of hatred etched across her face. She pushed him backward, and he tumbled over in pain. The other guards drew weapons.

Alaji's gaze turned to Minot-Rin.

"Wait," Yemerik said to her. Then he turned to Minot-Rin. "My offer stands. We still need a ship."

The guards began to step forward, but Minot-Rin raised a hand to stop them. "How did she do that? I have seen demonstrations of all the magic known to man and—"

In response, Yemerik turned to the startled Imi, who was still shaking. She was staring at Alaji, wondering where the blood that covered her clothes had come from. Alaji was uninjured, and the soldier had barely bled. "Tell him. Tell the regent-lord of Hathari where I'm from."

The Imi looked up, in shock. "They are not from this world," she replied.

"A ship," Yemerik said, once more. "And a crew, of course. We can help you outrun death for centuries. Millennia."

Minot-Rin motioned to a guard on the other side of the table. "Take Jier-Tollith to a healer." The guard sheathed his blade and hurried to the fallen soldier. He helped him up and began towards the door. Minot-Rin followed behind him. "I must consider this," he muttered.

3

"They killed her," Alaji said, fighting back tears. She hugged Imi, closely, which of course left Imi even more shaken. It would have been worse if she'd been able to understand Alaji, but she was speaking her own language again. "The guard, he… he drew his knife and—"

"I'm sure he did," Yemerik said. "And me, as well, eventually.

For the time being, though, this version of us is alive. And, with luck, we'll have a ship at our disposal, as well."

"You said they'd know you here, that they'd be able to contact the Citadel and send me home."

"I know. And I'm sorry," Yemerik said. "Something's gone horribly wrong. This era isn't right. They never learned to master time, never even discovered it was possible. The damage done to the timeline is much more severe than I'd expected. It's become increasingly unlikely that the ones responsible were Hatharian."

"You mean the old woman, by the lake."

"Yes. Her and her accomplices. They're... they're something else. Something worse, I fear. Yemerik paused and reached for a glass of wine left on the table. After a sip, he continued. "There was always another possibility. A more likely possibility, perhaps. I have a theory – for years, I've believed that there's something else like the place I'm from. Another magically advanced civilization existing somewhere in time. I came to your time looking for them. I had... reasons for thinking they might be there. I'd always thought they'd have the same goals as the Gathering at the Citadel, but that was before all this. If they did this, if they lured me here, introduced time-travel to your people, destroyed a talisman of the Citadel, and reduced Hathari to a petty city-state ruled by shortsighted men... the damage done to the Gathering's work may be catastrophic."

"Is there anything we can do?"

"The Citadel can still set this right. It's just... getting to them will be considerably more difficult than I'd expected. I have no idea what they've managed to piece together about what's happening. I'd hoped if I waited I'd run into a traveler here to investigate. But I've been here a lifetime and found nothing. It may be time to try a new approach."

"We need to go there, don't we?" Alaji asked. "We need to travel to the Citadel itself."

"That's impossible. Not even the gates were built to last that long. But there may be ways of sending messages. If we're lucky, we might find a civilization that's discovered temporal magic. Either way, it won't be an easy journey, one I'm far too old to make. But you will need my help. Do you understand?"

Alaji rubbed her forehead. "I think so. We need you younger. We need to travel back and find you before you were lost."

Yemerik nodded slowly. "It's the only way. I'm sorry to ask this of you. I'm sorry to have dragged you on this whole twisted adventure. But this is the only way to set things right."

"I'll do it," Alaji said. "But I want something else. My brother. I want to save him."

Yemerik took a deep breath. "Time doesn't work that way," he said. "There's no way to guarantee that...." He shut his eyes and pinched the bridge of his nose. "I will do what I can. It's not a promise, but... I'll help you in any way I can. Tell the younger me I said as much, and he'll understand."

"What do we do first?" Alaji asked.

"First, we wait and see if Minot-Rin lets us leave his palace alive. He's in a difficult situation. We've shown him he can't keep us here safely, but he can't kill us without risking his chance at immortality."

"Immortality?"

"He thinks you're two hundred years old. One of his men says he saw you years ago, and you haven't aged. So he thinks you're carrying the secret of eternal life."

"I've never been here before."

"No, of course not, which is even more troubling. It might be nothing, just another version of you in an alternate timeline. That won't make sense yet, will it? There are... sometimes complications. Do you remember all those years ago on the plains? I'm sorry, it wasn't long ago for you, at all. Do you remember how I wanted you to make sure you always carried all the shards if you were... what did you used to call it? Stepping back? They're objects of the Citadel, attuned to its energy. In a sense, it perceives them and protects the continuity of anything connected to them. If you have one, someone can't go back in time and hurt you. Or rather they can, but it won't have any effect on you in the present. But this has consequences when attuned objects cross paths. When you step back while I'm holding one of the shards, there's a chance a version of me will be maintained in a timeline you've vanished from."

"You told me you'd die. Is that... like what happened to Imi? She died, then I saved her."

"It's complicated. You saved her, and you didn't save her. There's a sustained timeline where you vanished, and the soldiers killed her. Then most likely tortured me to death. And there's no telling how many times I died on the plain. It's not a pleasant thought, but I was trained to look past it. It's a reality of time-travel sometimes. A price."

"There are other versions of me out there?"

"Perhaps," Yemerik replied. "Almost certainly, now that I think of it. You crossed paths with another traveler when you were attacked. If she had a talisman... yes, that should have created variant iterations. Either of us could have been duplicated if a traveler from the Citadel crossed our path in this era, too. The guard could have seen a different you entirely. But there's another possibility, too. A circle. You go back to find me and – forgive me for being blunt – get killed after running into that guard. Yes, that might do it. A simple loop. It should be easy enough to break, at least. You just need to reach me before I reach Hathari. You need to find me in Elsimi."

"What about the other... me's? What should we do about them?"

"Nothing. It's best to stay focused on your goals: you can go mad trying to figure out your own fate, only to wind up in an alternate line of causality anyway."

"If another version of us reaches the Citadel first, what happens to us?"

"If that happens, the Citadel will fix everything. I spent every day of the past thirty years hoping for just that. But we can't count on it: we have to assume we're on our own."

Alaji nodded. It wasn't what she meant by the question, but she let it go. "Then we need to get back to Elsimi."

"Before the younger version of me has a chance to leave. It's a short window, I'm afraid. A little less than a year. If you can reach me there, we can simply sail on to the next era. Hope for better luck then."

"I'm not sure I can open the portal that specifically."

"That's okay. I'm not even sure we're going to get out of here alive."

Before Alaji could respond, the doors opened and several guards entered. They were better armed than before, but Yemerik didn't seem concerned. Behind them, stood Minot-Rin. "I have made up my mind on how we will proceed," he proclaimed.

4

There was wind and seawater in her hair, sunlight on her face, and around her was the ocean in its eternity. The ship was massive, at least compared to any she'd been on before. Even the ones in Elsimi were small in comparison. The sails overhead bore the insignia of Hathari, a deer standing before a setting sun. Or perhaps the sun was rising: she'd never gotten around to asking, and it didn't seem important, anyway.

She looked up at the mast of their ship, then at the others. Theirs was the smallest of four that had left the harbor. Furthest out was the largest, the massive white boat that carried Minot-Rin. She'd understood his presence was strange even before Yemerik said it aloud. The regent was supposed to remain in his city, with certain exceptions made for state functions and occasional voyages into the provinces. But for him to leave on a quest was in violation of several laws. The idea that someone like Minot-Rin had anyone to answer to was baffling to Alaji, but Yemerik assured her there were powerful families and churches in the city that would attempt to have him overthrown. But, with a wry smile, Yemerik added that none of it would matter, anyway.

Alaji, Yemerik, and Imi were all stationed on this ship, along with two dozen sailors, all of whom were armed and all of whom would look at her from time to time. They looked at her the way a hunter might look at its prey. She wasn't sure what Minot-Rin had told them, but she knew they were dangerous. Still, she knew they wouldn't hurt her for the time being. They were here to murder her and Yemerik if they betrayed Minot-Rin, or perhaps simply after he had what he was after. But he wouldn't get any sort of immortality elixir from them, and they hadn't betrayed him yet. So, for the time being, the sailors could do nothing but imagine how they'd kill her, and she might as well enjoy the open water.

They sailed south towards a southern coast Alaji's people never knew existed. The shape of the world joined a growing list of ideas her parents and village elders had been mistaken about. In the water, she gazed upon fish larger than the boat itself, though Yemerik assured her they were harmless and not rightly called "fish," at all.

Yemerik spent several days adjusting to the feel of the sea. After that, he began teaching Alaji everything she could grasp about time, the Citadel, and the world. There was a great deal to cover.

"Remember what I said about creating a circle in time? It's one of the two primary modes of temporal interaction. It's actually the preferred mode, unless you're protected by the Citadel. The concept is simple: a traveler goes back in time in continuity with events in their own past. Sometimes the events they cause are even related to why they went back in the first place. The other mode is a cut line or contradiction, a future timeline which exists for the duration of one's stay, only to be replaced with a different timeline once a traveler goes back and makes a change. These are dangerous unless you know what you're doing. Well, not for us, because we've got the shards. But without those, there'd be nothing to protect us from the changing lines of causality. There are plenty of cases of early time-travelers destroying themselves or even their civilizations. You used to worry about that, back on the plains, I recall. Regardless, it's actually what we want this time, to utterly cut away this whole timeline."

Alaji ignored what she didn't understand and focused on the aspects that made sense. "How do you choose which happens? Whether you close a circle or cut it?"

"Sometimes you can determine the pattern and maneuver out of it. The guard who recognized you is a good example. It's likely that a version of you traveled back to find me in Hathari and met the guard. By going back before I leave for Hathari, we're altering the chain of events."

"Couldn't I have met him outside the city?"

"Of course. We'll have to take precautions. But then I was going to do this anyway." He removed a small bag from his side and handed it to Alaji.

She could feel the shards of the talisman echoing through the cloth. "They're different," she said. "They're...."

"They're older," Yemerik interrupted. "I was hoping you'd be able to sense that. The fragments I was carrying will be out of sync with yours. In theory, there should be a way for you to use that. Like a tuning fork."

"Tuning fork?"

"Never mind. Just... see if you can make sense of the energy patterns or pulses or however you perceive them. Maybe hold the shards close together and see if there are differences. The truth is, I've never really understood any of it. When I'm from, there's simply too much knowledge to try and learn it all. Everyone chooses a topic and tries to master it, and those topics can be extremely specific. I'm no different: I only have a basic comprehension of temporal magic theory, at best. But you found your way this far, and I'm betting you can get those pieces to align." Yemerik smiled. "Take this, as well."

He removed his pendant and handed it to Alaji. She held it, and he motioned for her to try it on. He started speaking, but his speech had changed into something she could no longer understand. Within a few seconds, it had shifted into something she could. On some level, she realized it wasn't a language she knew, and if she focused on a specific word, that word became unclear. But, so long as she simply focused on the conversation, it made perfect sense.

"Do you understand me?" Yemerik asked.

"I think so," Alaji said. The words contorted in her lungs and chest and seemed to warp her mouth and tongue on their way out. It felt wrong, even gross in some ways, like she was eating something with an unpleasant texture.

"Good, it's working. Congratulations. You're speaking a language that won't evolve for hundreds of millions of years. It should work with anyone, though there may be a delay if it's a language the Citadel hasn't encountered."

"Like the city on the river," Alaji said.

"Yes, the dragon-head village," Yemerik said.

"Will you be alright without it?"

"Yes, yes. I can speak their language well enough to get by. I've had decades to practice. We just have to make sure you're comfortable with the pendant before we reach Ilpinthi. Oh, and make sure you don't address the sailors or any of Minot-Rin's people. The last thing we need to do is try and explain why you're suddenly able to converse with them. Just use it with me, and we should be fine."

Alaji looked over her shoulder at Imi. "What about her?"

Yemerik considered this for a moment. "It's dangerous," he decided. "She might say something that gets back to Minot-Rin."

"She'll be discreet if I ask her," Alaji replied.

"There's really nothing useful she can tell us. Her people think we're from another world, some magical sea or something. There's no reason to involve her further."

"I'm going to talk to her," Alaji said at last. "She got me to Hathari. I owe her the truth."

"You don't owe her… Alaji?" But by then she'd already started towards the girl. Yemerik considered hurrying after her, but decided he was far too old to try. Besides, he doubted he could change Alaji's mind. Silently, he cursed himself for giving Alaji the pendant so early in the voyage.

5

The Imi was thinking of Elsimi. It was easy enough to pretend she was back there while she stood at the side of the ship. She'd spent plenty of time on fishing boats tending the nets and gutting the catch to feel at home on a boat, even the large, eastern ships of the Hathi.

When she saw the woman from the Sea Beyond the Sea approach, she bowed her head. Alaji placed a hand on her shoulder and asked, "Can we speak for a moment?"

The Imi was momentarily caught off guard. Alaji's accent and pronunciation were flawless: she spoke as if she'd grown up in Elsimi. The Imi nodded, wondering if Alaji could always have spoken like this, if perhaps her apparent confusion had simply been a test or game of some sort. Regardless, she nodded her head while Alaji led her to a relatively secluded spot on the deck.

"Can you understand me?" Alaji asked.

This made the Imi even more confused, but she replied, "Yes."

"Good. There's a lot we need to discuss, Servant." Alaji heard the word leave her mouth but was unable to catch it. She panicked, apologized, and tried once more, but she said the same thing: "Servant." On the third time, she focused on the word and caught it. She placed a hand over her mouth. "I'm so sorry. All this time, I thought… I thought that was your name. I didn't know."

"I am a servant," the girl said, more confused than ever. She seemed a little embarrassed, though she wasn't sure why.

"I never… your name. What is your name?"

"I am the servant called Giora," Giora replied.

"Giora," Alaji repeated it. "I'm sorry. I heard them use it, didn't I? Back in Elsimi, people would say that word when talking to me."

"It isn't improper to refer to a servant by title," Giora said, before realizing she was telling an emissary of the gods what was and was not proper.

"I won't call you that again. I don't care if it's proper here or not."

"I'm sorry," Giora said. "Clearly, I should have specified earlier."

"No. It's not…. You didn't do anything wrong. At all. I don't think I could have gotten to Hathari without you. I mostly wanted to thank you. And also, I want to tell you the truth about me, about where I'm from."

Giora suddenly looked concerned, but Alaji continued. "I'm not what you think I am. I mean, I don't really know what you think I am, but I don't think it's right. Yemerik said something about an ocean. He said you thought I lived there. Is that right?"

"The Sea Beyond the Sea," Giora said. "We have only vague stories. I know they aren't all true. It is said that nothing from my world can live there, but nothing can drown."

"I'm not from any Sea. I'm from a valley that holds five lakes. Do you remember those mountains we passed, about halfway through our trip to Hathari? The ones shaped kind of like a fish's fin? I think those are near where I'm from. If we'd travelled north instead of south there, I think we'd have gone right through my home. Or at least whatever's left of it."

"But we saw the door. We saw the grey world open. The morning you arrived."

"Grey? Oh, the clouds, of course. That wasn't a different world. It was just another time. I should have died hundreds of years ago. Maybe thousands, I'm not sure. I was taken out of my time and brought to yours. It's not entirely my fault, but I'm not blameless, either. When I got here, I couldn't understand anything you were saying, but I figured that you thought I was someone important. I took advantage of that, and I'm sorry."

Giora didn't entirely believe or disbelieve Alaji. There were inconsistencies about her people's stories about the Sea, after all. In secret, she'd doubted its existence at all until the night she stood on the shore and stared at the open hole in the world with others from her village. Still, it seemed just as likely that Alaji was lying: the people from the Sea Beyond the Sea were said to do this. "What... what do you want from me?"

"Nothing. I just... I owe you so much. The people we're trying to reach, Yemerik's people, are very powerful. Maybe I can ask them for something for you. Is there anything you want?"

Giora thought for a moment. "I just want to go home," she said, before quickly adding, "But I will go where commanded."

6

"Are you adjusting to the pendant alright?" Yemerik and Alaji were seated in the small cabin she'd been given. It was almost evening, which usually meant Alaji would be on deck to watch the sunset, but the storm clouds which had hung over them for the past three days made that impossible. They were somewhere far to the south. The world, Alaji decided, was far larger north to south than east to west. It was also lined by strange peninsulas and harbors, most of which they sailed near enough to keep in view.

The four ships were all anchored in a bay waiting for the storm to pass, and there hadn't been much to do beyond spying on the sailors, who were still unaware Alaji could understand their speech, and working with the pendant and shards.

"It's fine, but I don't like your language," Alaji told him. "I prefer Giora's. Yours makes my jaw sore."

He laughed. "There are worse. Trust me." He cleared his throat and withdrew some rolled up pieces of parchment from his bag. "You might as well get used to these." He unrolled one and handed it over. She recognized the map at once: Yemerik had checked it periodically when they were traveling across the plains a millennium before. He tapped a cluster of symbols in the upper left corner. "Go ahead. Try to read it."

Alaji shook her head. "I don't know how."

"Just look at the writing. At the... the symbols... and try speaking them aloud. The translation pendant will do the rest."

She stared at the paper, and none of it made sense to her. But she breathed in and spoke, and – once again – the words came on their own. "Northern Bay. This, right here, it's the Northern Bay." It strained her eyes, but the effect was well worth it.

"Yes. Good. You should spend some time studying–"

"This says Ilpinthi!" she exclaimed. "And over here–"

"Yes, yes."

She studied the document, drinking in the symbols and mouthing the names of cities, rivers, seas, and nations.

"You should reach a point where you don't have to say them aloud. Don't worry if it takes a while. You can do that later, though. Have you made progress with the fragments?"

Alaji reluctantly released the map and took out the two cloths containing the shards of the talisman and opened them. "You gave me all of them," she said.

"It's better I don't have them anymore. When you get back, they'll overwrite the versions I had."

"Then... the shards you'll have – the younger you, I mean...."

"They'll seem to vanish."

"What about you? Won't you be... 'overwritten?'"

Yemerik smiled. "You always were clever. I'm not going back with you."

"Won't you be killed here?"

"There won't be a here," Yemerik replied. "As soon as you go back in time, this whole timeline will be replaced with something different. It's the only way to get the younger me back. If I went, the shards would overwrite the younger me, along with the earlier versions of themselves. That becomes the dominant past, and this timeline ceases to.... What? What is it?"

"Wait. If we overwrite everything, what happens to the people who are here?"

"Well, that depends. It'll be a world without my involvement for the past two and a half decades, so I suppose a great number of people will miss out on the stories I've been telling."

"What about Giora?" Alaji asked.

"That's complicated," Yemerik replied. "I mean, possibly nothing. She wasn't born when I passed through, so. Oh. Never mind."

"What?"

"People aren't destined to be born. It depends on how the line progresses and a million factors, but ultimately it's more likely than not that she only exists because this timeline was created."

"She won't be born?" Alaji's voice rose.

"It's not really like that. Lives aren't like that. There's... did your people believe in a spirit? Everyone has a spirit, a soul, that's born into one body after another. Well, almost everyone. There are eras where... never mind. I'm sorry, I'm losing focus. The servant – sorry, Giora – she has a spirit. Like you and me. We're not entirely sure why they exist at all, but we have theories. Whatever causes them, they move from body to body. They don't remember previous lives, but they're shaped by them. We've proven they retain strong emotional states and these impact.... Listen, Giora and everyone else in this time is living in a world that lasts for hundreds of millions of years. That's... that's longer than anyone can really imagine. They'll experience life after life. In the grand scheme of things, this one life doesn't matter. Not when you look at the big picture."

"We owe her, Yemerik."

"The only thing that matters is that we reach the Citadel, so they can correct the timeline and continue the work. Believe me, that will help everyone, including Giora."

"There has to be a way to do both. What if we went to a time after she was born instead?"

"By that time, I was already in Hathari," Yemerik said. "And it sounds like you're getting dangerously close to the time loop we're trying to avoid."

"Why are our lives more important than hers?"

"Maybe they're not. But our message is. Because each minute the Citadel is left without this information is a minute they're not working on what matters. If you're so worried about Giora's existence, just bring her with you."

"She doesn't want to come. She thinks–"

"Oh yes, eternity beneath an ocean or something. I forgot. But, wait. That's a good metaphor. She doesn't want to suffer for eternity. That's what we're trying to prevent. That's… yes, it's perfect. Listen, the world lasts for eternity, at least as far as you understand the concept. In that time, she's going to be born into good lives and bad ones. There will be lives where people like… what was his name? That warlord on the plains you were after? Oh, yes. Hollik. There are always people like him, making war and conquering lands, and most are much stronger and less merciful. There are monsters a hundred times worse than those dragons in your time. There's magic and torture and horrors you can't imagine. Then there's the Gathering Before the Falling Stars. It's impossible to eliminate those bad things. It's simply impossible, because of trends in human behavior and statistical probability. But there are ways to minimize them, to reduce the overall amount of suffering. That's what the Gathering does, that's why the Citadel exists. That's our purpose. To adjust the flow of history to make the world better. To work towards the best world we can create, with as little hatred and pain as possible."

Alaji grew silent for a moment. "I understand. I think I do. But there has to be a way. Didn't you say sending me back with the shards will change things, even if I go a little later?"

Yemerik sighed. "It's extremely dangerous. Without knowing the causal incidents, you could be entering the same dangerous situation with an incidental change. Or we could simply be generating a double-loop, where events from one timeline cause those of another and vice-versa."

"I can be careful," Alaji said.

"Someone saw you in the past, and this isn't an acceptable future state: that alone suggests you weren't careful enough. We need to be changing variables, not marching towards them. I'm sorry, but it's too dangerous."

Alaji stared at him and crossed her arms. "Are you able to open the portal to the time you want?"

Yemerik leaned against the wall and buried his face in his hand. Between his fingers, he whispered, "Don't do this, Alaji."

"It's the right thing to do."

"No, it really isn't. It's a stupid and reckless thing to do, and you have no idea how many people could pay for your decision for eons and eons to come."

"Then it's decided. I'll go back and find you between when you arrived and now. I'll just have to make sure I don't die."

Yemerik sighed. "This will make matters considerably more difficult. There's no telling where I'll be living or what I'll be doing. I was in Hathari for almost twenty-five years. I doubt you'll be able to fine-tune it to a specific year. I was hoping you could simply match the frequencies between the shards I'd carried and the ones you had and step out a few months after I'd arrived. Without that as a guide, this is going to be incredibly imprecise."

"I've been working with the pieces of the talisman. I think I can manipulate the energies close enough." It was more lie than truth. She wasn't even sure she'd be able to do what Yemerik had originally wanted, let alone split the difference between past and present. But she didn't want to fight over that detail, as well.

"Fine," Yemerik said. "I'll prepare a list of places I lived and visited over time. Just... think about this. This really isn't your decision to make."

"Yes, it is." With that, Alaji left the cabin to get some fresh air, even if meant getting wet in the rain.

7

Alaji found Giora in tears the next day. She was sitting on the deck, while a number of sailors moved around ignoring her altogether. The rain had stopped the night before, but the sky remained grey and the wind rocked the ship in its harbor. Alaji knelt beside the scared girl, sighed, and asked, "What did he tell you?"

Giora looked up and climbed to her feet. "I apologize. It is not my place–"

"If he said you had to do anything, you don't. You don't owe him. If anything, it's the other way around."

"I am... I only–"

"Come on," Alaji interrupted, grabbing her arm. "We'll talk to him together." She led the girl through the ship to where Yemerik was waiting.

"I'm glad you're here. I was thinking about our discussion yesterday, and I think I've found–"

"Did he tell you that you had to go through the portal?" Alaji asked Giora, ignoring Yemerik entirely.

Giora looked at both of them. She opened her mouth, as if to speak, then, catching a look from Yemerik, looked away silently.

"You told her she had to go with me but that she wasn't allowed to tell me," Alaji said. "My mother used to give similar instructions to me when I was a hand's age. Damn you for making me do this. Giora: which of us were you told to serve?"

"You," she whispered.

"In that case, my last instruction… my… order… is for you to ignore any instructions, requests, or demands from either of us that you don't want to follow. Do you understand? If he tells you that you have to go through a gate or fend off a dragon or fetch him something to drink, and you don't want to do it, then I'm ordering you not to. Do you understand?"

Giora nodded fiercely.

"Thank you. Now, if it's alright, could you give us a few minutes alone to talk?" Alaji asked, and Giora nodded once more and hurried off to another spot on the boat.

"Do you feel better about that?" Yemerik asked.

"What's wrong with you?" Alaji screamed back.

"Calm down. I was trying to find a better solution."

"I already found one," Alaji said. "I found the one we're going to use, and that's that."

"You have no idea what you're doing," Yemerik replied.

"Between the two of us, I'm the one who's able to step back and use the shards effectively. I'm the one who got to this time and found you. And I'm the one who's going back to fix all of this. I'm guessing you spent most of your time trying to feel the energies coming off the shards, and you never figured it out. So, the way I see it, I have a better idea what I'm doing than you do."

Yemerik breathed in deeply. He watched while a sailor passed by, eying them both suspiciously. He leaned on his cane, then looked around. "I wish… I wish there was something I could say," he said. "You're right, in a way, about us. I don't know as much as I pretend to. When I was young, you'd have been even more right. I knew so little, I lost the talisman to a child using a rudimentary temporal trick. But even then, there were some things I knew. And I've had a lifetime to go over the possibilities and risks and everything else. I promise you, I'm not trying to hurt your friend. None of this will even…. Please, can you trust me once?"

Alaji didn't hesitate: "No." Yemerik laughed first. A second later, she joined him. She didn't know why it was funny, but she couldn't stop.

"No, I don't suppose you can," he said. "Alright. I've got no way to stop you, so we'll risk everything over a whim. Just... when you reach the past and find me – assuming you do – this is exactly the kind of thing you should listen to me about. The way time works and history develops. It's just about the only thing I understood back then, but it's what I devoted my life to." He looked away towards the sea. "But other things... you might be right to trust your gut. I knew how time works, but I didn't really understand how the world works. You saved my life a half dozen times back on the plains, and I didn't always thank you or even realize it."

"I'm going to save Giora and find you," Alaji said. "You'll see."

"Well, a version of me will," Yemerik said, shivering. He smiled in an attempt to conceal it. "There's so much we still have to go over first. The dates and events and all that. Then there's the sailors." He smiled at one who passed by on the deck, unable to comprehend the language they were speaking. "I'm worried at how they'll react once you're through the portal."

"They probably have orders to kill us if we try and escape," Alaji said.

"Yes. I imagine they do. I doubt their orders will cover this, though. Still, they might interpret the events badly. They may turn on you."

"I know," Alaji said, then added, "I'll kill them if I have to."

"Oh. Good. Good. Are you sure you're ready?"

"I'm sure," Alaji said.

Yemerik nodded, though he seemed less relieved than Alaji had expected.

8

The weeks passed quickly while Yemerik went over the details of his entire life in Hathari, including where he could be found on any given year, who to ask for that might know him, and places Alaji could go for help. Then, of course, he had to cover the years themselves and what they meant, followed by a basic overview of the calendar. He told her about several city-states and small nations, some of which might be at war with Hathari, depending on when she arrived, a fact which required her to learn more dates. He gave her advice on how to speak to guards and how to deal with others who pestered her. He tried to provide her with information on how to shop for food and beer, though she already had a good sense of that from watching Giora make similar decisions.

Most of her remaining time was spent experimenting with the pieces of the talisman. She did this in her cabin, so the sailors wouldn't notice and try to take them from her. When she held one of the fragments she'd brought near one Yemerik had given her, she felt a discomforting sensation. It wasn't painful, but it was dizzying. The feeling reminded her of what she'd felt at the lakes, when the old woman cracked the supposedly invulnerable stone. This was nowhere near as bad, but there was an unmistakable similarity.

When she wasn't toying with the forces of time or learning the history of an era she hoped to visit only in passing, she paced the deck of the ship and enjoyed the spray of the sea, the setting sun, the breaking waves, and everything else this bizarre new world offered. They'd sailed far to the south, navigating around islands and waiting out storms in harbors and bays. On a few occasions, they even stopped at cities for supplies, though she was never permitted to leave the ship herself. It occurred to her at one point that they'd have been able to make the journey over land just as quickly. But of course their captors would have had a more difficult time controlling them.

The weather grew warmer and more humid as they went, until they rounded the southern tip of the continent. She spotted numerous birds and fish unlike any she'd seen. When she asked Yemerik for their names, he'd simply try and turn the conversation back to her upcoming journey through the portal, so she quickly learned it was best to go to Giora for such things. The biggest of the fish were whales; the next largest were dolphins or sharks, depending on how often they jumped out of the water. The strange half-dog, half-fish creature she first encountered months before at the gate was called a seal. One evening, she saw a dragon swoop down and pick one of the seals from the water. The dragon was a bit larger than the ones she'd known and colored differently, as well. The sailors didn't seem concerned, so she decided they probably weren't in much danger. Indeed, the dragon didn't come near the ship; it simply headed back towards shore with the seal struggling in its claws.

The crew caught fish using nets. The cook wasn't much good, but the food was always fresh. She tried to keep her distance from the sailors, but eventually they began to approach her or point out various objects in the distance. Over time, she noticed the way they looked at her changing, until they seemed sad or regretful. They were starting to like her, she reasoned, and were growing conflicted by the knowledge they might have to kill her. It made her uncomfortable too. She didn't want to kill them, either.

Occasionally, their ship would be visited. All of the vessels had a couple of smaller boats on board. These were far closer to the ones she'd known growing up on the lakes, though their construction was different. They lowered the small boats into the water, then a couple of sailors would climb down the ropes themselves.

Minot-Rin never came himself, but he sent Imn Orith several times. The old man would usually bark a few orders to the captain, then hurry excitedly to Yemerik and question him about philosophy, medicine, and history. Alaji rarely stuck around to listen to the debates, but knew Yemerik well enough to tell his responses were utter nonsense.

Imn Orith tried to engage her in conversation on a few occasions. He'd approach and begin to ask a question slowly, making sure each syllable was pronounced clearly. They were usually about her father or her home on the lakes, which he'd somehow come to assume was literally built on floating pillars on a lake. She almost never answered him. Instead, she'd simply smile or look at him confused. This worked for a time, until he found her near the front of the ship and began with a question about the knife she'd had when she'd come to Hathari. It was already a touchy subject for her. It had been the greatest knife she'd ever seen – far better than those the sailors had – and of course it hadn't been given back. Her face must have betrayed some recognition, because he sensed an opening and began pressing the issue, repeating and rephrasing the question again and again. Fortunately, Yemerik found them and stepped in, interrupting Imn Orith mid-sentence.

"Oh, good. I was hoping to catch up to you before you had to leave. You remember earlier, we were discussing rock formations in the south? I was thinking about that, and it reminded me of a study of clouds I read years ago. It claimed they shouldn't be understood as carriers but as conduits for water. I wish I could remember the name of the treatise. It was one I read during my time abroad. I think it goes a long way towards explaining how the sky and sea can occupy the same space in the same instant during a rainstorm. It would surely explain why philosophers in Huryi have been able to demonstrate the presence of cloud crystals in the feathers of some large birds. I wanted to get your thoughts on the matter, though."

Imn Orith was reluctant to turn his attention away from Alaji, but Yemerik was unrelenting, and eventually managed to entrap the philosopher in a debate on rain, clouds, dirt, sand, and the ocean that amounted to nothing more than an endless train of words and disjointed ideas. But for some reason, Imn Orith became invested, and Alaji had a chance to slip away. After that, she resolved to remove her pendant whenever she saw him coming. It would make it easier to behave as if she had no idea what he was saying. Besides, she could actually answer him without danger of accidentally doing so clearly in his language.

It made little difference, though: Imn Orith's next trip to their ship would be the final one. At the end of two months at sea, they spotted the gate to their left and Elsimi to their right. They'd reached their destination.

9

Alaji shivered and gazed out at the distant arch. It seemed much smaller now than when she'd first seen it.

"Just like before." Yemerik coughed and cleared his throat. "It was autumn when we last arrived. Do you remember? Those tiny boats from the village on the shore. It was just like this."

It wasn't like this, at all. When they'd arrived together, the sky was covered in dark clouds. Despite the cold, this was a bright and sunny day, as nice as any they'd seen in the last phase of the moon. But she didn't correct Yemerik, who was much further from that day than she was. So she simply nodded and said, "I remember."

He was sadder than Alaji had ever seen him, though he was trying to hide it. "There's still a great deal to do. I don't believe I've told you about the uprising in Virath."

"Settlers fighting because of a wheat shortage in the year of landing fifty-three. Or six-hundred fourteen on the Virathan calendar."

"Oh. Oh, yes. Good. It probably won't come up, but if you wind up in that year and don't know which side to take–"

"The Virathans west of the mountains and the Hathari east of the Iritaith River. And anywhere in between I'm supposed to laugh and say I hope they hope they all starve."

"Yes, that's...." He looked back towards the gate. "You're sure you can align the patterns?"

"For the hundredth time, no," Alaji said and laughed.

Yemerik chuckled as well. "As long as you're sure," he added.

"We've stopped," Alaji said, realizing the boat was standing still.

"I'm not at all surprised," Yemerik replied. He then turned around and, speaking in the Hatharian tongue, shouted, "Captain! Captain! The archway is just ahead. What are we waiting for? We should stop in Elsimi for supplies and make haste to the island."

The captain of the ship stared at Yemerik and Alaji stoically. Most of his crew did the same. After a few moments, the captain looked to his side at the sails behind him. Then he said, "We need to wait."

"Wait? For what?" Yemerik demanded.

The captain shrugged and pointed to Minot-Rin's vessel. "Orders."

Yemerik smiled and nodded, then turned back to Alaji. "We'll want to keep an eye on them," he added.

"They're sizing us up. Deciding how to kill us." It was only a guess, of course, but she decided it was best to err on the side of caution.

Yemerik pretended to smile again, then he waved at one of the sailors who was staring at him. "Minot-Rin wouldn't have brought us here just to have our throats cut. He wants to see what we're after, so he can take it. Then he might want us killed."

"He's worse than Hollik ever was," Alaji said.

"Hollik. The old warlord, right? Did I ever tell you I looked him up?" Yemerik asked. "Years ago, soon after I arrived. I found him in an old history of the plains. He was barely mentioned in passing, just one of a handful of lords from the north who tried to conquer the continent."

"Was there anything about my people?"

"I'm sorry," Yemerik replied. "There was barely anything about him. And what there was…. It doesn't matter."

"It's okay," Alaji said.

"They used a… I guess you'd call it a favorable title. Someone thought he was just or wise or something. It doesn't mean they knew what they were talking about."

"The northmen probably found him just," Alaji said. "And they probably thought Arahm was deceitful and ruthless. Like him," she motioned toward the ship carrying Minot-Rim. "His people probably love him."

"Some do. He's done a lot of good for them, considering what he had to work with. The Hathari were supposed to control time and unite… and conquer… the world. They will. Not in this line, but once we reach the Citadel… I'm sorry. I'm babbling again. We should be getting ready. Going over the plan. Once we've activated the portal, once it's open–"

"I know," Alaji said. "I have it."

Yemerik sighed and nodded. "I hope so," he said. He looked out at the water and saw a small boat approaching.

—

Imn Orith clapped his hands together for warmth when the sailors finished pulling him up. Six guards climbed up after him. Alaji didn't recognize any of them – these men weren't ones Minot-Rin had sent on any of his advisor's earlier trips.

"It's a brisk morning," Imn Orith said, excitedly. "I'm eager to see this."

Yemerik smiled. "I think we're all glad to have reached our destination. If we make for shore now, we can replenish our supplies and be back before nightfall."

The advisor took a deep breath and paused. "I'm afraid there's been a change in plans," he said. "Nothing to be concerned about, but our Lord was most insistent we're to sail on now."

"That's impossible," Yemerik replied. "Once we open the door, we'll need to sail onward for a month and a day before we reach the island I told you about. With our present stores–"

"I assure you, we have more than enough. There's plenty of food and fresh water on the other ships to last the remainder of the journey. They'll send some over once we're through."

"Even so, there's no reason not to rest our feet."

"Our lord has asked us to push on. He's anxious to reach this island, I think. And, besides, he's concerned that his presence here could lead to confusion with the locals."

"I see," Yemerik replied. "So we're to sail on from here. He understands we'll have to prime the gateway?"

"If I understand correctly, the girl can accomplish that on her own. That's true, isn't it?"

Yemerik paused for a moment. "Yes, but… it would be safer if–"

"I'm afraid the matter has been determined. You will join Minot-Rin on his vessel. As his guest. And Alaji will make the preparations necessary for us all to sail through. Oh, there is… another matter. It is something of a delicate point, and I would not bring it up if my Lord did not press the matter–"

"He'll have me tortured to death if he's denied entry," Yemerik replied.

"I would hesitate to put it in such terms. He merely said he would hold you responsible for the actions of the girl. But there's no need to fret about the girl's well-being. I'll remain here to look after her."

Yemerik smiled. "I don't think I have anything to worry about, anyway. Alaji!" He turned his attention to her and, speaking in his own language, said, "You know what to do. Don't take chances. If any make it through with you, kill them all." He turned back to Imn Orith and patted him on the shoulder. "Him, too," he added, though he maintained a warm smile.

Alaji swallowed. She wanted to respond but didn't know what to say. Imn Orith, however, was faster.

"That language," he began, "it isn't the same as before. It's...."

"Oh, an old form of Gruim. Still spoken in the hills. I'll tell you all about it when we see each other again." Yemerik chuckled and began towards the boat.

Imn Orith watched him go and looked concerned. He was bothered by the tone in Yemerik's voice. But his concerns were ultimately meaningless: he was as bound by Minot-Rin's decree as the rest of them. So he turned his attention to the captain and began pointing towards the gate.

Alaji pulled her cape close to fight off the cold. She followed when they led Yemerik away, looking for an opportunity to speak to him, but several of the sailors stayed between them. They lowered him quickly to the boat and pushed off. As soon as they were away, Imn Orith ordered the oars lowered, and the ship began to drift forward.

10

Whether or not they were planning to kill her, the sailors made Alaji's journey to the top of the gate far easier. Four of them accompanied her and Imn Orith, who stayed close to Alaji and observed her every movement. He seemed equal parts intrigued and frightened of her. The sailors brought a number of ropes, far stronger than the one she'd had the last time she came this way, and were experienced climbers.

Giora had come onto the small island but stayed behind when Alaji and the others climbed the rocks. It had taken a great deal of effort to convince Giora to come that far: she was clearly terrified of the whole area. In the end, Alaji had whispered to her that the ship would be going through the gate, and that this might be her last chance to remain behind. She practically fought her way on the small boat after that.

Alaji returned to the center of the arch and knelt down. She wasn't surprised at all when Imn Orith did the same. He watched as she removed a shard of the talisman and lowered it into the indentation in the stone.

"What is that?" he asked, staring at the object. Alaji ignored him. She would have ignored him even if the energies of ages weren't spilling over her and if it didn't take every ounce of concentration she had to maintain some focus on the situation. She inhaled briefly and removed a second shard, one of the pieces Yemerik had given her. She held this in front of her, between herself and the indentation.

It was madness. Impossible madness. The second shard felt as though it was about to vibrate out of her hand, or perhaps rattle until the bones in her fingers shattered. Her hand shook, and her face twisted.

Imn Orith reached for her, but she screamed, "Stay back!" and glared at him with bloodshot eyes. A spot of blood dripped from her nose to her lip, and Imn Orith leapt away. Only luck and a quick-thinking sailor kept him from going off the edge.

Alaji turned her attention back to the shards of the talisman and the waves of force that seemed as if they could fling her off the bridge into the seas below. Her fingers ached – her whole hand did – as she pinched the second shard. It was shaking, rattling, scraping against her…

She shut her eyes and began to count. That the count was wrong did not surprise her. Everything was wrong. Everything was moving and shifting and turning. But she forced herself to find the first number. She felt it, anchored herself to it as if preparing to step back. Even this was wrong: it had an echo that reverberated through her. But she focused on it nonetheless, echo and all, and moved the second piece of the talisman.

A millennium earlier, in the village where she'd been raised, Arahm kept a number of crystals, artifacts which had been passed down from elders for generations. Some said they'd come from the holy caverns; others that they'd been won in a game of chance against a passing trader. He would bring them to town gatherings and hold the largest up to catch the sunlight. It would cast light to all sides and in all colors.

She thought of this, and how the slightest movement would redirect the light. She directed time the same way. She focused on the count in her head. Each number appeared twice. But as she moved the shard, the mirroring moments shifted, coming closer together or farther apart. As they moved apart, the pain in her head increased; as they came close, it subsided. The quivering of the shards dwindled as well, until she realized they were never shaking at all, not really. The energies weren't moving the shards: they were moving her perception. The pain in her hand was from clutching the piece of jagged stone.

She forced herself to relax her grip and move the pieces until the energies were perfectly in sync. She found what Yemerik had spoken of, the difference between them. If she opened the portal now, it would lead to Elsimi a few a months after he'd arrived. The difference would be the same as her stay in this time to the day. To the second.

But that wasn't what she'd decided. Slowly, she twisted the two shards, turning them as one. She did not go far. She was fairly certain the smallest change would mean years. Maybe more. She pulled the shards back when she was fairly certain.

And she collapsed to the stone bridge. She felt like she'd been running for miles. Each breath burned and her head ached from the strain. She pushed herself up to her knees and looked around.

Imn Orith and the sailors stared at her. Their expressions were a mix of shock, fear, and respect. Alaji looked down at the stone floor in front of her and saw the two shards. Imn Orith did, as well. He reached for the nearer of the two.

"If you take it," Alaji began. As soon as she spoke, he froze and met her gaze. "If you take it, I'll kill you," she said, finishing her thought. She grabbed both shards and returned them to their pouches.

"You can talk," Imn Orith whispered. He was more startled than frightened; the sailors, on the other hand, seemed scared. They traded glances, then moved their hands to rest close to their knives.

Alaji stared at them for a moment and wondered what they thought she'd overheard on the boat. She'd never actually overheard them say they were supposed to kill her, but they might have spoken openly about it before she had the pendant. Perhaps they were simply wondering if one of their shipmates had said something too close to her.

She looked below the arch she was standing on. The small boat they'd taken to the islet. She locked eyes on the sailors. There were just a few here, armed with knives and accompanying an old man. It would be easy. Easier than dispatching dozens. She could step back and push them off before they realized what was happening, or perhaps grab one of their knives....

But her head still hurt and she ached all over. She didn't feel much like murdering anyone right now. And she doubted they were supposed to murder her yet: Minot-Rin's gate to an imaginary island which contained pools of elixirs or trees with magic sap or whatever they'd glossed from Yemerik's lies wasn't open. And, as far as anyone knew, she might be the only one who could open it.

"Let's go," she said.

"The gate is...."

"It's ready. But not open," she reminded them.

"How do we open it?" Imn Orith asked. "I thought you were–"

"Like I said, I was making it ready," she snapped. "We'll take the ship through. I'll open it as we go through."

The sailors and Imn Orith whispered back and forth. Alaji ignored them and began moving back towards the way down. After a moment, she heard them following.

Two of the sailors boosted her up the stone wall, and in return, she helped them up the rope. The absurdity of it all never left her mind, and she doubted it did theirs, either. They'd likely be enemies soon, but for now, they remained partners in this expedition.

Once they'd helped Imn Orith up, they began down the boulders. "I'd like a word," he said to Alaji.

"As soon as we're through," she replied, pointing back to the gigantic arch.

"It may be important," he said. "It's… why didn't you say anything before? Why the secrecy?"

"As soon as we're through," Alaji said, again. "I need to concentrate if I'm to do this right." It was a lie, of course. She had every intention of leaving him on this side of the gate and would likely kill him if he came through.

They reached the bottom soon. Two of the sailors hurried ahead to ready the small boat. Giora sat quietly to one side. Alaji went to her and helped her up. She said nothing but hugged the woman who'd helped her survive and communicate for months. She spoke softly, so the sailors wouldn't hear. "You'll be safe here," she said. "Once we're through… the people from Elsimi will come." It was another lie. At least, Alaji was fairly certain of that. Once she was through the portal, the past and present would change. But her only alternative was to command Giora to accompany her. If Yemerik hadn't fought for that, she thought she might have done it. But he had, and it felt more wrong now than the alternative. So she released Giora and stepped away.

"Th… thank you," Giora said. "If there is…."

Alaji smiled. "You shouldn't see us again, I don't think. But if you do, if you ever see anyone from the… the Sea Beyond the Sea… you don't owe them anything. Tell them I said so, then just walk away and let them torment someone else. You can say I commanded it, if you want." Alaji hurried back towards the boat, where she bluntly informed Imn Orith that Giora wouldn't be joining them.

He tried to debate the point: things were already deviating from Minot-Rin's expectations if not his explicit orders, but Alaji refused to discuss the matter. The sailors didn't seem interested in trying to press the point – or even to speak in Alaji's presence, for that matter – so Imn Orith had no choice but to give up the debate and return to the ship. If Minot-Rin wanted the Imi taken, he'd have little trouble sending some men to reclaim her. Otherwise, it all seemed too minor a detail to squabble over. Before the hour was through, they'd all be through the portal or the girl would be dead. He could imagine no other outcome.

11

She considered it a dozen times between the rocky island and the ship. There were only four of them; five counting Imn Orith, and despite the fact they were watching her, they'd have little chance of stopping her. It would have been easy to take one of their knives and finish them. Then, alone, she could have made for the portal long before the ship could reach her. It would still have been risky, but less so than the alternative.

But whether it was the wiser choice, the thought sickened her. It wasn't so much the idea of killing: she'd done that and felt little guilt. But she knew Giora would be watching, and the idea that the last act she'd witness Alaji commit was murder horrified her. Besides, she didn't really want to kill these men at all and hadn't given up hope she could avoid a fight. She imagined how horrified Yemerik would be that she was letting this opportunity slip away, but that thought didn't bother her in the least.

When they reached the ship, the sailors helped her up, once more. A glance around revealed Minot-Rin's ship had inched closer to theirs. He may have accepted theirs would have to be the first through, but he clearly had every intention of following directly behind.

Alaji made her way to the bow of the ship. To either side, rowers strained to move the vessel onward towards the archway. She took stock of those around her and noted every glance and expression cast her way. The sailors were more concerned than before. She noticed them whispering and realized they'd all know her inability to speak was an act by now. She wasn't sure whether it was good or bad they'd have no way of knowing it hadn't always been.

Imn Orith had taken an even greater interest in her movements. He gave her some space, but was clearly curious. Was he angry, as well, that she'd lied to him all along? Or perhaps it troubled him more that Yemerik had misled him. Had he really trusted either of them enough to feel betrayed?

Alaji sat on the deck and closed her eyes. The sailor's shouting, the rushing wind, the glaring sun, the ringing in her head from opening the portal, the sick irony that the sailors who'd spent the last few months helping her could soon be trying to slit her throat and she theirs… and, above it all, the knowledge she was leaving people she cared for behind. It all weighed on her. Giora was the larger loss, of course, but she felt like she was losing Yemerik, as well. And she was. Even if she got another back, he wouldn't be the same. The old man who'd taught her about the flow of history and the use of the translation pendant would be gone.

Gone or dead. The notion she was killing them was certainly hard to ignore. Yemerik had dismissed the idea on several occasions, but he'd seemed terrified as this day approached. And whether he saw it that way or not, she found the alternatives unconvincing. To exist then cease existing wasn't the same as a knife in the back, but the end was the same. In some ways, she thought it might be worse.

But what choice did she have? She could run to Imn Orith and demand they return for Giora. Or she could leave the portal open for Minot-Rin's ship to come through with Yemerik. But there were prices to be paid for either of these. For the first, she'd be endangering everything and – in a real sense – betraying Giora more than if she let her die. For the second, she'd be saving one Yemerik to kill the other. And, in all likelihood, she'd guarantee that she never returned home to save her brother.

And that was the final straw. She opened her eyes and stood up. She shook her hands to get her blood moving. And she focused on two things and two things only: the approaching gateway and the count running through her head.

12

From the shore in Elsimi, they saw it. They were already watching the Hathari ships, of course, unsure whether they'd come for war or trade. They did not know the vessels carried the visitor from the Sea Beyond the Sea or the Imi they'd sent away with her. Nor did they realize Minot-Rin, reigning lord of Hathari, was a passenger. But their presence near the ancient passage was already a subject of concern. When the doorway opened, it was far worse.

From the deck of his ship, which held a number of open boxes containing growing flowers from his court, Minot Rin saw, as well, as did his magicians and entertainers and even his guest, Yemerik, to whom he continued to extend every comfort and courtesy and had every intention of continuing to do so, as long as the power he'd been promised was delivered to him.

And from the smaller ship, Alaji stood on the precipice and felt the waves of energy divide. Ahead of her, stood the past; to her back, the future world she was leaving behind.

She was staring at a storm of ice and snow. She was surprised to see this, though she should not have been. Twice she'd opened the portal to find spring: it was only fitting that her luck not last.

For a moment, the sailors panicked. A few screamed; others simply stared in awe. The ship, caught by the wind, veered to one side. The force threw Alaji to the deck and left her momentarily dazed. Behind her, the sailors began trying to right the ship.

The cold wind struck her, and she climbed to her feet. Then she began the count. She looked around at the madness. Imn Orith was shuffling towards her, gazing around with a bewildered expression. Others were charging towards the sails or the rudder or the oars. A few were fleeing towards the back end of the ship, which still extended into the time she was leaving.

She stepped back in time a few seconds, and the connection between the gate and the fragments of the talisman broke. With a crash, the breach between times closed shut, and the bright world behind them was swallowed by dark clouds, driving wind, and flakes of ice.

Boards and beams creaked, and the screams began at once. There was no time to figure out what caused this before the boat dipped forward, sending buckets, tools, and men tumbling. Alaji caught herself on the railing, just as the boat began rocking backward.

She turned, gripping the handrail for support. She saw men slipping away. Imn Orith cried out in fear and confusion as he slid backward on the tilted deck. Beyond them, lay the open sea, its surface littered with sailors, planks of wood, and crates.

The back half of the boat was gone. She'd closed the portal around it, and split the ship in two. Splintering boards spilled out of the hull, along with boxes of apples, barrels of fresh water, and other supplies.

The ship rocked forward again, and sailors lay sprawled out on the floor. Some called to their gods; others cried out for their companions who'd fallen overboard.

Briefly, the ship seemed to stabilize, but it was resting low in the water. Alaji glanced around and saw several of the men were glaring at her. One, lying prone on the deck, opened his mouth to say something, but she didn't wait to hear it. She gripped her belongings close and hoisted herself over the railing,

The wind shrieked and, for an instant, she was weightless. The icy waters engulfed her, and she bobbed to the surface gasping. In the back of her mind, her count began, and she began swimming towards the island. Shifting back in time wouldn't help her with the cold, but it would allow her to reach land before the sailors.

Behind her, she heard a cracking sound, like thunder. She tread water and looked back to see the ship leaning towards her once again. The mast leaned, buckled, and snapped, crashing down onto the deck. A bloodcurdling scream from a sailor pinned beneath it echoed over the water.

Alaji swam as fast as she could, shifting back in time as she did so. She heard sailors hitting the water and wondered how many could swim. She couldn't yet deal with the idea she'd be better off if they all drowned. She fought currents and wind alike. The water was freezing, colder even than the last time she'd been marooned here, but despite the pain, she knew what was happening and what she had to do.

She reached the island dragging two pieces of wood out of the water. There were more around her, as well: the tides were covered in them. Her teeth were chattering as she set the first piece ablaze and dropped it to her feet. She lit the second and tossed it down as well, then ran to gather more. Wet or not, the spell of the hearth lit one after the other, and she had a fire burning in seconds. She soaked up the heat and stepped back in time, then repeated the action. When she decided she wouldn't die, she grabbed a final piece and waited by the fire.

The ship had all but sunk, and the sailors who didn't go down with it would be here soon.

Sure enough, they began to arrive, clawing over each other to escape the water. Alaji held her board but gave them space. Eight men closed around the fire for warmth. They looked like corpses, with blue lips and pale skin. They were covered in cuts and scrapes. A few drew weapons and stared at Alaji.

"You killed them," one said, spitting a wad of blood and seawater on the rock. He was shaking, as were they all, Alaji included, and his voice quivered. "All of them!"

"I didn't!" Alaji shouted back. But of course she had. She had no idea how many had been pulled down with the ship or were unable to swim. And the ones left behind were no better off, save that their end had been instantaneous.

"Good men," one of the sailors said. He spoke solemnly, with reverence but anger, as well. "To the last. Good, honorable men."

"I didn't want them hurt," Alaji said. "It… it all went wrong. This wasn't supposed to happen." But of course, this was exactly what was supposed to happen. The plan she'd worked out with Yemerik hadn't included breaking the ship in half, though he'd likely thought it a possibility. But this was the goal, wasn't it? Her in the past with only a handful of sailors.

"You've lied to us from the beginning," another said. His knife was in his hand, and he began to approach. "You lied to us and to our lord." All true, of course.

"Minot-Rin has no power here," Alaji said, stuttering. She edged backward to buy time. "He's–"

"He is our lord!" a sailor yelled. "And this insult will be avenged!" They were all moving now as a group. Alaji was running out of time.

"Stop!" she demanded. "This is the only warning–"

They didn't let her finish. The sailor who was closest lunged forward, swinging his knife. Alaji stepped back in time.

"Honorable men–" the sailor was saying, though he cut off mid-sentence. To his perspective, Alaji had vanished and re-appeared a few feet away. The sailors froze.

"Listen to me! I'm giving you a chance," Alaji said. "I don't want to kill you, and I don't think you want to kill me!"

"It doesn't matter what we want," a sailor said. He was the same who Alaji remembered accusing her of lying. But that was a time he hadn't experienced. His demeanor was different – the sight of her moving without moving had left him more frightened than angry. For a moment, Alaji thought she might reason with them.

Until he charged. He came at her quickly, and she let him approach, waiting to step back until he was nearly upon her. She only traveled a second, arriving at just the point to strike him in the face with the splintered end of her board.

Then she moved backward to buy a bit more time. His pain and confusion blinded him, and maneuvering behind him was easy. She made sure the others never saw her swing the board. To their eyes, it simply appeared, her in tow, behind their reeling companion. He fell against the rock. Before he could even try to stand, Alaji's foot was crushing down on his wrist. He released his knife with a scream, and a second later it was gone. It took their eyes a moment to take in the new scene. The knife was in Alaji's free hand, and she was standing several feet away from its previous owner.

Alaji studied them as they studied her. She looked them in the eyes and waited. No one spoke, but the ones who hadn't been armed before drew blades or picked up rocks. One coughed, and all were shaking in the cold.

13

When Imn Orith saw Alaji approach the front of the ship, he did as well, though he did not know what he hoped to accomplish. Perhaps he merely wanted to ensure she did not somehow slip through the portal and leave him behind to face Minot-Rin's rage. An instant later, when the world went dark and cold, Imn Orith looked again to Alaji, hoping for some sort of explanation. Instead, he found himself thrown to the deck, as the ship rocked back. There were screams blending together as he felt himself falling backwards along the wet floor.

He managed to grab hold of an oarsman's seat and held himself while the ship tilted further and further. A sailor tumbled over him and struck his head against the seat. Imn Orith craned his neck and watched the unconscious man tumble back then drop off the edge.

Only then did he realize that when the gateway closed, it had taken half their ship with it. Whatever became of that other half was beyond imagination. Perhaps it had been left behind in the world he'd come from: there was no telling. He held on for dear life until his fingers went numb. Just when he thought he couldn't hold on, the ship rolled forward.

It was even more violent than before. He was thrown towards what had been the front of the ship. Others were, as well. Sailors formed a human chain in an attempt to remain onboard. But there seemed little point: the ship was sinking. He caught sight of Alaji looking back at him before leaping off into the water. She was hardly alone: several sailors were diving off the boat, and this seemed as good a plan as any. Imn Orith considered this himself, but he never had a chance. Before he could reach the side, the ship turned and tipped again. The deck slipped out from under him, and he turned as he fell, sliding along the floor once more. He tried to grab for one of the seats as he had before, but the force was too great. The wooden edge smashed his hand like a club, and he slid by.

The edge of the deck was even less kind. Jagged boards sliced his leg, side, and arm as he went over. Then the water took him. Ice cold and dark, he dipped under, and the salt water filled his mouth and nose. He forgot everything else and fought for the surface. He crawled his way into the air, pulling himself up using a barrel, then he tried futilely to wipe the salt water from his eyes. He looked around as best he could, but his vision was blurred. All he could make out were the things around him – barrels, crates, and other objects which had spilled out of the open hull, broken pieces of wood littering the sea, and several bodies bobbing between the waves.

Somewhere, back on the ship, there was another crash, followed by more screams. But he was preoccupied by the cold sea and by the salt water against his wounds. He tried to pull himself up, but the barrel simply turned and dumped him mercilessly back in the water. He panicked and tried to grab it, but it was turning now. He realized he'd die here if he didn't find something better. He considered going for the ship, but he retained just enough sense to realize that, too, would seal his fate. Instead, he released the barrel and grabbed ahold of a large plank of wood. It kept him afloat, but he could feel his legs turning numb.

A moment later, out of the corner of his eye, he saw a flicker of light. Fire. Instinctively, he swam for it, clinging to the board to stay afloat. He struggled for what seemed like hours, until he grabbed hold of solid rock. He could barely move, but found the strength to pull himself up. Through blurry eyes, he saw Alaji surrounded by sailors from the ship. Someone was speaking, but Imn Orith's ears were too full of water to parse out the words.

One of the sailors charged. Alaji's stance and location changed, though she did not move and time did not pass. Now something she was holding had struck the sailor. Again, she was not where she was, and her weapon met the back of his head. Imn Orith blinked, and she was elsewhere. Now she held a blade in one hand and a club in the other. She did not give the men a chance to regroup: she charged ahead, and they moved to meet her. But they hadn't taken two steps, and she was in their midst.

The next fell back bleeding, and an instant later a third's nose was crushed beneath Alaji's club. Alaji appeared in front of him next, and for a moment Imn Orith thought she'd been caught. But she turned away just as fast, and the man's body slipped to the rock and rolled towards the waves.

Alaji's knife was gone, but she flickered and her club was

burning from one end. She flickered again, and the end on fire was inches from a sailor's face. He leapt back, but she was there, as well. He leapt back a third time and tripped back into the larger fire behind him. He screamed in pain, rolled, and made for the water.

But Alaji appeared, crouched to one side of him, holding a blade in his calf. It was his blade, too: he'd had it only a moment before. He screamed and fell face first into the shallow water. He struck a small boulder too hard and floated away.

There were three left, and they panicked, swinging their knives about madly, as if they'd hit her as she appeared. But these attacks fared no better: Alaji appeared in the air a moment after one of the men sliced it, her blade already at his throat. She cut quickly and deeply, and he was gone just as fast.

The last two stood back-to-back and held their knives ready. Alaji was standing several feet from the first, watching. Slowly, she moved towards what was left of her fire and traded her broken board for one that was turning to charcoal. She set her knife in her belt and took a second board.

The sailor facing her watched and whispered something to the other. Imn Orith didn't know if they were trading plans or saying a prayer. Whichever they chose, it did them no good. Alaji vanished and appeared twice, and she was beside them. She struck the logs together, and cinders rained into one of the sailors eyes.

He swung and stabbed and screamed, and when he regained his sight and senses, he found the other sailor gasping for breath in his arms. It never even occurred to Imn Orith to call out and warn him that Alaji was now behind him.

The two bodies fell together. Alaji turned and saw Imn Orith. Red ran down her right forearm, hand, and over her knife. She was panting, and her breath appeared like smoke. She looked at him, and he pushed backward. He kicked at the rock desperately to get away, crawling backwards into the freezing water.

Alaji came at him. She didn't vanish or run, but walked quickly. He rolled over onto his stomach and tried to raise himself into a crouching position so he'd be able to leap off the partially submerged stones and reach the deeper water. But his legs were numb and he slipped and she was standing over him.

"No! Stop!" he shouted. He tried again for the water, but Alaji grabbed the back of his shirt and held him. She dragged him back out of the water and led him back to the fire. She half threw him beside it, then hurried to gather more wood washing up around the island.

Imn Orith covered himself as best he could, then turned to watch Alaji return. He watched her cast wizard spells and light the boards on fire, then add them to the pyre. Through the flames and still-blurred vision, he could see she was crying.

14

They were picked up by a fishing boat, like she'd been in the time that would never come to pass. The fishermen were confused and horrified by the bodies in the water; bodies, no doubt, they assumed had come from the Sea Beyond the Sea. They seemed horrified at the prospect of touching the corpses and were elated when Alaji told them to leave them where they were.

Imn Orith was half-alive by the time they were rescued. Alaji wasn't doing well herself, but he was far worse. The sailors gave them blankets and beer, and rushed them to shore. She looked at the buildings in Elsimi as she approached and marveled at how small they seemed now. She wondered how the huts of her own time would seem to her now, if she ever returned to them. The village gathered and greeted them in the same manner as her last visit, though they were even more scared of her now that she was covered in blood. Some prayed, some cursed her, and others came forth with gifts. A few of the gifts were the same ones she'd received before:

heirlooms the village had parted with twice, through the strange twists of time. She thanked them but said all she wanted was hot water and a warm room.

Imn Orith didn't ask her to explain what was happening, and she didn't volunteer any information. He was able to understand the people of Elsimi when they spoke slowly and in simple terms, but anything more and he was lost. He was shivering violently, and he pushed away anyone trying to force necklaces and carvings on him. Alaji asked them to bring him medicine, hot water, and dry clothes. If he lived, they would have much to discuss. In the meantime, she had questions of her own.

She cleaned herself and waited until she could move around without an excess of pain, then called for Yuval, the Imi who'd been assigned to care for her. At least this time she'd managed to acquire the woman's name.

"Have your people met a man named Yemerik?" Alaji asked.

"Yes," Yuval replied. "He was a… traveler, like yourself. He visited our village eleven years ago, then left for the east."

"Eleven years," Alaji replied. She converted it into numbers and counted in her head. "Then this is the six-hundred and sixteenth year, isn't it?"

"Yes," Yuval replied, plainly.

Alaji nodded. "Good enough," she decided. "There's something else. Is there… a girl in the village named Giora?"

"My nephew has a daughter by that name," Yuval said. She sounded worried, but offered to send for the girl.

"Thank you. I would like to see her," Alaji said. Yuval excused herself to make the arrangements, and Alaji took the opportunity to gather her belongings and verify she hadn't lost anything of importance when she fell into the sea. Some of the documents Yemerik had given her were damaged, but she still had all the shards of the talisman. She stretched her legs and arms and checked to ensure she could feel her fingers – there were rumors Imn Orith was going to lose at least a digit. Fortunately, nothing seemed amiss with her, though she was still sore. It seemed a low price to pay for the lives she'd taken, but she was long beyond thinking the world was balanced or just.

Yuval returned with a man and young girl. The man was much younger, but Alaji recognized him. She'd seen him on the day she'd left Elsimi when he gave her his daughter. He seemed more concerned now, and he fawned over the girl at his side.

The girl was a child. Alaji tried to determine her age – four or five, she guessed. She seemed afraid, but not nearly as scared as her father. "This is Giora?" Alaji asked.

"This is my daughter," the man said. "Her mother and I are teaching her to attend the elders. She is to be given to the temple to serve."

"No," Alaji said. "She shouldn't serve anyone. She should be waited upon all her life. The temple should honor her."

The father nodded. "I can discuss this with the elders," he offered. "It is... unusual for one born a servant to become something else."

"She wasn't born a servant," Alaji said. "She was born to be important. I came here to tell you this. If you'll send for the elders, I'll explain it myself."

The girl's father held the child close. Then he thanked Alaji and asked if there was anything they could do.

"Nothing. Just remember what I said. And bring me anyone who won't believe you." Giora's father took her out of the room. She'd never spoken to Alaji and still seemed scared. She didn't seem to have any idea what had happened or what it meant. But that was all right. Alaji had repaid her debt.

More than that, she'd changed the girl's fate. Alaji smiled to herself. It had taken only words to give someone a far better life. Words and the knowledge how to use them. What else could she accomplish?

15

The winter months passed slowly in Elsimi. Alaji spent her time practicing until she felt she'd mastered her time stepping spell, her count of five. She began considering what else it might do. She experimented with stepping back twice in quick succession, moving from five to three then one. It was dizzying but possible. Then, she tried stepping from her fifth count to her first, then forward to her fourth. Even harder, but still doable. None of these were as difficult as trying to move forward to time she hadn't experienced; starting her count at one and immediately stepping forward to five. She'd discovered it was possible, but she could do it only with great focus. With practice, perhaps she'd get better.

When she wasn't toying with the fabric of time, she made preparations for her journey to Hathari. As soon as she'd arrived, she'd told the villagers she would leave in the spring. When the time finally arrived, she was surprised how sad the idea left her. She was growing to like the town and its people. It was beginning to feel like home, but she knew better. Her home was by the lakes, weeks away by horseback and hundreds of years gone. The villagers in Elsimi provided her with everything she asked for: food, drink, and comforts she'd never imagined in her own time. They gave her warm capes and blankets woven from the fur of animals, beautiful decorations crafted with skill or magic centuries beyond what she'd known, and stones painted colors she'd never seen.

Also, there was a boy she liked. His name was Krelch, and he was brash and kind. She'd seen him swimming in a river once and found the experience far more enticing than she'd have expected. She found excuses to speak with him, asking his opinions on a number of subjects she didn't otherwise care about. She'd have chosen him over any of the boys of her own village, certainly over the one her mother hoped to marry her to.

Of course, Krelch was deathly afraid of Alaji: the whole village was. The things they did for her, they did out of fear, and she didn't trust their actions would always be so generous. They thought her some sort of prophet from a timeless place, but they didn't think her immortal. After all, they'd found her half-frozen to death and surrounded by corpses. A hand's count of bodies laid out on the rock, more bobbing in the waves, and two that drew breath.

Imn Orith had lived, though his time in the icy water had cost him two fingers off his right hand and given him a pale mark on the left side of his face. For a full phase of the moon, Alaji had expected him to die.

When he began to recover, Alaji was more relieved than she'd have expected. If she'd have had her choice, she'd have selected almost any of the others to live in his place. But they hadn't given her that choice. She had liked the sailors. They seemed like honest men, after a fashion, and they had sufficient reason to want her dead. In her darkest moments, Alaji would ask herself if she should have let them kill her. But it was only a passing thought. She knew perfectly well she'd kill the same men again if the situation demanded it. And, given the nature of her journey, it very well might.

She hadn't even liked Imn Orith. If he'd attacked her, she'd have killed him with even less regret than the others. But he'd been far too scared to come after her. He remained afraid of her now, though he went to great efforts to conceal it behind gratitude for saving his life. On more occasions than she could count, he'd found a way of slipping into conversation that he'd been forced to do Minot-Rin's bidding at pain of death, as if this would make them allies.

But, for all that happened, they were both out of place in this time. It had taken her a while to appreciate that: his twenty-year displacement seemed insignificant compared to the centuries she'd lost, but, in some ways, he was far more lost than she was. Thanks to Yemerik's charm, she could understand the inhabitants of Elsimi as easily as if they were speaking her native tongue. But while Imn Orith's language bore many similarities to the western speech, he'd yet to fully overcome the differences. He could hold simple conversations about fish or the weather, but in depth conversations about philosophy, politics, or metaphysics were beyond the boundaries of his vocabulary. And Imn Orith had little interest in fish or the weather.

He caught up with her a few days before she'd planned to leave. "If it's not too much trouble," he said, "I was wondering if we could talk a bit more. I have some questions about what would happen if… if I were to meet myself here."

"I'm not sure you are here," Alaji said. "Yemerik didn't come with us, because he said the talisman would destroy the younger version of him. It might have done the same to you. If so, I'm sorry. I meant to go through the gate alone."

"Just… destroyed? Perhaps it would be better. Otherwise, there's a younger version of me with equal claim to my property. Still, it's a harrowing thought. That an older me could pop up from a further future and suddenly I might not exist."

"It's disorienting," Alaji admitted. "I'm not really sure that's how it works, though. The younger Yemerik would have had the shards of the talisman. They seem to connect with people at close distance, so maybe the younger version of you wouldn't be destroyed unless you were both near part of the talisman. I haven't really figured it out yet."

"I suppose I can inquire about myself in Hathari. If… you're still willing to help me return home."

Alaji shrugged. She hadn't completely decided what to do about the old man yet. He'd slow her down and, despite his calm disposition, posed something of a threat. Still, he knew a great deal about this world and could come in handy. But more than that, she didn't want to travel across the distance alone if she could help it, nor did she want to command anyone from Elsimi to accompany her. Not even Krelch.

"Have you gotten the hang of riding?" she asked.

"I can ride," he replied. "I still have a little difficulty climbing up, but I can manage. Alternatively, we could take a wagon, couldn't we?"

"No. It'd take too long. But if you're willing to ride, you can come to Hathari with me."

"I'd like that," Imn Orith replied, though he couldn't hide his disappointment at hearing the wagon wasn't an option.

"I want to leave soon. I was talking to one of the town's... one of the wizards. He said the weather will hold. At least, he thinks it will."

"I understand. I'll gather supplies."

"I've already asked Furnea to pack food, beer, and money. I'll let him know we'll need a second horse and extra supplies."

"Thank you," Imn Orith said. "I'll practice my riding. You'll let me know if there's anything I can do? Organizing the supplies or plotting the trip. That sort of thing."

Alaji nodded. "I think we're fine," she said.

16

They didn't leave the day after the full moon, but the delay had nothing to do with Imn Orith's riding. Whatever augers the town's wizard had used to predict the weather had been faulty; a storm cloud rolled in during the evening and it rained for the next three days, even hailing briefly. They could have pushed through regardless, but there was no sense starting their journey under such conditions.

The rain subsided on the fourth day, and Alaji told Imn Orith it was time to go. The village came out to wish them farewell. She saw Krelch in the crowd and briefly entertained the idea he might charge forward and beg to accompany her. But of course he did no such thing.

The village presented them with numerous gifts, only a handful of which could possibly be stuffed into their already overfull sacks and saddlebags. It did present an opportunity for Imn Orith to demonstrate his use, when Alaji leaned over to him and whispered, "Which of these will get us the most in trade?"

They made decent time on the first legs of their journey. Conscious of his age, Imn Orith rushed every morning to ensure he didn't keep Alaji waiting. Perhaps he was worried she'd leave him behind. He wasn't accustomed to cooking, but he had a knowledge of herbs that proved useful.

"How did you learn that?" he asked one evening, after they'd been traveling for a week.

"Learn what?" Alaji asked, rotating a rabbit she'd caught and killed earlier. Fresh food was a welcome break from the dried fish and stale bread they had left over from Elsimi. "To hunt?"

"No. The... the spell. For the fire. I've never seen anyone who wasn't a wizard use magic."

"My mother taught me," Alaji said. "Where I'm from, it's a woman's spell."

"Woman's spell," Imn Orith said in a tone that seemed at once intrigued and amused. "I've never heard of such a thing. How long did it take to learn? Wizards train for years to do that sort of thing."

Alaji shrugged. "I spent at least a finger each day practicing the five spells. I'm sorry... a finger is a fifth. So about three of your hours, sometimes more. As long as I can remember. Some of my earliest memories were of my mother berating me for not working hard enough. It was the same with my brother, but he was taught by our father. When we turned a third... when we turned fifteen, we were allowed to relax. We were still supposed to practice, but the timing wasn't as important."

"That's a long time to focus on just five spells," Imn Orith remarked. "Wizards learn dozens, including versions for invoking fire. But not many cast them as quickly as you do."

"I never knew there were so many spells," Alaji said. "We just had the ten."

"If you don't mind me asking, is the spell you used to... the spell for... 'stepping back' in time... is that one of the women's?"

"No," Alaji said. "That's different. That's something I learned on my own. Maybe someone manipulated me into learning it – that's what Yemerik thinks. I don't know. I just kind of figured it out."

"It's an incredible thing to stumble upon," Imn Orith said. "If you'd be willing to teach me, I'd do my best to learn." For a moment, he seemed younger, more energized. Though he also looked scared.

"I wouldn't know how to start," Alaji said. "I don't even think I could teach you the fire spell, or the mending one. With the time spell, it's all about feeling. It's like a heartbeat, a pulse. I just concentrate and match it, then sort of take hold of a specific instant and pull myself there. I don't know how to teach it."

"Of course. I don't know what I was thinking. I'd like to hear more about it, though. Maybe understand the theory, at least. I'd also like to hear more about your people. There's not a lot that's known about the plainsmen before the Hathari came and... I'm sorry. I've probably said too much."

"They wiped us out, didn't they?"

"Not completely. But, yes. For the most part. They swept across the plain and conquered most of the continent in a few years. The armies here weren't really armies. Just groups of villagers fighting without real strategies."

"What did they do with us?" Alaji asked.

"This was almost a hundred years ago," Imn Orith said. "Please remember that. Most of the warriors were killed in battle. The ones who lived were conscripted into the armies and made to march on the next group. By the end of it, there weren't a lot of men from the plains left. Those who did survive were assimilated, welcomed into the empire, the scribes say. It's not inaccurate. There weren't orchestrated slaughters, or at least there weren't many. The lands were conquered and the survivors joined the greater kingdom. There were treaties, political marriages, and all that. The empire was expanding. It had already crossed one sea, overtaken a new continent, and there was talk of it continuing until its tail reached its head. But the problem was no one could really agree which side was the head. The Eastern and Western Empires declared dominion over the other. There was a brief war, and it became apparent the Empire couldn't maintain its territories inland. They pulled support, and the regions fought each other for land and resources. Then, about thirty years ago… no, no. I'm sorry, that would only be ten years ago now. About a decade ago, Tikt-Minot tried to retake the continent. He gained some strongholds, but that fell apart. Just ten years now. I don't expect people will like my accent much out here. We may want to err to the north, if possible. Most of those wars were in the south. I mean, if that's alright."

"It's fine," Alaji said. "I want to take one of the northern paths, anyway." She fished a map out of her bag and unrolled it carefully. Then she tilted it, so it caught the light of the fire. "This one, here. Do you know it?"

"I've never been there," Imn Orith replied, "but it should keep us clear of the southern lands. At least the ones that will hold a grudge. It will cost us a little time, though. We could keep south for a bit longer, until we reach Urgothe's Pass."

"No. I want to go this way." She traced the line northeast, where it passed through an area labeled Serjathm. She tapped the region, which encompassed five elongated lakes.

17

She'd expected things to be different, so when they were, she was prepared. What Alaji wasn't expecting was for things to also be the same. The buildings and dress, of course, were nothing like what she'd known. The people in the village now called Kirpalith wore clothes all but identical to those she'd seen in Hathari, and their larger buildings looked like those in Elsimi. But the small huts where the poorer families lived were similar to what she remembered, and a hundred other details called out to her. The woven reed nets for fishing were just like the ones her people had used, and she felt like she saw echoes of her town in the mannerisms and expressions of the new inhabitants. The tree line had changed dramatically, and there was vegetation growing along the waterline that hadn't existed. But the shape of the land and the lakes were largely the same; certainly less altered than they'd been when she'd traveled into the distant past.

Most of the boats on Boars Lake were larger than what her people had made. And, of course, they'd changed the name of Boars Lake. Now it was "Irith-Li Lake." She'd asked a woman selling bread who Irith-Li was, and she'd gone into a long tale about a maiden from the area who one of the Hathi princes had fallen in love with. The story ended with the woman and her lover falling through the ice and drowning, and the prince's brother decreeing the two had been married in death. Irith-Li, the breadseller explained, was the name the woman would have had if she'd married the prince.

Alaji preferred the old story. She doubted this one held much more truth, anyway.

She considered finding the place where her family's hut had stood, but decided against it. The experience was already disorienting enough. Instead, she left Imn Orith in the town center to tend the horses and went for a walk alongside Boars Lake. The sun shone down on the water as it always had, and she looked out at the strange men on strange boats catching familiar fish with familiar nets.

When she returned, she discovered Imn Orith walking beside a rotund man about his age. They were struggling to communicate but seemed to be making headway. When Imn Orith saw Alaji he called out for her.

"There's someone I thought you'd like to meet. His name is Tir Jerot. He's a historian who lives around here. I told him you were interested in the region's past."

"Do you know what happened at the battle here?" Alaji asked at once.

He chuckled. "There have been several battles fought not that far from here," he said. "I'm sure they group them all together when they talk about us out east. There were numerous fights and skirmishes when the Hathari first arrived. The most famous involved an attack on an encampment of the Emperor's men in the dead of night. The lakemen came across the water, but they were betrayed by a startled duck which drew the lookout's attention. Or at least that's the story."

"I'm more interested in the older wars. The battles between the northmen and the lake people. There was a conflict between the people of the lakes and a warlord named Hollik. Have you ever heard of him?"

"Yes. I'm surprised you have, though. He's not well known in the east. Have you spent some time near here? You speak as though you've lived here your entire life."

Alaji smiled at the irony. "I had a teacher from the southern hills. I picked up his accent."

Tir Jerot nodded. "I know a little about Hollik, though I'm afraid there's not much left to be known. This was before the written word reached the area. Before the Hathari civilized it. Did your teacher tell you about the people here?"

"Not that I recall," Alaji responded.

"They were without the grace of the gods. In the time of Hollik, most lived underground, in deep caves."

"Underground?" Alaji asked.

"Not all of them, but most, we think. They certainly came above ground to scavenge for food and to gather water, but they spent their time in caverns. We're not sure whether it was to stay warm or if it held some primitive religious significance, but we've actually found one of their dwellings. It's really something to behold: the walls are covered in elaborate paintings depicting dividing lines. It must have meant something to them, but whatever that was has been lost to time."

"Probably nothing important," Alaji whispered.

"It's hard to say. To the primitive mind, the simplest symbol can appear profound. The people of this time… did your instructor tell you about their numbers?"

"I don't think so."

"It's truly fascinating. They had only rudimentary mathematics. They couldn't work with numbers greater than five. They had no word, no concept for anything they couldn't count on a single hand. I'm sorry – is this bothering you?"

Alaji forced herself to smile. "No. It's just… you were telling me about Hollik a moment ago."

"Yes, the second North King. That's how the stories refer to him. His name survives in just a handful of legends. He's commonly associated with spirits. They say he traveled with one for a time, and that a second appeared on a hilltop in the midst of a battle. This was far in the northlands, back at the beginning of his campaign. It's an odd story for the era, actually."

"But there's nothing about the battle here? Whether he left survivors or enslaved his enemies?"

"I've never heard of him having a battle at Kirpalith. It's possible, of course. He was ruler of a large stretch of land between the northern mountains and the eastern sea, so he likely had to contend with revolts and the like. But there's nothing important enough to have made it into the histories. I'm sorry to tell you this, but it's likely your instructor was confusing Hollik with one of the other north kings. Maybe Gurint. They say he swept across the land and won the land by spear and bow. But that was generations after Hollik died and his kingdom collapsed."

"Do you at least know what happened to him?"

"To Hollik? He died, either from disease or in battle. The histories differ. His sons tried to rule over his kingdom, but there were too many of them and too few willing to relent. Barbarians are never able to maintain a kingdom."

"Do you know anything about what happened to the people who lived here? Did they move somewhere after they left their... caves?"

Tir Jerot grinned. "They didn't leave. They're still here, in a sense. I'm descended from survivors of the Hathari Expansion on my mother's side. I consider the history of the land my own."

Alaji looked over his face. His skin was indistinguishable from Imn Orith's, noticeably paler than her own. His dark golden hair was also a hue she'd never known in her time. If he carried the blood of her people, he carried very little. "I see," she said. "Thank you for speaking with me."

"I'm glad for the opportunity. Not a lot of interest in the distant past these days."

—

"I'm sorry," Imn Orith said, after the historian was gone. "I only caught a little of what he said." They'd rented rooms at an inn and were sitting in an open patio waiting for their food. Beside them was the lake, reflecting the setting sun and rising moon. A handful of boats were still drifting towards shore with their catch of fish.

"It wasn't true," Alaji said. She was tired, despite spending the day in the village. Perhaps because of it.

"It didn't think it was. History... it isn't written by people like... like...." he trailed off.

"Like mine? No. My people couldn't write."

"Or count, it seems," Imn Orith added.

Alaji turned to correct him but saw a wry smile on the old man's face. She began laughing, and he did as well. She sighed when she'd finished.

"You could correct him," Imn Orith pointed out. "Maybe even tell him the truth."

"He wouldn't have believed it. Besides, what would it accomplish?"

"Men like that – like me – we talk to anyone who will listen and most of those who won't. Think of everyone he'd tell. At least your people could be remembered as they were."

"I don't know that they deserve to be remembered." Alaji felt bad as soon as she'd said it, but it still seemed true. "Besides, it wouldn't last. Anything I could tell him would be forgotten just like before. Forgotten or mangled again. The future will change everything."

"Alaji. Have you… seen it? The future, I mean. I'll understand if you can't tell me if you have, but I've worked my entire life to build upon the world's knowledge, to increase our rate of development."

"I haven't been further than your time," she replied.

"But… you know there are ages beyond it. I only ask, because there are those who think… it's stupid, really."

"That the world will end?" Alaji asked. She laughed again. "No, Yemerik told me that this – all of this, your time and my time – is the beginning. The world goes on far longer." She gazed out across the lake and wondered how much of the world and the future she'd see before returning to her own time. She was surprised to find herself hoping she'd see a great deal.

EPILOGUE

When I was a child, I dreamed nothing more than becoming as my father, Timin-Laur, who conquered lands and people and sought an empire that could reach its arms around the world. This was my grandfather's dream, as well. The great emperor-king, Cilea-Timin, who conquered the eastern coast, as his son would claim the rest of this continent. For me, they dreamed I would push on further into the west, and while they would never say the words aloud, their eyes told me to overthrow the old empire and rule over all. Or perhaps they'd merely hoped for me to pass this task on to my own son.

This was my dream. To be as they were, or greater. But they were men as strong as the bronze they wielded. They were fierce and unyielding, warriors who'd spilt blood and taken their enemies' wives as their own.

I am Laur-Alem, king of Hathari, and I am no great warrior. Let any who says otherwise face ridicule. If a poet claims I performed feats of courage and a child laughs at him, let them call that child a scholar and that poet a fool. In my travels, I have seen statues of me raised where I held high great weapons. I have heard stories of great exploits. I have heard of this Laur-Alem, the warrior-king who fought bravely and slew his enemies, only to learn the futility and emptiness of death upon the battlefield. It is has a lovely ring to it, I think, but it far from the truth.

When I was young, I was a coward. I was weak. I tried to make myself more, and had I succeeded, I think I would have never looked back. No words can I speak more proudly than these: that the world is richer for my failure.

I turned away from warfare not because I understood it but because I did not. And I looked instead to scholarship, hoping at first to find an edge that would help me in battle. It was there, in my readings, that I found an animosity for combat. It was there I found a love of learning, of building, and of peace.

And it was there, in the philosophies of the ancients, I found an understanding of time.

I learned to focus my attention, to see the passing of moments and of years as a sailor sees the waves breaking upon the bow of his ship. And I learned to chart a voyage across that sea, to move in time.

Using this magic, I have traveled hundreds of years into the future. I have gazed upon marvels I could never have thought to behold. And I read books of philosophy, of science, of history.

I even gazed upon a tale written by a king who'd come to rule an empire beyond his father's father's dreams. One claimed not by sword or spear, but by friendship and invention and magic. I cannot tell you the awesome fear I experienced reading that tome – this very tome I now write. I saw words change before my eyes and realized that the act of reading my future transformed it. The words transformed me, and so now I write them differently.

Already Hathari is grander than I'd ever hoped. Already, we have pipes to carry water into our cities. We have metals unimagined by our fathers, and sculptures and paintings plucked from dreams. The barbaric practices of old are gone. Slavery is no longer practiced in any land aligned with Hathari. We have come to understand the value inherent to all human life. We understand the philosophy of ethics, the highest of learnings yet discovered by man.

But these are nothing to what we can yet accomplish. When I first traveled into the future, I saw a world beyond any I could have hoped for. But each time since, I come upon one far greater. As we learn from our future, we make it better. We become better.

I have passed on my knowledge in this craft and this philosophy. Our future can be changed by our actions, and we can be changed by our future.

As I grow old, I wonder whether there is a limit. I wonder if there is a future we can make where suffering is not known and joy is eternal. This is the quest I pass down to my children and to future generations of scholars.

We must go forward and gather the knowledge and wisdom to make a better world. A perfect world, if such a thing can be created.

– *From the writings of Laur-Alem, the inventor of time-magic, the Emperor of Hathari, presented by the Emperor himself upon his 90th birthday to the first visitors from The Last Gathering. It should be noted this is one of more than a hundred distinct versions from different iterations and timelines.*

The scholarship on the variations between editions is extensive.

ALAJI'S JOURNEY CONTINUES
TO A NEW LAND,
A NEW GATE, AND
AN AGE OF STEEL AND BLOOD.

A TIDE OF ICE
NOVEMBER 2015

ERINLSNYDER.COM

www.ingramcontent.com/pod-product-compliance
Lightning Source LLC
Chambersburg PA
CBHW030914120626
46554CB00001B/148